2020

Random Summer Storms
Book Three – Family

Denise Ann Stock

Strategic Book Publishing and Rights Co.

Copyright © 2020 Denise Ann Stock. All rights reserved.

No part of this book may be reproduced or transmitted in any form or by any means, graphic, electronic, or mechanical, including photocopying, recording, taping, or by any information storage retrieval system, without the permission, in writing, of the publisher. For more information, send an email to support@sbpra.net, Attention Subsidiary Rights Department.

Strategic Book Publishing and Rights Co., LLC
USA | Singapore
www.sbpra.net

For information about special discounts for bulk purchases, please contact Strategic Book Publishing and Rights Co. Special Sales, at bookorder@sbpra.net.

ISBN: 978-1-952269-47-9

Book Design: Suzanne Kelly

This book is dedicated to my nephew Adam Brooks. I miss you.

ACKNOWLEDGMENTS

I have many people to thank for helping me with this book. People who let me use their life experiences. My characters are fictional. The real places and true events are for effect only.

Thanks, Jack Strandburg, for putting up with me the last two books. I owe a special thank you to Connor Cornell, the professional photographer that took the pictures I use on my cover. Connor was born and raised in Florida, and an avid surfer and skateboarder who's extraordinary photography is known in many countries.

INTRODUCTION

Cheers to those beautiful summers past and present; the summers we all look forward to, and the ones we spend much time reminiscing. Summer time when we kick back or cut loose, enjoy perfect weather to do just about anything we desire. The days of beaches, boats, and barbeques, we enjoy all summer long. Those blissful days spent with family and friends doing what? Something good, or were we in the middle of something terrible?

Something we chose to tell everyone, or was it so terrible we hid it for most of our lives? Because we only want to share the right things, avoiding sharing when things go wrong. So, cheers to what you choose to share with your family, whether good, bad, or indifferent.

We all are simple families that become complicated at times. Mostly a group of people living life to the best of their ability. We all have our best and worst attributes. In this life we are living, we find ourselves standing in judgment of ourselves as well as one another, often holding back the cruel realities we wish to keep secret. Comparing the trials of our siblings' lifestyles to our own, but not comparing it honestly. We see things happen and point our fingers, saying that would never happen to me. Does it not?

While other people's drama unfolds, we stand tall, pretending we're better, and would never experience anything of the kind. Some of us are professionals, and our families are living a good life due to our accomplishments. Funny how most of us consider our lives to be perfect.

You've probably experienced it—the judgment meant only for others. Because who really wants to admit they have family problems, failures, and ugly secrets? We show what we wish to our friends and family, while hiding those things of which we are ashamed or embarrassed. Putting on that happy family face, when inside, we know we all deal with many of the same struggles. We call them our dirty secrets.

Ian and I have saved up many secrets; countless ventures through the years we bury for fear of sharing with others. We always boast the good and celebrate the things we champion in life—our great successes, such as palatial homes, expensive cars, and a luxury life.

As time passes, do we ever really bury the wrongs from our past? We spend time worrying those deeds will show up at the most inopportune times. It's Karma, and might not come today, but it will come. Will you ever receive it yourself, and can it pass from your generation to your children? No, you never really get a pass. Deep down, you know you won't escape it.

We keep shutting the closet holding our skeletons, hoping no one remembers what we did. We hope it is forgotten, especially by Karma, but it isn't. What you do now is accept that payback. Karma never forgets and will always deliver.

I hope some of that Karma isn't ours. We hope it instead is given to the criminals we crossed paths within our younger days.

I will retrace the steps bringing me to my Karma fear, where everything in the past resurfaces, some in the next generation. As the Bible says, "in the end, what once was will be again." Our youth of today is just a mirror of our past youthful discretions. I pray our children will not follow in our footsteps, but instead forge a new path above the complete carelessness of our youth.

Ours is the generation of hippies, preppies, and ordinary folks and neighbors, all who seemed harmless. Our parents were conservative about life; but back in the seventies and eighties, we approached our actions with neither political nor calculated fear. We lived; oh boy, did we live.

We avoid discussing our devil-may-care youth with today's generation. Life in California was wild for Ian and me, along with many others. John and Darryl, Ian's brothers, were there with us. I hope it's just history, a time that passed for all of us.

We all grew up. Perhaps those days are truly forgotten; or are they? Then again, why us? Should we truly pay for indiscretions from our youth, a time when we were free of responsibility? After all, we were learning then.

As I reflect, we enjoyed sunny days and endless summers; surfing trips caravanning down to Mexico with a select group of friends. The nights were warm, and the sky was deep shades of purple. I don't think about the consequences of our actions, rather consider it a process, our rite of passage drawing us along. Right or wrong, we walked that path, and our actions led us to who we are today.

We approached life with no boundaries. We unashamedly snorted cocaine and drank all night on some weekends. It was just fun, right? No wrong. It happened over twenty-five years ago, and people listen to our history with mixed reactions, so perhaps it's best to forget the wild days, and avoid discussing.

We believed that by avoiding discussing our history, we'd dodge the Karma we created. We don't feel ashamed; it's nothing more than memories. I believe we've become different people, knowing that lifestyle is no longer acceptable, and might damage our careers.

The question arises of whether we can keep those skeletons in the closet, or will they come out on their own? Will our children be as wild and careless as us, destined to repeat our every foolish act? None of us know what the future holds, we can only wait as it unfolds. Good or bad, the experience is ours, and our children will make their own choices—right or wrong. My story is about our summer storms.

Summers Past

CHAPTER 1

Some will empathize with my story; others will find it absurd. When I recall some of our actions as kids, I'm amazed how we ever became adults and parents. I believe most people feel the same way, and either admits it, or believes it of someone else.

My name is Dee (short for Dolores after my great grandmother), but I never admit that in public. (sorry, Mom). My family called me Dee Dee until college when my friends shortened my name to Dee. I am married to Ian Connor, who I first met in our teens while living in Huntington Beach, California. We didn't start dating until we were in our twenties. Our past was rocky at best. We eventually worked through our problems and setbacks to become a couple. I know—boring, but this is a situation where you needed to be there to witness the ups and downs to understand.

Most couples struggle with bumps in the road, but we were hard-headed, so it took us longer. Ian and I couldn't stay on the same plane; but it's our history, and it defines us. Even with those rocky times, our past is no less than extraordinary.

When I met Ian, I was a simple surfer girl living at the beach, looking for the next best wave. Ian lived in the affluent Huntington Harbour and hung out with the same circle of friends. The story of our meeting is basic enough until we experienced unusual situations while getting to know one another. These situations caused the ups and downs, creating a twisting and turning road we traveled in eventually developing a relationship. Sometimes our actions weren't legal, yet we never thought about the consequences.

Ian and I and friends approached life as free spirits open to trying new things. We traveled, surfed, and hung out in our back yard that was the California Coast. Had those innocent and normal activities been the extent of our actions, we'd have no cause for regret. Unfortunately, our past involved much more.

I don't regret everything, just a few side paths we took along the way, and indeed, regret might not be the correct word for my emotion. It's difficult to convey a lifetime of misdirected opportunities or just plain crazy choices that lead to adventure and excitement we otherwise would never experience.

Water skiing with Orca's was fun and exciting, mostly due to not knowing whether we would be attacked. Fortunately, despite sharing the same waters as a pod of Orcas, averaging 10,000 pounds each of hungry whale following a tuna troller off the back coastal waters of Catalina Island, we survived. The fisherman warned the killer whales were following behind their big fishing boat; and a pod was looking for a handout. They could easily mistake us for food. We could have chosen the safe route and went back into the cove while they passed, we chose to stay in the water; figuring we'd share the ocean with its creatures. Dumb? Maybe, but most certainly the experience of a lifetime.

Oh, let's not forget the accidental mushroom trip in the hills of Ortega. I say accidental, because most of us had no idea we ingested them until it was too late. A couple of our friends thought it a funny joke and a new experience among friends.

Although I didn't regret it, tripping on mushrooms in our campground, with the band America singing on the radio about alligator lizards in the air as we looked up at the trees whose leaves shone with a fluorescent glow, was something we learned not to repeat.

Yes, we survived that unforgettable camping weekend too.

Meeting people on our surfing trips up and down the coast was memorable. The runs up to Northern California at Half Moon Bay, where big wave surfing extremists went for the chance to say they surfed Mavericks on a thirty-foot day. The waves are no phenomena, the commonly large waves of that particular location are created by a combination of weather, gravity, and the undersea bumps and lumps on the ocean floor, uniting to create an enormous wave. We cheated death on several occasions.

Oh yes, those were great times. Mavericks is outside of Pillar Point Harbor a little north of Half Moon. Back in our days, it was the best-kept secret surfing spot. Legendary yes, regrettably, never. My first surfing competition was up north at Half Moon. Placing third felt better than I imagined, not a bad alternative to winning.

The locals discouraged outsiders. We made friends in the town on our visits who let us stay with them each time we came, and we returned the favor when they visited us in Huntington.

Jeff Clark surfed Mavericks long before it became the famous big wave location. Jay Moriarity was the youngest to challenge what is referred to as the deadliest waves on earth. Shawn Dollars holds the record of surfing after a paddle-in on a fifty-five-foot wave. This occurred long after we stopped making the trip.

We also frequented San Onofre, San Diego, and Tressels, known by every surfer in California. We traveled on many weekends to experience these awesome breaks. On any given day, we carved with some of the best surfers of the seventies and eighties. We spent summers camping and surfing all weekend with guys and girls coming from Hermosa, Manhattan, Venice, and Newport, to name a few.

I also experienced one eye-opening summer of exploration, where I dated three different guys. Ian was one of the three, who I dated off and on, never knowing he'd be my soulmate. Ian dated his own group of girls as well. I didn't regret the time, because without having relationships with others, Ian and I would've never known we were meant for each other.

Finally, we decided to befriend and spend our evenings drinking with criminals, the perfect time to regret; to step back and remove ourselves from the situation; but we chose not to. The pretending and infiltrating their group as friends was crazy dangerous.

Until you set a course to undermine someone, you don't know how it feels to get the upper hand. The feeling that won't let you back off was all-consuming. The criminals, murderers, and thieves got what they deserved, and swallowed the bitter taste of their own medicine. These Cartel men would do anything to make money and stopped at nothing to build their illegal business of drug trafficking in the United States.

One summer, three of us put a kink in their plans. Initially, I felt good, but I regretted the decision we made, which unintentionally put our families in danger. We made the mistake of not knowing our actions on the island would adversely affect our lives.

My father always told my siblings and me to "be careful what you do in your life. The little things you do in youth have a way of resurfacing and coming back around to bite you in the bum."

We laughed, thinking that funny, then dad went on to say, "beware, all the things you left behind or thought you buried will show up on your doorstep when you least expect it. Do something you and your family will be proud of." He told us these are the things you want your loved ones to remember. Don't leave your family full of bad memories because memories are all they will have of you after you're gone.

I was thinking about skeletons we might put in our closet. Dad was talking about us getting jobs where they might have to investigate our background. Perhaps Mike's career with the Swat team. Maybe Kathy's. Although she's a stay at home mom, her status in her husband's world could possibly be affected by past indiscretions she might harbor. Knowing her penchant for perfection, that didn't seem likely.

We would always remember the good in my father, such an honorable man, we knew he wasn't talking about his past. He was a decorated military career man for 35 years. Everything about his life sparkled and shined. My mother, well, she was a saint, and everyone adored her.

I felt through the whole conversation he was talking directly to me about skeletons in my closet. That is how I perceived it, and rightly so, knowing what I knew. I didn't think my father knew my skeletons even existed, but I could have been wrong. Dads are funny like that.

While he spoke to us that day, I thought it useful advice for someone else, but much too late for me. I'd already started collecting my skeletons. Ian and I had already done some idiotic things we regretted, yet we both believed we'd gotten away with them.

Think about it. Do you ever really get away with something you did? Even if it doesn't physically hurt you or someone else, you must live with it. Knowing sometimes is the hardest part. The haunting of the facts. Flashbacks of days and specific events that were bad, *really* bad.

Maybe my dad wasn't talking about Karma, "the sum of a person's actions," but in the back of my mind, I was sure thinking about its fate. As it turns out, our actions adversely affected some bad people, and we believed it to be their bad Karma. Maybe we shared this Karma with money launderers and drug traffickers. Either way, there were consequences from our actions.

Although they were the bad guys, and we got one over on them, I worried about the Karma for stealing. We stole from crooks who obtained their goods illegally, but does that justify our actions?

Karma scares me. I feel as though somehow, and sometime, it will find me. I don't know when, but I know the bitch is coming, and the notion scares the hell out of me. I have no way to stop it.

Blame might lie in the era we grew up, days of sex, drugs, and rock and roll. Hippies were prevalent Yuppies, not far behind. That lifestyle made the quiet little beach town of Huntington Beach the perfect place to be whatever we wanted. Most of us were surfers, some were hippies. Our lives were just getting started, and the sky was the limit.

Little did any of us know at the time we would eventually leave the simple life and become professionals living miles from our homes. That seemed so far off. Back then, being the carefree youth wasn't the problem; we enjoyed beach life and adventures. Our prospects boiled down to what we would do with our lives as responsible adults.

For most of us, surfing was the center of everything. Although skateboarding was gaining popularity. It was mellow in those days. This small town offered horseback riding, bike paths, parks, and beaches for miles. Expansive oil fields circled the city. The schools were excellent, and neighborhoods were full of kids of all ages.

That time would never return. I know all generations say that, but somehow, I feel this was the end of the small town. The next generation would never know the relaxed, easy-going society we were privileged to live. Kids played outside from morning until night and walked or rode bikes for miles to buy a five-cent ice cream cone.

I find nothing better than being with friends sitting on the curb eating ice cream. Building on lifelong friendships. No one ever expected it to change, and for many years, it didn't. Bright sunny mornings turned into beautiful clear star-sprinkled nights. The smog line of the city so far from where we lived, here in our clean little beach home. I remember thinking its ugly grey would never touch us here.

As youngsters, we lived a simple life. Having a best friend and bicycle was the ultimate for our neighborhood, until one day we added surfing, meeting new friends at the beach, extending the boundaries of our world. Is there anything better than learning how to surf and hanging out with others that loved the same thing? Nothing I can think of beats friends and discovering new places and new ways to have fun.

As we aged, our lives became more complicated, although at the time, we didn't think we were the cause. The drug trade quietly infiltrated our country, but we weren't aware of the pending plight.

We smoked weed and snorted a little cocaine, sensing no danger; simply a way of cutting loose on the weekend; a form of entertainment, also practiced by celebrities and the rich and famous—a secret society of decadent beings enjoying the unspoken indulgence. No one died, so no one cared. Not yet anyway. We experimented with all things, a crazy era where we were making memories and history.

Huntington Beach and its townspeople were oblivious to the drugs and trafficking in its own back yard, let alone that drugs might be flooding the neighboring cities as well. No one worried about it until decades later. In the future, drugs would become an epidemic. Back then, it wasn't a part of average everyday lives, and didn't affect the mainstream society, the good people of the neighborhoods. Perhaps they should have paid more attention. Even if us wild children had known then what we know today about drugs, we might have been more cautious in our pursuit of fun.

Life was not all illicit or inappropriate behavior, and it was mostly good for us in our beach town where the surfing was, and still is phenomenal. We knew everyone in town, and the people in town all knew our families. Your neighbor was your doctor. The other neighbor owned the gas station. And down at the end of your street, Mrs. Barker was your high school English teacher. A tight-knit beach community.

We knew people that sold weed the same as the next person sold furniture. Others sold cocaine, which we knew was a little dicier, but still didn't pay it much attention. They handled their business quietly, blending in with society. They were comfortable, living the "good life," and nothing much ever really happened. They lived in our neighborhood, harmless in the pursuit of their lifestyle, and we accepted that. People didn't stick their nose into the neighbor's business as long as they kept their grass cut and took in their garbage cans. Funny, they kept their grass cut- a little play on words.

Changes were coming, and although I believed we were none the wiser, perhaps it was because we didn't care.

People were growing their own marijuana, and weed growers in the hills of Northern California tried to get their foot in the door of what would become big business. They called it "progress." Besides, who would care about some surfers and hippies smoking weed? Certainly not us. Eventually, it would all become legal anyway. The subtle hints suggesting we heed warning were there—we simply refused to see them.

Trafficking was happening behind the scenes, from South America up the border into the United States, where cocaine was sold in powder form. Although no proof existed, many believed the government allowed it in, but there were telltale signs of a bigger picture than we realized. Millions of dollars passed hands, and life went on day by day with no one the wiser.

Back then, cocaine sat on the table at most parties of the rich and decadent; common as offering someone a drink in many circles. Cocaine was the gateway drug they should have talked about, but how could they know? It would become so much more than weed would ever be, yet they didn't see that marijuana was not the most significant problem until they did.

Not everyone was aware of the drug trade. We hung out with great people back in those days. Many friends we grew up with became a significant part of the community. Doctors, lawyers, mayors, and business owners. With these Community leaders, progress flourished, as in any city. The beach town began to grow and change, and became a city that was the perfect picture of modern society. I'm not pointing fingers but speculate that some of them smoked weed back in the day too.

New developments were sprouting up everywhere, and the oil age of the 1940s faded into the past. Large condominiums replaced the small single-family dwellings along Pacific Coast Highway. Where a hundred people once occupied the land, now a thousand would replace them in million-dollar homes built on every available space from one border of Huntington to the ocean. Traffic, schools, and the beach all packed to capacity.

The cost of living was increasing daily, and if you weren't making money, you moved. The entire state of California was on the same track. Homes inland from the beach areas were more affordable; yet growing and booming with the rest of the state. Still, it remained beautiful, with its lovely modern architecture of Southwest stuccos and manicured lawns.

Some things, like the traditional gatherings, never changed at Huntington Pier. Events we all love managed the test of time. The U.S. Open Surf Championship was hosted every summer without fail. I never missed that competition. I was lucky enough to compete in it back in the eighties. I will always remember that period, surfing, and meeting some of the greatest men and women surfers of all time.

I spent my time with cool guys, my friends Jimmy, Mike, and Steve. Jimmy was the only one of the guys to go pro, making a living for years, and he talked me into competing for a couple of years. Although it was tough yet fun, I learned I wasn't cut out for it. Surfing on islands and in other countries was an unforgettable experience. My pro surfing life, though short-lived, was one of my fondest experiences growing up. I surfed the United States from coast to coast. I surfed the famous North Shore Hawaii as well as other hot spots for competition, travelling down to Bells Beach Australia, where I finished first in an International Championship. Then there is Teahupoo, a surf so treacherous, I will always remember as I nearly drowned, yet still managed to walk away with a title. Although the competitions were exciting and the experience unforgettable, traveling all the time wasn't for me. I'm a small beach town girl at heart and traveling to strange places for the competition became too much. In the end I chose to surf at home.

If you walk out on the Huntington Beach Pier during a good swell, you can see many of the same guys I surfed with still to this day, catching waves in their favorite spot. I say a good swell as if there aren't many. Huntington has the most uniform wave size of any place I've ever been. Bluewater rising and falling, forever amazing. So are the guys and girls that frequent this place. They were called the local boys and remain local boys today. I enjoy seeing the same faces out there, cutting it up, twenty-five years later.

Many other events still take place in H. B., like the massive Fourth of July parade and celebration that occurs every year with a bang. I had to throw that in there; I'm goofy like that. Anyway, we'll never forget these fun and special times. People lined up on the street early to watch, then stayed late into the evening for the fireworks display. I remember that from a young age.

They created the Surfers Hall of Fame in the nineties long after Ian and I moved away. People come from everywhere to see those honored here. Renowned surfers and industry leaders all represented in the most appropriate place in the world, Main St. Huntington Beach, California.

The board shapers and surf shopworkers from my youth are still representing Huntington on Main St. and Pacific Coast Highway. Those people are the surf shop and business owners of today. The place offers great memories and history.

I've always felt interest in the history of this town. The original Huntington Pier was built in 1902, then extended a few years later, and has been rebuilt several times since then. The Huntington pier was nearly destroyed in 1988 when an uncommonly large storm came through and ripped the deck from its pilings, throwing the café down into the raging sea.

Huntington Beach rebuilt the pier, and the city continued to flourish. Growth and all, it remained home in our eyes no matter how long we have lived away. That special place was everything and the start of our lives. All memories, good and bad, would never change how we felt about this place; we had the building blocks for great futures. Yet many of us made wrong decisions when we had all the best opportunities in this beautiful town, we called home.

CHAPTER 2

Unfortunately, we did make those decisions; choices that changed our future forever. We became acquainted with unsavory characters. I suspect that happens to everyone at some point in their lives. Why do we not turn and run away as fast as we can? The most dangerous people to encounter in a place least expected—a Country Club on the backside of Catalina Island. The Catalina Yacht Club, a place where elite individuals parked their yachts and hobnobbed with other wealthy people. But wealth doesn't sift out the bad, and they infiltrated the elite.

Nobody ever expected to find criminals working in such a beautiful place, but there they were, secretly conducting business when we uncovered their money laundering operation. That was back in the mid-eighties. A multi-million dollar business, operating right under the very noses of upstanding well to do citizens from different parts of the golden state of California, the land of opportunity and wealth. Who would ever imagine that kind of behavior in a paradise such as Cat Harbour, let alone California? It appeared the rich had either turned a blind eye or were simply naive.

The Cartel and a Los Angeles lawyer were doing business together when we crossed paths. They had everyone fooled in the beginning. Affluent boaters were staying the weekend in a secluded harbor; drinking cocktails at the pavilion, and swapping boat stories, not aware some of the people they were conversing and sharing stories with were scary traffickers and highly paid criminals. The criminals were good actors, as they never discussed their business. They played the game well, keeping the illegal side of their business under cover of night. They handled their secrets in the dark, and although they thought they were slick, we figured out what they were doing. We were watching from our boat.

Ian, Shelly, and I watched them for most of the summer, witnessing money drops every weekend. So, we planned and plotted, and stole one of the money drops, but they tried to kill us and take it back. It was all over the news back then. But the news thought they were pirates, and we never let on that wasn't the case at all. There was so much more to the story.

Our assailants weren't pirates, but Colombian Cartel killers trying to retrieve a bag of money they expected to have washed clean through legitimate business in the United States. That is where Attorney Anthony, their money laundering connection, entered the scene. We took money from his boat, and he would be the one to tell them to get us, and they did. A boat of Cartel assassins attacked us to recover the money, but the money was on the island, and those goons would never have found it. We weren't stupid enough to bring it with us on the ship we were traveling on but were dumb enough to think they wouldn't come for it.

The entire world thought that pirates attacked a yachting family out on the ocean between Catalina and California in hopes to steal the boat. Society was appalled at how crazy the pirates were to try something like this, in these gentle waters. A single-family defended themselves with guns out on the open sea that everyone in the United States considered a safe area. The story dominated the news for weeks.

Airing on the World News, over fifteen countries wanted to help control the pirate problem. An attack as brutal as this one was uncivilized to everyone, and something that doesn't happen to people like the affluent Connor family, certainly not off the coast of the United States.

The U. S. Coast Guard is America's maritime first responders, and they weren't about to be ousted by small-time no good pirates from a third world country, so after that night, they beefed up the patrol in those waters. The story caused great concern for the protection of the United States as well. If pirates could get away with this, how far would they go, and what else would they try? It was a breach of security in America. The scariest part was, we stayed quiet, not acknowledging we knew the real story. What would happen to someone for not telling the truth? Prison perhaps? Not for these three people. We would take it to the grave.

This situation might be one of those evil deeds my dad was referring to when he told us to "take care what you do." What made us think this would unravel any other way? All those crazy sayings like "take on a bull, you get the horns." We ripped off the Cartel! They kill people, and we knew that. We had no proof, but we believed we heard them shoot someone in the dark of night that summer on the backside of Catalina Island. We never saw a body, but we heard the gunshot from their boat. Not actually seeing anything, we couldn't call the authorities. As it was, we had no proof, only speculation, and so didn't call anyone.

Youth is the culprit. We thought we were invincible and could do anything. We, meaning two small-town surfer girls and a med-student who believed they were smarter than any crook. If you think about it, we were, because we beat them at their own game, and at least *appeared* to have defeated them. They couldn't prove we did anything, and they'd have to expose themselves to declare we stole from them. We counted on them fearing exposure more than seeking revenge on us.

Anthony, the money laundering attorney, stood to lose his practice from disbarment, not to mention his affluent lifestyle in the community. I don't know what the Cartel would lose besides money and face, but I know that made them mad, and they would want revenge. Hopefully, they'd become the target of an investigation on their business in the U.S. and it would be enough to make them go away.

Back then, nobody knew much about the Columbian Cartel, other than being a South American problem. The Cali Cartel worked with them, landing under the radar with the DEA in the late eighties and early nineties as big city distributors, most notably Los Angeles. I'm not sure they knew we weren't after their business, because they kept coming hard at us, day after day.

They spent hours a day watching the apartment we fled from shortly after we picked up the money, we stashed on Catalina Island. They staked out our old neighborhoods and watched our families. Scary guys sat in vigilance in cars outside our homes, and we're fortunate they didn't attack us or our families.

We never admitted to anything and never said who we thought was involved, hoping the bad guys would leave us alone. But we couldn't deny we had their money.

We never entertained the idea of returning the money after all we went through, and that caused a problem. Still, we wouldn't let them win, so we kept our hope that hiding the truth about the money and who we stole from would keep everyone involved anonymous. Maybe even make the Cartel consider not come after us anymore, a silly assumption on our part. But there was always the chance they would write off the money and abandon the chase. We knew it was a gamble but decided the best course of action was to remain silent.

Our situation reminds me of a song, The Smugglers Blues lyrics, "it's the lure of easy money its gotta powerful appeal." And the part that says, "You stay cool for twenty hours." Of course, we needed to stay cool for much longer than the song suggests.

The whole thing seemed simple at the time, and we thought they'd get over the loss of one duffle bag. We saw so many bags dropped off behind the Island of Catalina that summer, so what's a million dollars to the Cartel, who had hundreds of millions? They would have to expose their operation to get to us. That was our ace in the hole. We all kept quiet, and slowly, silently moved away; sacrificing the life we knew for our safety.

We didn't tell anyone where we were for years except our immediate family and Shelly; she always knew, since she also needed to move away. We let people believe we were avoiding the pirates. Shelly played a big part in the "Catalina Caper" and the danger. "Caper," what a funny word, but that's the name we secretly called it. Frankly, it was more a foolish undertaking than a caper, and no one thought it was funny when they came after us and shot Ian.

Shelly was staying on the boat with us when we decided we were going to steal from these guys. I think back on it now and wonder what we were thinking. We voted in favor unanimously, as we all wanted in on it. We stashed the money for a long time, then chartered a boat to retrieve it.

We tied down the money with weights off the shore on the backside of Catalina's Cat Harbor. We planned to split it equally between the three of us, making a pact not to spend it right away, keep the spending inconspicuous, and not all at one time to draw attention to ourselves. Ian and I didn't touch ours for years.

Shelly must have done the same because no one ever questioned us about our money. We've all been successful in our lives and careers, and didn't need to steal the money, but we did it more for the sport; the idea of beating these guys at their own game. We wanted to win. We, at least Ian, had another reason. He wanted revenge on them because one of the traffickers, a man named Ruben, attacked me one night. If Ian hadn't arrived when he did, Ruben would have raped me. Ian couldn't let that go. He wanted them to pay for Ruben's attempted rape. As for me, all I wanted was to forget that night, forget the pain and disgust I felt. I needed to forget Ruben ever existed, but I hated him, so in the end, we all agreed to seek revenge. It was a long time ago.

Ian and I moved from California to Florida, hoping to leave our past behind and start a new life and family. During our visits home on holidays, we learned the people involved in the money laundering continued for nearly a year to look for us.

Still, we kept silent, not telling anyone what they wanted from us. We believed if no one knew, the criminals would have no reason to hurt anyone in our families, and maybe leave us alone. They never managed to contact us after that night on the sea.

Thankfully, we never ran into any of them on our visits. Eventually, they gave up their search for us and their money.

The real reason they backed off was drawing attention to themselves as we had hoped. Our families talked with different men who came looking for us, and threatened them with the police and news media, which turned up the heat on the Cartel goons. Since no one they were watching had any details, they couldn't say anything to our families without incriminating themselves.

They tried to intimidate our families, but their actions were reported to the local police, and every time they came to the house, patrol cars cruising the neighborhood scared them off.

All the questions and poking around never provided the Cartel with helpful information in finding us, and without us, there was no money. Anthony and the Cartel hit a dead-end.

Everyone assumed they had a connection to the pirates, and in the end, I think they realized the benefit of everyone believing they were pirates and not drug smugglers or hired killers, worked to their advantage. Almost a year later, they stopped coming around. Ian and I, Shelly, and Keith moved on with our lives and had a family. Our new responsibilities took over, and we all left that "caper" behind. Not one of us wanted to share the real story with anyone.

Shelly couldn't continue to carry the burden, so finally told her husband, Keith, although we never discussed it among each other. I don't even know how Keith took the news. We all agreed to close this chapter in our lives, to bury it, never to bring it up again. Short of taking on new identities, we changed everything about ourselves. All three of us became responsible adults and parents in every way.

CHAPTER 3

The transition from irresponsible to responsible emerged after we moved, and we lived a healthy family life at the beach in Jacksonville, Florida. Ian, my husband, became a surgeon at Mayo Clinic. The move and Ian's job were an incredible opportunity for any new surgeon. We were so grateful they chose him.

The Mayo boasts a top-ranked cardiovascular department. Ian started there immediately after we moved to Florida back in the eighties. He took his place among the exceptional surgeons performing heart surgeries and critical transplants. He is well known throughout Florida and respected in his field. Saying I'm proud of my husband is an understatement.

The facility was brand new and state of the art with an extensive research center for many diseases and transplant specialties. Mayo was located close to the beach, so Ian's commute was less than ten minutes. He quickly settled into his role as a cardiologist, becoming an integral part of the team.

I worked hard for years to earn an enviable position at the local news station as the producer of the morning show. I love my news team; an incredible group that prepares the early morning traffic and news. The job is always a challenge yet rewarding as well. Our traffic broadcast is essential to our viewers in the morning, preparing them for a safe commute to work. My forte is my creativity to present strong stories impacting the community, and I keep this segment interesting to keep viewers coming back. My workday mornings consist of several hard-working hours.

Ian and I have three children. Ian VI, full name Ian Christian Connor, the sixth of the Ian Connor men, who we called

Christian from the time he first started walking. I'm not sure why we started calling him by his middle name, but it stuck.

Taylor and Anna, the twins, were born 4 ½ years after Christian. We have a golden retriever named Mercedes, and a cat named Edward (King Edward) who we learned early on believes he's the king of our domain. Mercedes got her name because she's a beauty, runs at high speed and probably the smartest dog I ever had. Mercedes and Edward get along very well, especially considering Edward's attitude. Our fish swimming in our saltwater aquarium, who remain nameless, rounds out our family members.

The kids all attend Bolles, a private school they've attended since kindergarten and will graduate from after twelfth grade. Bolles is well known for sports as well as academia; and the short commute is a welcome convenience.

Our daily lives are nothing if not normal. We live on the beach and stay active in our community and church, and the entire family is involved in fundraisers for our church, the Mayo, and the sea turtles. You can't live here and not care about turtles; our whole neighborhood is interested in their survival.

We lead busy lives. Work, school, and sports; we all go in different directions while trying to stay connected as a family.

The twins play tennis at the country club, and only Anna enjoys playing on the team of girls. She's our competitor. She plays USTA and is ranked 12th in the junior league in the state of Florida. Our family travels for some of her away games. Though she enjoys playing, she made it clear she has no intention of playing tennis for a living. The sport is too hard on the body she tells us. She's our free spirit who has no clue what she wants to do when she grows up. She says she'll know when she gets there.

My other daughter Taylor would much rather stay home and hang at the beach. Tennis to her has always been a hobby. She's more focused on academics and grades, an Honor Roll student who loves earth sciences; and a big reason we hold fundraisers for sea turtles. Taylor has changed what she wants to be when she grows up many times. When she was a child, she wanted to be a nurse, until she realized there was blood involved. Of course, that changed to aspirations of becoming a firefighter nixed for the same reason, which turned to, "I want to be a medical research specialist," at Mayo with her dad. After writing a school paper about turtles, she now wants to be a marine biologist. She's been talking about this for almost two years. Maybe she finally found her niche.

Christian is academic as well but has played basketball since he was six. We initially thought our little grom would be a pro surfer. He's an athlete who excels at any sport he tries. He enjoys surfing, baseball, football, and skateboarding, but basketball is his favorite, and he's played as a point guard since he was little. He chose his own path.

In the seventh grade, his school took an interest in his game and started preparing him for the Varsity team at Bolles, grooming him as a star point guard. They won the state championship every year he played. He played with several outstanding kids on his team. They all liked hanging out at our house every day after school, shooting hoops out in front of the house. Everyone on that team was a star.

We were amazed and proud of Christian and his leadership skills. He landed a basketball scholarship at the University of North Carolina, where he's earning a degree in finance.

Christian applied to several colleges at the end of his Junior year. He was offered scholarships from several colleges, including the University of Florida and Florida State University. The day he called the University of North Carolina to inform them he was accepting their offer was exciting for all of us. Since we were University of Florida Gator fans, we hoped he would choose that university, but in the end, he told us, "if UNC was good enough for Michael Jordan, it's good enough for me!" Goodbye Gators and the University of Florida.

Our lives seemed perfect, but a storm was brewing. I wish I would have seen this one coming, but I ignored all the signs and let it happen. With everything going along so well, I couldn't imagine anything going wrong, especially not from my children who all excel in school and behave well in public. As much as I knew, I was still ignorant of the possibility something was amiss. I'd never believe my stellar child would walk the wrong path, but we're not there yet, so I'll continue the story.

I think back to when we moved to our lovely home almost twenty years ago. A three-bedroom two-bath brick home on two and a half acres of land; we found the perfect place right on the oceanfront. We built a wood beach access shortly after moving in that goes over the sea oat, and Passiflora covered dunes.

The dunes are full of cactus hiding in with the sea oats, making the beach access build completely necessary. Amazingly enough, we grew out of the twenty-two-hundred square foot home, and after living there for ten years, gutted, renovated, and remodeled it during a summer when we took the kids to Ireland.

We had a wonderful trip. We flew into Dublin, the Republic of Ireland's capital, and stayed a week in one of the beautiful hotels on the river Liffey. We toured the beautiful countryside and visited Dublin Castle, followed by two weeks at the lovely quiet island of Emerald Isle. The village shops and taverns offer musicians playing the local favorites. We took a country ride and learned it's the roots of Celtic, Viking and Anglo-Norman cultures. A fascinating place we'll always remember.

We couldn't leave without visiting the historic Moors. We walked them for miles and witnessed the incredible beauty previously seen only in pictures. The visit seemed surreal. It's difficult to put into words how something this magnificent affects you when you are there in person.

I don't know why, but for some reason, every time I reminisce about that trip, the song sung by Sting, "Fields of Gold," comes to mind. Although it doesn't reference Ireland, it plays in my mind every time, when I think of how our family enjoyed the beauty of the place so different from our country.

The house was far from complete when we returned, given the usual construction problems like rain and permits, so we stayed the rest of the summer in a rental, located a few blocks from our house, which allowed us to frequently ride by and note the progress. We added a second story and expanded the two-car garage into a three-car. In the end, a twenty-two hundred square foot home became the eight thousand square foot home made of cinder block we live in today. We renovated it to withstand winds up to 185 miles an hour, the result of the hurricanes that sometimes pound the east coast.

The upgraded home served our needs well. My father lived out his golden years in the mother-in-law suite we built over the garage, until he passed two years ago.

I often wondered if he gave up being without my mother. He moved out here after she died of cancer, no longer able to live in our family home in Huntington Beach without her. It broke my heart to sell the house where I grew up, knowing I'd never again set foot inside.

The day we put our mother to rest was worse. I thought we'd all never stop crying. Dad and my mother were high school sweethearts and married young. My father, such a strong man, took her loss so hard. The sorrow of her passing was so heartbreaking, I thought he might not recover. They were married for nearly fifty years when she died, but I take comfort knowing they are together again. I miss them both so much.

Having my father living here while my kids were growing up was a good experience for my family. He never overstepped as an authoritative figure, but offered his views and opinions freely. My children respected him completely, although they never stopped trying to bring him into the twenty-first century of tablets, cell phones, computers, etc.

Dad never really got it. He struggled just to turn on the smart TV. Simplicity was one of the beauties of his era. He was accustomed to turning a knob, not trying to figure out which of the three remotes worked the "on" button of the TV. Still, he was good-natured regarding his inability to adapt.

Christian now stays in the suite when he comes home from school on holidays and summer break. The suite is similar to a one-bedroom apartment with a small kitchen, bedroom, bathroom, and sitting area. It covers the entire three-car garage that completes the L shape of our house. A door in the upstairs hall of the main house provides access, and an outdoor staircase leads down the side of the garage to the driveway. This setup provides Christian his privacy.

The rest of the house consists of our master on the first floor at the back end of the house, with French doors opening out to the wood deck, spanning half the length of the house facing the ocean. The bottom floor consists of a living room, library office space, formal dining room, and dividing walls in the kitchen. This changes with a casual eating space that opens into to a large family room. I love this room, as it provides an all-glass view of the beach. I can see from the kitchen to the shoreline and watch the children play in the yard. Oversized glass windows in our formal living room and dining room face the ocean. The idea was to assimilate being outdoors when you're stuck indoors, and I think we achieved our objective.

Our second floor consists of the girl's bedrooms, looking out over the front yard, each with a connecting bathroom. The rooms are basically the same, but the personal styles are entirely different. Anna's is modern with sharp corners, where Taylor's are comfort and ruffles. We converted Christian's old bedroom to a guest room, and a large bonus room for games, toys, and television, sits at the end of the hallway. The bonus room has a large screened balcony and is one of my favorite places to lounge and read.

The game room was Ian's idea and the best part of the renovation. One wall is all shelving and cubbies for the organization of all the kid's toys and things. The kids can play upstairs, and the mess stays up there; perfect when we entertain guests, because we don't hear the roughhousing. The toys and mess made by the children are invisible to the guests.

Entertaining is a big part of our lives. We love regularly inviting friends and business acquaintances over for dinner. The kids had their friends over every day. I was the Kool-Aid mom, and their friends were always welcome at our house. Besides, when the kids were home, I could keep an eye on them and not worry about them getting into trouble.

Jeff and Susan, our best friends, live directly across the street. Their two kids and our three play well together. Usually, if our kids weren't at our house, they were across the street.

Jeff and Susan's oldest was Darius. Darius was a couple years older than Christian, and Thomas, a year older than Taylor and Anna.

Our families did everything together. During the football season, we swapped hosting game day. Their family that lives in Duval county were part of the package, so on any Saturday, the Jones family would sometimes consist of ten guests.

We also alternated hosting New Year's Eve parties every year. We all liked to enjoy the holiday without leaving the kids out. We had a blast and never left our street. The Fourth of July was always a big production on our block as well. All the neighbors joined in shooting off fireworks together and having a street party with food and drinks. We set folding tables out, and everyone was welcome. This tradition started with one of Ian's childhood neighbors, who hosted a huge Fourth of July street party every year.

One New Year's night, I found out that when Susan and I drink too much champagne, we dance the macarena in the middle of the street. At least ten kids and several adults joined in, providing Jeff and Ian with a good laugh. I hate to admit it, but we knew all the moves. Thank goodness back then nobody carried cell phones with cameras.

One memorable Fourth of July gathering, we hosted a rib cookoff. All the neighbors, the Jones family, and some of their cousins, joined Ian and me, cooking ribs all day to find out which neighbor made the best ribs. If I recall, it was a toss-up, all the succulent meats were delicious. Darryl, Renee, and their kids visited that year. Darryl's entry of ribs was a Caribbean twist on the southern ribs everyone else cooked, and simply delicious.

The night was so much fun. Everyone enjoyed the food and neighborhood camaraderie. The fireworks display spun out of control, and the local sheriff's department came out to make sure we were responsibly shooting off the projectiles and nothing caught fire. The display created so much smoke, you couldn't see the houses across the street. They let us continue until 10:00 p.m., then asked us to shut it down because of a city ordinance. Considering the amount of smoke and mass of people, they were civil.

We let the smoke blow away, cleared the street, and hung out until the early hours of the morning. That night, Mr. and Mrs. Smith, an elderly couple in their early eighties living next door, joined us for the first time. They enjoyed themselves, and I'm glad they came out. We quickly became friends and learned many interesting things about them, including where they lived before they moved next door.

They both hail from Louisiana and speak with a hint of an accent. A bit of Cajun charm.

Mr. Smith worked for the electric company for thirty-five years before he retired and moved to Jacksonville beach only a few years ago. They didn't know anyone but always wanted to live here, and over time, joined many of our gatherings.

If they didn't show up, one of the kids would take over a plate of food for them and make sure they were doing well. The kids all loved them and enjoyed listening to their "old fashioned" stories. I was glad to see the kids take an interest in them. I believe there's a lot to learn from people of their time. Mixing generations is beneficial for everyone.

Most of the people we live around are friendly. Some we've never met, but the ones we have are decent, hard-working people, with busy lives like ours. We run kids to school every day, to soccer practice or dance every evening—a regular suburbia in our beach town.

We're protective of our beach and neighborhood, pitch in to keep it clean, and all work together to keep it a safe environment for our kids. The neighborhood watch is comprised of vigilant men and women living in the area, and take the responsibility seriously. We watch each other's houses, the beach area, and the neighborhood. Once a year, all the families unite to pick up trash on our stretch of the beach to keep it clean. This allows us to enjoy the community spirit and care for our environment at the same time.

It reminds me of the beach town I grew up in, Huntington Beach, California. My kids started their lives in the same extraordinary way as I did. This town is similar to my hometown in so many ways.

Located far from the crowded city, the clean air is ideal for beach life and surfing, but as in most cities, is changing. New homes are built daily, as thousands of people relocate to Jacksonville every year. Thank goodness they don't all move to the beach, and Jacksonville Beach still boasts a hometown quality. The closeness of the neighbors to each other is heartfelt.

Originally Jacksonville Beach was incorporated as Pablo Beach in 1907, changed to Jacksonville Beach in 1925. With a boardwalk and restaurants along the dunes, it was considered a coastal resort. Beach boardwalks on the Atlantic coast were popular in those days. A pavilion and amusement park were part of the town and driving on the beach was permitted up until 1979 when they deemed it too dangerous. I'm glad we moved here after the law was passed, because I don't believe the idea of people driving on the beach while children are playing in the sand is smart.

Today those restaurants and shops are being replaced by condominiums with 16 to 18 floors. Once again, progress changes the landscape of things; and there's no stopping progress. Yet, it remains a great place to live. The condo towers are built with taste and designed elegantly but detract from the hometown effect and aren't my idea of beach town living.

The Beach Pier, where we like to ride our beach cruisers to see what people are catching off the pier, is close to our house. The record catch is a 14-foot 4 inch Hammerhead shark a guy caught one evening back in 1975.

The Hammerhead wasn't the last giant shark to swim in these waters, but knowing this doesn't keep us from spending most of our free time in the water. What I love about the places I've lived is the history, and a big part of why we live here. Of course, avoiding getting eaten by a shark all this time is a bonus.

When the twins were little, we attached child seats to the back of our beach cruisers. Ian and I each peddle our bikes with one of the girls buckled in on the back, and Christian rode out front of us on his Diamondback BMX bike. We did this most weekends, and it was one of our favorite activities.

The ride down First Street is picturesque, and Christian jumps curbs and performs tricks the entire way to the pier for entertainment. He seems to be fearless, unfortunately has been to the emergency room so many times, the nurses all know his name. He's broken his leg, an arm, cracked his skull, been stitched a number of times, and sprained and scratched himself more times than I can count. Frankly, I'm surprised DCF (Department of Children and Families) hasn't come to my door and demanded to know the reason behind Christian's various injuries.

Those of us with sons understand completely. I know it's not funny, but we're at the hospital far too often. I think the nurses secretly enjoy his stories on how the injuries occur, and we learned Christian is quite the storyteller.

The song "Skater Boy" by Avril Lavine runs through my mind as I watch him do his thing. I'm amazed that he's good at everything he tries—surfing, skateboards, and the BMX bike Ian ordered made especially for trick riding. At five years old, I wondered whether the extra frills and gadgets on the bike was more for Christian or Ian. Christian mastered it in a short time and knows many tricks for a little guy.

The girls are happy to be out on the road, talking and pointing at birds and dogs. They were content to people watching as we passed others on the sidewalks and enjoyed this lovely day. As babies, they were always happy, never needing much to make them laugh and enjoy the moment. Strangers would never have known that because if these two little girls didn't know you, they'd give you the most severe scowl possible.

Tourists, and the locals line the pier fishing. The surfers in the small swell below shredding for every inch of wave paints the Pier as the perfect picture of summertime fun. The water is a light olive green with a foamy finish. On a good day, the waves maintain a constant three feet. If the wind continues to blow in the afternoon, it creates sets a little more impressive at four to five feet, and glassy, sometimes producing a coveted barrel of surfers' dreams. I always felt these surfers here in

Jacksonville Beach were innovative, creating great rides from smallish waves.

Summer, being outdoors riding bikes to pier, hanging out on the beach and in our back yard, is by far my favorite time of the year. I taught the kids to surf at an early age. Christian was riding a surfboard at three. When he turned four, we ordered a custom board made for a child. We took him to California in his younger days and let him ride the bigger surf with our local friends. He was happy to be the center of attention with the local surf crew.

He taught himself to ride a two-wheel bicycle at three and a half. I remember when he wanted to skateboard at two, and my friends were so against it because he was little. Ian and I let him learn to tic tac on the carpet, and once he mastered that, we let him go outside to conquer the streets. We encouraged him and always let him explore his limits. He showed interest in many new things early in life, and we loved it.

Taylor and Anna started learning to surf at about five years old. Both had excellent balance and loved surfing. They continue to surf to this day. All the kids are good at teaching surfing to others who visit. Their cousins have all learned to surf and enjoy staying with us. Watching them all together is a good feeling. We spend hours out in the ocean together, and it's satisfying to share a passion.

Sometimes in the evening, after work, Ian and I would take the kids out to surf for a couple of hours before dinner. Ian is a bodysurfer. Sometimes we all would bodysurf with him; he has a way of making everything more fun for the kids. Most of the time, Christian, Taylor, Anna, and I use surfboards. The kids show me new tricks, and I try to imitate them. Ian is learning to surf.

One year, a professional photographer created a photoshoot of the family, standing on the beach, holding our boards. The best shot of that day hangs in the family room. Ian and I love the awesome five by eight-foot photo of the family with a beautiful sunset in the background. The photographer was phenomenal, and all the images came out perfect. He captured the essence of our family, doing what we love best.

CHAPTER 4

My sister Kathy lives in New York. She visits and stays with us almost every year, and we travel to New York in the winter and snow ski with them. When they stay with us in the spring, we make the usual trek to Disney World. Spring is the best time for that adventure.

We cherish great memories of Mickey, Goofy, and Winnie the Pooh. The rides have changed progressively from year to year; still, all the kids are excited to stand in line for hours to ride as many as possible in a day. Although it's chaotic, I always enjoyed taking the large group. We had a blast when the kids were young, and they'd never let us talk them out of going to Disney. We could add other stops to the trip, but never omit it entirely until they were all in their teens, when trips to Disney were replaced by beach resorts and crystal springs. We swam with the manatees one summer down in Crystal Springs, Florida in water as clear as glass. The manatees were swimming among the green underwater plant life. We swam with dolphins the following year in an open ocean excursion just as spectacular, although the water wasn't as clear.

The first time we all went hot air ballooning in New Mexico was spectacular. Both families met in Albuquerque, reveling in gorgeous scenery while driving to the site where the balloons would launch. The view of the terrain from the hot air balloons was breathtaking, with so much color in spring. We saw a large grouping of buildings off in the distance, in a hugely populated area, and learned the city was named in honor of the Viceroy, the tenth duke of Albuquerque. The entire family enjoyed an excellent adventure.

Everyone loved that vacation together, and we'll never forget the ride, followed by a picnic lunch. The song by Hoku, "perfect day," always reminds me of the road trip to New Mexico with our kids, "on this perfect day when nothing can go wrong."

My sister's kids are a little bit older than mine, but they get along so well, the deep knit bond between the cousins is evident. We expect our house to get very crazy with them visiting. The situation reminds me of the movie "Home Alone," although I don't know why, because we never left anyone behind. We have just so many kids and adults engaging in different activities under one roof.

Kathy and Michael have three boys and a girl, all born within a few years of each other. Brook is my niece, and how she remains sane growing up in a house with three brothers is beyond me. She's sweet and funny, and my girls look just like her. The boys are Darin, David, and Daniel, all great guys, but that house has too much manliness for one girl and her mom. We love spending time together at one another's home.

My brother Mike still lives in California with his wife Jill and two sons. The oldest is Mike Jr., a couple of years older than Christian, and Sean, the younger one, is the same age as Christian. They all live in Norco on a horse ranch. Norco reflects a western theme. Known as an equestrian town, it's rural, but perfect for people who own horses and love horseback riding.

We have such a good time visiting them. We aren't horse people, so it's comical to watch us ride and interact with Mike's horses. My girls are probably the best with horses. They're gentle and love to pet and talk to the big creatures. I was surprised they weren't afraid as toddlers to be around the horses.

Those horses follow all the kids around in the field like big puppies. They live in a beautiful country and visiting is such a treat for us. Hills and mountains as far as the eye can see, with trails leading in every direction winding up into the hills behind the house. The neighboring homes are set up similar to Mike's. We come from flat Florida land, with no hills, and definitely no mountains. Visiting them is the ideal getaway.

Growing up, I would have never pegged my brother as a horse guy. He didn't like kids in his early years either. He always made fun of what he called "squalling babies," referring to the neighbor's kids on the street where we grew up. I thought he'd never have children, then he goes and has two boys, four horses, and two dogs. Family members often surprise us that way.

Ian's brothers Darryl and John still live in California as well. Darryl and his wife live in Northern California about 300 miles north of San Francisco, and John remained in Huntington beach in the home they all grew up in, where he cares for Mrs. Connor, now in her late eighties.

Darryl and Renee operate a multi-million-dollar operation just outside of Humboldt County, where they grow medical marijuana for dispensaries. I remember occasionally noticing a random pot plant in the family yard when we were teenagers. Darryl's handiwork, I'm sure. I know the boy's parents never knew what it was back then when it wasn't legal.

Darryl holds a degree in Horticulture from the University of California. I'm sure no one in the family expected him to use it this way. Renee, his wife, balanced the books and ran the marketing in the beginning, but it has grown too large, and they use an accounting firm now. Becoming a legal grower was a long hard road. They worked for years to complete the paperwork and obtain proper documentation, allowing them the fields to grow the marijuana. Darryl bought 10 acres when he started growing for a government project years ago, and over the years, it grew to 1500 acres.

He needed to hire security to patrol the land and keep trespassing thieves from stealing his crop. I remember when they first started growing, the neighbors protected each other. The criminal element surrounded the area, knowing there were no cops to protect them. We heard horror stories on the local news about crime and murder in the town. If you look it up today, many people who were transient workers disappeared, and family members put up signs looking for them—terrible stories about disappearances.

However, Darryl said they never suffered any altercations. They were aware of the bad around town, yet fortunately, didn't become victims. With the legalization and dispensaries, that changed, and the criminal element was no longer as prevalent.

They started with a travel trailer when they first bought the property, and now they own a big sprawling ranch style house and three kids: two boys, Trevor and Alan, and the youngest girl, Sherry.

Sherry and Christian kept in touch over the years more than the others, talking regularly on the phone. She's older than Christian by a few years, but that didn't matter; they still shared much in common, talking about their school, sports, and friends.

I love the fact they all reach out to each other, calling and checking in. A close family relationship is essential to me. I would like them all to remain close throughout their lives. When I think back, I should have asked questions about the conversations. They're all good kids, and at the time, I never thought they could get into trouble, living so far from each other. After all, what's the harm in just talking?

Ian's youngest brother John owns a large computer software company that creates systems for banking. He and I talked about computers when he was in his teens, and I knew one day he would be successful. He's the most technically savvy of the bunch and has been since he was young.

John lived in Newport for years until he moved back into the Huntington Harbor house with his mom when we realized she couldn't live on her own. She refused to sell the house and move into an assisted living community. Her companion stays with her during the day while John's away, but he works mostly from his home office now.

They sold the Trinity, a seventy-foot Hatteras that just sat unused at the dock, when Darryl moved up north. He was the last to use it regularly, a sad reminder of Dr. Connor's passing. We came back to California a few times and sailed it to Catalina on family trips when Christian was young. The rest of the time, it just sat at the dock.

Mrs. Connor had no desire to hire a Captain to take it to Catalina or out on the coastal waters. She left that task to Dr. Connors, and without him, the trips became less fun and meaningless to Mrs. Connor. The kids had grown, and no one was there to use it. We all loved the boat and its great memories, but a yacht that size must be run regularly to keep the engine functioning. None of the brothers had the time to run it as frequently as necessary, and when the boat inevitably fell into disrepair, they decided it was time to give it up. They moved it to a large Marina in Long Beach and sold it quickly.

That left a one-hundred-foot floating dock sitting idle. Mrs. Connor requested changes to it, and now it has beautiful flowerpots, with benches to sit and look out at the harbor. Grandma Connor has a landscaper who changes the flowers out every season to keep the dock looking beautiful. Thanksgiving is always Chrysanthemums, Marigolds, and Zinnias. And Christmas is still Poinsettia, as it has been for years.

We all make a pilgrimage to go home to the Connor house every Thanksgiving and spend four days with Grandma Connor. John's an excellent cook, and we all have a good time. We all pitch in to prepare side dishes, and John cooks the turkey, dressing, and asparagus wrapped in Prosciutto; his specialties, and they are by far the best dishes of the day.

The house looks the same as it did when Ian lived there, with beautiful traditional furniture. Grandma Connor always had good taste. When the boys moved out, she redecorated the rooms but retained the ambience. She replaced the old televisions with large flat screens.

The house offers plenty of room for our group of five, Darryl's five, Grandma and John. Since the grandkids were born, she changed from Mrs. Connor to Grandma Connor. She loves being a grandmother. She's sweet and kind, and the kids all naturally gravitate to her. To see her reading to them when they were young is a pleasant sight. She let them choose a story, and all gathered around while she read.

The first time we went for Thanksgiving, the kids were all twelve and under. Ian laughed when I told him "Darryl's kids smell like weed," then told me Darryl was a cannabis farmer. No wonder he's so mellow. I had no idea for years, and curious no one told me. They must have felt it was just a job and not significant.

Thanksgiving was so special that year, and with so much family bonding with the kids and Grandma, we decided to do it every year. Even though it was November, the kids spent most of the time in the pool, while the adults sat around and reminisced.

Darryl reminded us how different times in their lives were growing up, with the entire family dressing up for church on Sunday with a shirt and tie as mandatory dress code. Darryl says he hasn't worn a tie since.

They always talked about bicycle rides for miles around Huntington Beach. Leaving in the early morning and not coming home until dinner. They fought over who would buy gas for the minibike. The mid-sixties were simple times. We all love to reminisce. Ian and his brothers seem to remember everything, in great detail, the family ever did, and we all laugh at the antics.

I reminded them of the summer in Cat Harbor when they won the Avon dinghy contest; and the altercation with wild boar on the island, and the buffalo on the tennis courts. We laughed until tears streamed down my face. The boats were a central part of the Connor family for many years.

They didn't always own a big yacht. The family started with a Boston Whaler the senior Dr. Connor would use to take them out to the flats off the coast of Huntington Beach to go halibut fishing. As the years passed, the boats grew bigger and more expensive. Before I started dating Ian, they owned a Grand Banks Trawler. Most of the great stories they told concerned that boat.

When I began dating Ian, his father was having the extravagant Hatteras custom made. We talked all afternoon about the fishing trips before I became a part of the family, and many tales after. We laughed and talked through our delicious turkey dinner.

That evening we piled into the rental van and went to the Huntington Pier to walk off our dinner. The sun was setting, and memories of our childhood growing up here touched each one of us.

We promised the kids we would bring surfboards on the next trip so they could all get out on the water. The waves at this pier are twice the size of the ones on our coast.

I pointed out the apartments on the beach where I used to live to the kids, and where their father and I lived for the first year we were married. I talked about my pro-surfing days. Darryl was a surfer back in the day as well. "I never cared for the competing aspect of it," he said, as he stared out to the north side of the pier. "It messes with the vibe of the ocean."

Many surfers felt the same as he did. He described how commercialism of the sport took out the good vibes created by the competition. I love watching the competitions and personally don't think that's possible, but I get what he's saying and don't vocalize my opinion.

We looked at the statue where Duke Kahanamoku, a native Hawaiian, is honored for his popularization of surfing. To all who know his story, he's a true legend. We named off many greats who surfed here. David Nuuhiwa, well known for nose riding in the 60s; Corky Carroll, five-time U. S. champion and big wave rider; and the Pipe master himself, Gerry Lopez.

We went on and on about the early surfers who carved the path of the surfing world. The kids chimed in with surfers of today, such as Kelly Slater and John Florence. Taylor brought up the girls of surfing today, like the soul surfer Bethany Hamilton, and you, mom?

I laughed, insisting my footprint in this area is minimal, insignificant, adding that the first female world surf champion in 1964, was from Australia, a twenty-seven-year-old named Phyllis O'Donnell. And the big wave surfing champion is Kaela Kennelly.

Anna insists my time in the industry was relevant, reminding everyone of my big wave trophies stashed away in the attic. "Mom won a bunch of competitions and championships."

I appreciate the fact they think my name belongs with these greats. Kids are our biggest fans, and I certainly appreciate that.

Taylor sings the words to a song as she does a little dance. The song comes from a Nikka Costa soundtrack from the movie Blue Crush, one of our favorites. "Everybody got their something..." Anna sings along, "make you smile like an itty-bitty child, "dancing and looking at me while I reminisced of the Pipe Masters, a competition in Hawaii. I put an arm around them, both smiling as we move to the pier rail. We all giggle at the tune. I guess that was my "something." My husband always teases me that everything has a song or relates to music with me. It appears it does for my daughters too.

Darryl and Ian loved to skateboard right below the pier where we stand, and some of the leaders in skateboarding got their start in that very spot. Ian and Darryl are both goofy foot, and not too bad in their day. Many of our friends appeared in Surf Magazine for their skating ability.

Darryl and Ian were into it for years for fun, as was most guys who grew up and skated here. I love the nostalgia this place breathes, and know the kids enjoy hearing about it as much as we did telling the stories. All the boys were into skateboarding, but the twins never took to it.

John showed us his favorite wine bar on Main St., still open for business, but we didn't go in. We continued walking down the other side, looking into the windows of the closed cozy little restaurants and surf shops. Jack's Surf shop initially opened in 1957, yet amazingly is still here today. The street would change over the next few years and receive a makeover, modernizing the entire block.

Back in the 60s, Huntington Beach had a population of 11,960. Today, 201,875 people live here.

Our great memories will remain unchanged. I'll always picture the old way Main Street looked, even though it is beautiful in a modern style today. We laughed and chatted about town and history on the drive back to the house. A song was playing on the radio as we turned onto Warner St., "How Bizarre—every time I look around; it's in my face." Taylor started singing, and we all joined in. "How bizarre, how bizarre."

It became our traveling song from that day forward. I find it funny how a song stays in your mind, and you relate it to an event. Just like Ian said, we connect our events to music. Sometimes the song reminds you of a person, a place, or an activity, and it produces a déjà vu moment. We're an odd . . . okay, a goofy musical family.

Each of us has our own stories. We delight in the memories of the ones before we met each other, and each one since we became this crazy family. We've enjoyed talking about old hobbies and the places we visited.

John is our world traveler; visiting five countries since he was in college. He and Anna discuss the places he visited. I can barely hear them as they are in the third row back. His first visit to Europe was Russia, where he went with some friends. I can't understand or hear why he was there, and I hear only the part that is was a cold trip, and they drank lots of vodka.

His business took him to France, Rome, Dubai, Philippines, Japan, China, and Australia. I can't hear where else his travels took him, and then I return to my conversation with Ian and his mother, sitting behind Ian, our driver. She doesn't care to fly, so if she can't get there by car, bus, or train, she has no interest in going. Darryl and family are following behind in their Lincoln Navigator. Christian rode with them. I wonder what they're talking about right now.

Darryl's family travels to Hawaii every year on business. Hawaii is beautiful, and I'm sure they find time to enjoy the islands. His business usually takes him to the main island of Hawaii, where he talks to fertilizer vendors and people in the farming business. The island's terrain is varied, perfect for hikers and everyone else. The volcanoes draw big crowds.

Darryl and family all like Maui and have great stories of the day hikes they've taken there. The family will backpack anywhere. Their explorations took them to many mountainous places in the United States. They pride themselves on camping in almost every national forest in the U.S., which I think is cool.

I used to like camping in my younger days, but now am more of a hotel room service kind of girl, and my daughters agree it's the only way to travel.

I join the conversation by talking about our trips to Mexico. We went on surf excursions and visited tourist places like Mazatlán and Acapulco. Ian and I have driven from coast to coast and been to almost every state. We drove to Florida when we first moved there. We went sightseeing for two weeks before settling into our new life.

The State Fair was held in Louisiana when we were passing through, so we stayed two days eating Creole Food and enjoying New Orleans. They served shrimp at least six inches long. Their specialty drink everywhere we went were blue drinks called Hurricanes. I drank one and knew I'd never drink another.

The kids boast of a train ride we took one year on a fabulous trip from New York to Washington State in the fall. The autumn colors of trees were magnificent, with browns, golds, and oranges. Then there were the ski trips to Colorado, New Mexico, and Utah.

We all learned to ski together on one of the first trips. We took lessons for the entire week. We learned snowboarding once it became popular, which included the inevitable bumps and bruises. No matter how well you surf, snowboarding is a different animal, and we all took our lumps learning. The entire family felt the effects for weeks after.

Ian and Christian mastered snowboarding the fastest, but I think Taylor is the best at control and looking professional going downhill. Anna and I, well, let's say we both can do it, but neither one would brag. I thought our time surfing would make it easy. I was wrong.

We all enjoyed Ireland, England, and Scotland. Nobody in the family were fans of the food. No mutton and blood pudding for us thank you. Sightseeing the Castles and their surrounding grounds were unbelievable, with lush countryside, green as anything we'd ever seen. I wouldn't trade the trip for anything.

Those places were the extent of our European vacation. Somewhere over time, Ian expressed concern over terrorism making travel abroad too risky, and we never crossed the ocean again.

John voiced his opinion, saying that was plain silly. He travels all the time. He'll soon be flying to Switzerland and has no fears.

Ian strongly disagrees, and the conversation dies with the agree to disagree comment.

The thing we don't discuss as we reminisce is how wild we were before kids when Ian and I lived in California. John and Darryl went through that time with us, and were just as wild, staying up all night and sleeping all day. We approached life during that time with no boundaries, but those wild escapades have passed. Maybe we all grew up.

No, we don't discuss our past indiscretions, especially in front of our children. Bad behaviors we share among each other back then. Big old skeletons in our closets.

Back during that time, we were "only" having fun. We ran into each other at parties and didn't think anything of it, but our lives today depend on no one knowing our past. Our professions require stability, and no illegal escapades would be tolerated or accepted. I never want my children to know how we behaved. Shame, yes, regret, very much so. I like to think it carved me into the person I am today, but that would be a bit dishonest. I'm making up excuses for our bad behavior.

Thinking back, I'd never want any of my kids in the situations we got ourselves into, nor would I want them to try the things we did. Not only was it all reckless, we also endangered our families.

No, we don't discuss some of the ways we spent our summers in the past. Those days are long gone and should stay that way. I put those memories out of my mind so I can enjoy the rest of the long weekend at Ian's mothers, which suits me fine. At this point in my life, I'd like to forget that time.

We enjoy football while snacking on leftovers the rest of the weekend, a consistent ritual on every visit. Usually, by Saturday night, we're tired of traditional Thanksgiving food. The idea of eating another turkey sandwich is more than we can stand, so we go to Mario's for margaritas and Mexican food. There's nothing like tasty authentic Mexican dishes of enchiladas or tamales, and everyone loves tacos.

Sunday morning, everyone packs up their suitcases, and we return to our separate lives until next year. We all promise to call each other to stay in touch until next year. We haven't missed a Thanksgiving at the Connor house yet.

CHAPTER 5

Christmas is a crazy time for us. Every year we alternate who hosts the party—our house one year, Kathy's house in New York the next, followed by my brother Mike's ranch. Each is special for the holidays, although the kids love the traditional snowy Christmas at Kathy's house.

We're fortunate with a sixty-degree winter in Florida when they make the trip to our house. The winter fashions are a one-day experience around our neck of the woods, but everyone has a good time. We still decorate the house and put up Christmas lights in the palm trees and around the outer eves of the house. We bake together and prepare all the usual holiday treats. I should be honest; my sister bakes and I keep her company and find her the correct utensils for each item she creates. My specialty is surprising them with what I'll create for Christmas dinner each year.

My brother enjoys smoking meat in his smoker at Christmas at his house. We never know what kind of tasty meat he'll prepare. Turkey, ham, beef, who knows? Jill is the casserole queen and prepares the best concoctions of vegetables all the kids love. She says it's how she disguises vegetables so the kids will eat them. Whatever the reason, they taste delicious and always the hit when we go to their house.

The weather at my brother's house stays quite mild, too, even if it gets colder than sixty. It never snows, so celebrating outdoors most of the stay in Southern California is the norm. We all enjoy sitting out in his backyard, enjoying the beautiful mountainous views, drinking hot apple cider in a temperate Christmas.

When we stay at my sister's, Kathy always cooks the Christmas ham, while I oversee making my mother's famous potato salad. My sister is a fabulous baker too, and she makes several different cookies and beautiful cakes. Kathy and her daughter Brook traditionally make a delicious fudge, something I talk about but never attempt. I can cook almost anything but dessert. I never got the chemistry down. I make sides to go with dinner, the usual casseroles, and anything with cheese sauce.

The rest of the week of the family visit, we cook very little, opting to order take out or dine at a restaurant, preferring fun over slaving in a kitchen. They live in the suburbs, where the streets have small hills. Every kid in the neighborhood is out on bobsleds. It truly is a winter wonderland. I hung up my sled several years ago when I hit a tree down at the bottom of the hill and broke my nose. Fun over, thanks, Aunt Dee. The blood covering my face didn't deter the kids; they still go out and sled every chance possible.

Kathy's husband, Michael, is an attorney for a large firm in New York City. I kid her all the time about marrying someone with the same name as our brother. No one thinks the reference is funny.

Her husband Michael is the reason they moved from Huntington Beach, California to New York when their children were young. The house they live in looks like it came directly out of a movie set; with twelve bedrooms, and I'm sure at least as many bathrooms. I counted three guest baths and know of several half baths downstairs. Why so many bathrooms are beyond my comprehension, but Kathy explains they entertain a lot, and a bathroom line is unacceptable.

I didn't think it was possible, but they entertain more than we do. The entrance to the home is a huge foyer, and the downstairs hallways are all marble, beautifully done. I don't know what I'd do with all that space. The dining table seats twelve, with a similar sized table in the kitchen. Kathy calls it more casual dining, but it's fancier than my dining room that seats eight, and I thought my set was pretty extravagant when I bought it. It would be too much for the average household. Taylor used to say when she was a toddler, "we are going to the schmancy house." She was right.

Kathy radiates elegance, charm and graciousness. I tease her about it since we grew up in the same house. Not to take away from my mother, teaching us good manners will take you farther in life. The way my sister exudes perfection and grace now is far from just well behaving in our family home. She acts more like the wife of a governor; perhaps a First Lady. She playfully swats me with her hand towel as she wipes the flour from her hands.

They have a magnificent sound system throughout the house, and Christmas music plays gently in the background all day, every day. I hear Perry Como's version of "White Christmas," my parent's favorite. When we first arrive, it's wonderful, but by the time we leave, I'm ready for Christmas to be over. One more version of Jingle Bells and I'll explode.

We spend one entire day shopping at the mall. I usually bring gifts from home because we have things in Florida they can't find in New York, like beach items and sunny things. I also like to get a jump on my shopping so everything I look at isn't picked over. As a visitor, it's difficult to buy for the kids. We all experience the same problem when visiting each other, so I can't complain. Taking all that stuff home presents its challenges, but as the kids get older, it's become easier. They don't want toys as much as they want electronics and clothes. That's when shopping in New York is excellent; they offer the latest fashions on every corner. Technology? Well, that goes without saying, it's New York.

My children love my sister's kids, idolizing them as they grew up. When mine were tiny, the older cousins watched out for them, but as the years pass, they can hang out together and talk about things they all have in common. It's weird how that happens. They somehow catch up in age and maturity. I watch as they sit and talk together about everything. My girls love Brook and follow her around, wanting to be just like her. They talk about fashion and hairstyles, and at the moment, they all have the same style of hair with the same thickness and length.

Darin, David, and Daniel take Christian with them and treat him like one of the guys. The fact he's not afraid to try anything helped him fit in from an early age. They show him how to ride dirt bikes and four-wheelers, taking him to trails not far from the house. Many broken bones on those trips. When it comes to sustaining injuries from goofing off and trying different sports, none of the guys are excluded. They love swapping scar stories. Even my husband, Ian, joins in and shows his gunshot wound; explaining how a pirate shot him while trying to take over the Trinity.

The boys all love that story, even though they've heard it a number of times. Ian tells them while he was fighting one of the intruders on the boat, a stray bullet hit him. He was in the dark, and the pirates fired from a low boat.

So, no one knows who or how the attackers shot him. The bullet didn't come from the guy he was fighting. Ian says the guy didn't pull out a gun. After he was hit, at first, he couldn't feel it. His body was in battle mode. He talks of his Kung Fu training and the fighting moves, how the guy clocked him a couple of times in the head and knocked the wind out of him. The next thing he remembers is waking up in the hospital; feeling the pain and remembering what caused it. The nurses tell him he'd been unconscious for days. The doctors induced a coma because of the internal damage and pain. All the kids got noticeably quiet for a moment, then all started talking at once, contributing fight stories of their own to the conversation and pointing out the scars from those battles.

Mike Jr. has a scar on his forearm, where he got struck with a baseball bat. Pulling his sleeve up, he shows everyone the place where they cut him open, describing in gory detail the procedure he slept through on the operating table. He was practice swinging while waiting his turn when the player at bat hit a home run and accidentally hit him with the bat he threw aside while running for first base. It hit Mike's arm and broke it. He required surgery to pin the bone back in place.

His father, my brother, pushes his hair back on his scalp and shows a thin scar on his hairline where he was doing a penny flip at school off the monkey bars. He hit his head on another bar as he spun, splitting his head wide open. Mom, of course, had to go up to the school and take him to the emergency room.

All the dangerous situations Mike encountered as a cop, yet his scar is from the playground in elementary school. We count our blessings, yet still laugh and give him a hard time.

"Well, wait till you see this." Daniel pulled up a pant leg showing a large scar across his knee; the injury from a fall off a motorcycle before he became a professional dirt bike rider. The knee injury was the first of many caused by another careless or inexperienced rider hanging out with Daniel.

Daniel competes in X-games and motocross. He sports a wall of trophies and a large bank account he earned as an accomplished competitor. He can earn over $12,000 per event. He also makes plenty of endorsements for clothing gloves and other cycle accessories. He's enjoyed an excellent career in something he loves so much. He has the most stories to tell. He's broken both arms, one leg, cracked several ribs, and sprained both wrists. Motocross stardom comes with a price.

That doesn't keep the others from trying to make their stories more elaborate and continue to argue which one is the worst. Men are funny when it comes to comparing who has the worst war wound. Quite similar to fish stories.

Kathy always says, "it's all fun and games until we make a trip to the emergency room," laughing because we've all had to do that so many times. The girls make faces at them because they have no scars, and that sort of thing doesn't happen to them. The girls call the boys clumsy because they to play sports and surf, as well as snow ski.

Sean seems to have come through unscathed, as he has no scars to boast of either. All the guys find this amazing. Sean shrugs, feeling as though he just won a battle.

The storytelling is part of the gathering, and we enjoy every minute of it, new stories and antics that continue for years. The kids all grow, and their tales grow taller with each account. We all agree their dad's stories seem so much more outrageous than those of the kids.

Well, back to the Christmas holiday. With old-time Christmas tunes like "Have a holly jolly Christmas" by Burl Ives streaming through the house and football games on the

TV, it's a regular family Christmas. Kathy's house has several fireplaces, providing a warm glow to each room. For such a big place it has a very cozy atmosphere. I feel happy and content among my fifteen family members. Representing only my side of the family, none of Ian's made this trip. When the entire family gets together, usually at our house, we have twenty-two.

We stay a week doing all the fun things we can do only during visits to this climate. The kids get their fill of building snowmen and bobsledding. Everyone enjoys ice skating, and some did better than others. On our last day in New York, we split up into small groups and had a big snowball fight. Running and hiding around the yard, we made piles of snowballs and fired on anyone who dared to come within range. The epic day ended with a big pizza and movie night. We slept hard that night, exhausted by our snowball war.

Kathy's house and neighborhood aren't what I typically think of when I think of New York in the winter. I always think of the big city. All the houses in the neighborhood are beautifully lit up with Christmas lights and children playing in the snow, representing my idea of a good old-fashioned Christmas. By the time we return home, we miss the Christmas feeling of family fun and craziness when we're all together in one house for the holidays. Hard to believe, but we can't wait to do it again.

CHAPTER 6

John Connor, Ian's youngest brother, leads a busy and complicated life. When I say complicated, I'm referring to how we perceive it, although I'm sure he doesn't view it that way. What do we really know about others and how they live their lives? I will learn as my life progresses through the years that what we see and what's real aren't always the same.

John's a briefcase and Armani suit kind of guy. His company is either producing something technologically innovative or improving existing products. He's an innovator in the computer industry. His brilliance and profound knowledge of his field are widely known and appreciated by many. Innovation is what keeps his company alive. He strives to be on top of the game.

When the first personal computer was introduced in 1975, it immediately piqued John's interest. He was in high school, but even then, knew exactly what he wanted in life. His father bought him a computer a few years later. He studied and researched all there was to know about how it worked. He wrote down his ideas and went on to study business and finance at the University of Southern California. He worked hard for years and finally started his business in software for computers. Not everyone was on board and considered it a shot in the dark, but it became one of the largest money-making industries in the world.

John now has a piece of it, and his business has been thriving for years. With technology today, the sky is the limit. He's no Bill Gates, but he's earned his place on the Internet, computer, and software business. His offices are in Fountain Valley in a small business district. When looking for a place to locate his business, he lucked out on a location so close to home.

He's joined the millionaires of the world.

John keeps us posted on the care of his mother, but we hear little about his personal life, his dating, or social interests. I've tried a number of times to pry out who he might be seeing currently, but he only smiles and either says, "no one," or changes the subject, preferring to talk about us. He says he hasn't found his soulmate, and also admits to commitment issues. I know exactly how he feels. I had the same problem when I met Ian.

John's hang out is the Balboa, where he spends any free time with his friends. The Balboa Peninsula is a finger that juts out of the land next to Newport Beach, and is unlike any place in California.

Sailboats glide in the harbor or on the ocean side. The view from anywhere on this little island is fabulous. I love the island feel with its ferry boats bringing cars back and forth to the shopping and restaurants on the water's edge.

John has always shown an interest in yachts over fifty feet in length. I still wonder why he doesn't just buy one and keep it at the house tied to the dock, the dock that's been the home to many boats owned by the Connors for many years. Heaven knows he can afford a yacht that size, but he remains quiet about that topic as well.

He's at the house so much, perhaps he needs time away, and Balboa Harbor must be that place. We don't all understand what it required to be a caregiver for a family member. We're sure it's a huge time investment, and his commitment to running a company day in and day out is a huge responsibility. His life is as busy as any I've ever seen, yet he never misses a family gathering.

All the cousins love John. He's their center of attention and boasts the best stories of success in business. The kids love listening to his stories. He's a connoisseur of all things expensive, John exudes style and confidence in everything he does.

John tells us about his travels, including meeting several Presidents, such as the Bushes, Senior and George W. He met Clinton along with some of the country's wealthiest and influential people.

Bill Gates and Steve Jobs top his list of exciting people he's met in his travels, and his stay with a prince in the Trump Tower. He tells the kids about the yachts of Balboa and who owns them. He also met celebrities living in Newport, such as John Wayne and the Sheik, who owns a 120-foot yacht that frequents the harbor in Balboa. The people he meets there are friendly, not what you might expect of celebrities and television stars.

John explains how the way to distinguish a fine wine from one commercially produced and the difference between wine and sparkling wine as opposed to champagne. Wine in French is "du Vin," he tells them. They all repeat the word. John takes the time to explain what goes into making some excellent yet inexpensive wines pleasing to the palate. "A glass of cheap wine can taste good, but be mindful they come with a hell of a hangover." Of course, he didn't start talking about wine until they were older. Always the proper uncle.

"Every man needs a good suit," he would always tell the boys. They rolled their eyes, but he insisted it's a requirement. As the boys got older, he told them charm and manners are far more important than being the richest man or the most handsome man in the room. "People remember you holding the door for them, and the fact you said please and thank you. That, boys, will get you the girl."

I smile when he gives them this good advice. They'd laugh at each other's expense. Sometimes the boys nodded in agreement, other times they didn't believe his advice would work.

John has a passion for art and music. He owns beautiful French paintings from the eighteen century. They're certainly museum-worthy and probably priceless, and I wonder how he acquired them. He talks about them occasionally, but unlike me, doesn't seem concerned someone might want to steal them.

Cooking is only one of John's many talents. With practice, he's proudly recreated many of his mother's beautiful recipes. One of the all-time favorites among the adults is Chateaubriand and roasted zucchini with garlic potatoes.

The kids loved his lasagna, and I was happy to let him take over the kitchen, content to throw together the salad right before we ate. John, the poor guy, would spend the entire day in the kitchen, creating the delicious masterpiece in a pan. He always listened to music playing in the background. One thing we share is love of eighties music. I can't listen to Hair Cut One Hundred without thinking of dancing with John and Ian at my wedding, to Love plus one "where does it go from here? Is it down to the lake I fear?"

We always have a good time when John visits. He loves movies as much as music. We always enjoy sitting down and watching something together. John preferred old classics like Humphrey Bogart and Lauren Bacall movies, but that was asking too much of the kids, so we'd find something we all agreed on. The family watched many a family flick while loading up on popcorn and candy. I suspect we watched every Disney movie in existence, not to mention The Goonies and Stand by me. Taylor's favorite is Mack n Me. We moved on to the Hobbit and the Twilight movies, not to forget Joe Dirt.

John never visits without bringing gifts for everyone. I tell him all the time it's not necessary, but he loves spoiling the kids. He puts thought into each gift, knows their interests, and buys accordingly. Sometimes he buys silly presents representing that person on the sense of humor side. I secretly love it, but the family bonding with the kids is essential with or without gifts. He tried to buy us another dog, but I talked him out of it with threats of bodily harm.

The business John is much different than the uncle John the kids know and love. He researches knock-knock jokes before he visits and tries to stump them with witty what-if stories. As they got older, his jokes matured. What a funny guy. Who else but John would put in the time to keep the relationships fresh and vibrant?

Ian, John, and I would spend many evenings drinking expensive wine and talking into the night. While he didn't openly discuss his dating life, he offered much regarding business and finances.

He offered tidbits about where to invest our money. He's quite knowledgeable and I respect his advice. I remember back when cell phones were introduced, he advised us to invest in wireless phones. At the time, we thought it odd, but he was adamant about the future of wireless. I'm glad we took his advice.

Our visits to California staying with John and Mrs. Connor were no less memorable. John always had a fun place to visit. We ate at many great restaurants while frequenting local historical sites in Huntington Beach and surrounding areas. He could go on about the history of the places we went on our outings. Ian and I know the history of the oil fields in Huntington, but John enjoyed talking about it so much, we let him tell us.

In 1920, the first oil well was brought in as a producing well. They grew from one well to fifty-nine producing wells. A conflict emerged over whether to produce oil or support a resort community, but all ended well, as they have both.

The offshore platforms for drilling oil and natural gas of the coast started as early as 1948. All very interesting. We love talking about our hometown. Now and then, John surprises us with information we didn't know. I crack up when I refer to him as a deep well of knowledge, but neither John nor Ian acknowledge my sense of humor and aren't amused by my comment.

We discussed places no longer in business. The Golden Bear night club, operating from 1923 to 1986, located on the corner of Pacific Coast Highway and Main St., was an icon, a place to watch our favorite singers perform. I reminded them of Villa Sweden, a family restaurant Main St. as well, in business from 1961 until 1990. A lot of surf shops once on Pacific Coast Highway and Main St. are no longer open. The little restaurant Egg Heaven where we occasionally ate breakfast has also closed down.

We all frequented the Surf theater that initially opened in 1925. It changed its name to the Surf theater in 1941 and closed its doors for good in 1979. I don't know anyone who didn't recall fond memories of watching movies at that old theater. As kids, we watched many surfing movies there, from the *Endless Summer* to *Five Summer Stories*, and every surfing flick in between.

Cruising in John's car, we listened to old tunes by Frank Sinatra and the Rat Pack and other music popular before the seventies. I always got a kick out of listening; the kids—not so much, but one look from me let them know we weren't going to argue about it. So, Mack the knife, "Oh the shark has pretty teeth dear," played through its entirety without interruption. Although Mr. Louis Armstrong was the original composer, we listened to the Bobby Darin version.

Aside from the music, the kids looked forward to the visits. Mrs. Connor was a wealth of knowledge as well. She talked us into riding to the Pottery Shack in Laguna Beach off the Pacific Coast Highway one day, just to get out of the house. Everyone except for the kids remembered the old guy who, for many years, stood on the side of the road and waved at motorists. Little shops and handmade pottery are included among the stores. We'd stand and watch beautiful vases and little characters created in my favorite, the glass blowing area.

History is a beautiful thing, and I'm glad to be a part of the beach culture. When we were kids, my parents used to ride out here with us and walk around for hours. We'd all pick out something and eat lunch in one of the beach restaurants on the way home, like The Ruben E. Lee, another historic site. The restaurant sat on a one-hundred-twenty-foot paddle boat tied to the dock in Newport Beach for decades. They served excellent food.

The restaurant was torn down many years before, so we would have to pick something else. We all chose Cantonese food at Li's. We've all been eating there since we were kids. Christian, Taylor, and Anna love it too. It's hard to beat Mandarin duck, noodles, and stir fry. All our visits to the Connors were similar. We ate at a nostalgic favorite restaurant at least once every visit.

John and his mother lived a quiet, peaceful life in Huntington Harbor, California. The beauty of the harbor and the homes on the water's edge never changes. Mrs. Connor passed quietly in

Denise Ann Stock

her sleep at ninety-two years old one evening during the twin's first year of college. We remembered her as a beautiful woman married in her twenties, who raised three strong, intelligent boys, and always professed her faith in God; she went home to be with Dr. Connor in heaven.

John remained in the big house on the water. He loved the house more than anyone, and we all agreed he belonged there. I'm glad someone is maintaining it. We all recall so many good memories and would hate to see it go to someone else. We continue to go every year and enjoy a traditional thanksgiving, forging new memories while reminiscing the past.

CHAPTER 7

Ian's brother Darryl Connor and his wife Renee raised four children in an environment most might consider strange. How they make their living is a constant source of controversy. The mystery took its toll on Trevor, the oldest of the four, who showed his discontent with the family business. When they were young, there were no problems. Kids didn't talk much about how their parents made a living; they didn't care, but it became the subject of gossip in Trevor's middle school years.

Answering questions as to what went on at their private home was too much for him. They lived a close-knit family life just like everyone else, and it wasn't anyone's business. For Trevor, it was different, and he was embarrassed by people growing marijuana who didn't care that it was illegal. Everything he learned at school told him marijuana was "bad." Darryl tried to explain why they grew the plants and the medicinal benefits. Hemp was useful in making industrial products, rope, clothing, paper, shoes, and much more.

He educated Trevor on how THC and CBD were beneficial to cancer patients suffering from nausea. Studies showed it helped patients suffering from AIDS and other illnesses to gain much needed weight. Pain sufferers found relief from this product as well. Darryl was disappointed Trevor approached this with a close-minded view. Nothing could dissuade the boy who refused to acknowledge anything good about cannabis or growing hemp, despite the many benefits.

The arguments continued until Trevor left home. Renee tried giving Trevor his freedom and be proud of his personal opinion, but he believed he was right about everything, and no one else's views were relevant. He would not see or understand anyone's point of view but his own. The fighting often got ugly, with Trevor saying hateful things.

He accused his parents of being "old hippie druggies," not connected to the real world. He often would call them other hurtful things. The name-calling got the whole family angry at each other. Alan and Sherry took their parent's side in the arguments. They told him he was being unreasonable and mean.

Being a hippie was kind of Renee's thing. She'd always lived a carefree lifestyle, never compromising with society and regimented life in the city. I never saw it as wrong. She loved living off the land and growing her vegetable garden. She was organic before it was popular. I can't help but think of the song "Woodstock" by Crosby, Stills, Nash & Young when I think of her. "We've got to get ourselves back to the garden." She's a mellow hippie and vegetarian, but was never addicted to drugs, and was against alcohol and never drank. She's a beautiful person inside and out, and I felt bad for her during this time with Trevor. She loved all her children, and her oldest son turning against her was sad.

So, what if she smoked pot on occasion? Everything in moderation. Renee always said, and believed, "it was a natural substance created by God." She, too, received a college education from Berkley. So, don't let the hippie garb and mellow personality fool you. Renee is an intelligent and educated woman. She didn't deserve the hateful treatment her son showed towards her and Darryl. She never presented herself to her kids any other way. She was open and honest, hard-working, and a good mother.

Renee was an extraordinary accountant and knowledgeable about finances. She was highly organized with the family business and had an uncanny mind for money; she knew where every dime in their household went. Her financial skills helped to grow the cannabis business and buy thousands of acres of land.

Alan and Sherry weren't bothered by the family business. Maybe they didn't care or buy into the questions and gossip around town and school. They accepted it as a farm and did chores like any other children growing up on farmland. Many of the families in this area lived the same style of life on the farm.

They had no problems with kids at school, but Trevor, on the other hand, got into fights telling lies about what grew on the farm, and then later over what was legal and what was not. We don't think he ever really understood it was a project at the beginning paid for by the government, and indeed, legitimate. He wouldn't accept it, and nothing would change his mind.

Trevor started talking about moving away during his junior year of high school. He wanted to be far away from this kind of life. The talk of moving continued until one day, he packed up and moved to San Francisco shortly after his eighteenth birthday. He became a merchant marine and was gone most of the time. We saw him occasionally on our visits to California, but he stopped making the family trips to our house. He met a girl named Cora not long after he moved to San Francisco, and spent his off time with her, and holidays with her family. We had the opportunity to meet Cora a couple of times. Her family was in the crabbing business.

Trevor and Cora both enjoyed life on the sea, and we felt good seeing him happy. Unfortunately, Trevor seemed to not want her around any of us. They dated off and on for years. Sherry told me bits and pieces of what he was doing. She made it her business to know everyone else's. She said it was an art.

Sherry's the most fun of my nieces. She turned into a party girl in her twenties. Always fun, always happy, with an infectious smile and contagious laugh. Her bright and sunny personality, evident from an early age, always drew attention, and does to this day. The girl made friends with everyone she met, and people loved to be around her.

Sherry was a typical girl interested in boys, horses, and her friends. She performed well in school, but never showed interest in going to college. She was happy to live a simple life out in the backcountry of Northern California.

Her goals were to marry a man just like her father, someone who owned his own ranch or farm, and wanted to mimic her parent's lifestyle.

Somewhere along the line, things changed, as they often do. Sherry got a job, and her life turned for the better. Happiness was in her future; she was that kind of girl. After graduating from high school, she worked in town at a local hotel. She started at the front desk, and after a short time, became the manager. The position fit her perfectly, and she met lots of people every day from everywhere.

Sherry spent her days talking and laughing with people from all over. She started traveling with the company as well. Her job took her to hotels in different states to assist the management set up at new locations. She would come and stay with us when her travels took her to Florida. She made great money after a few quick promotions and without a degree. She'd found her niche.

Sherry's life was perfect. She had a fantastic career and traveled frequently; nothing compared to the life of living on a farm with a husband and a bunch of kids she thought she wanted. We were all so happy for her, and now we find it funny how we accepted the picture at face value.

We never questioned a girl her age working at a Holiday Inn would move up so quickly and travel to places like Jamaica, Mexico, and South America. She even traveled to India and Amsterdam. By the time she was twenty-five, she said she wanted to buy a house. From nineteen to twenty-five years old, she'd built a successful career in the hotel business.

She moved into an apartment not long after she got the promotion to Manager. Her life was busy and satisfying. She had a boyfriend, a Rastafarian who seem to be enamored of her. She, of course, was crazy for him. He was as mellow a soul as Sherry's mother, Renee, and was interested in the family business. He voiced his opinions on the benefits of Ganja in almost every conversation.

Sherry's life and career moving along as it should all looked and sounded perfect. Why, when it comes to our children, do we not see the signs? We accept everything at face value without question. Our family painted a pretty picture around every scenario, without a clue that maybe something else was going on during her travels, like, perhaps she was making a little too much money managing a hotel. Ask no questions, you get no answers. We put our heads in the sand and proclaimed success.

Yes, we're all fools of our worlds. We didn't know it, and certainly didn't want to think the worst of our perfect lives, so we laughed at the funny antics of Sherry's travels and marveled at all the places she went on business with the Holiday Inn management team. Life was great because we believed so.

Alan, the youngest of Darryl's boys, was happy to stay at home. His friends grew up in the same lifestyle. Many cannabis farm families in this small town attended the same schools from elementary to high school.

In 1988, a judge ruled that the DEA hindered cannabis research and allowed them to use the drug claiming it was therapeutic. In 1992, San Francisco recognized marijuana for medicinal use. Things were happening, and Alan started in the family business at this point. Seeing the headlines in the paper and the word around town, he took an interest, and it became his future.

He followed in his father's footsteps and worked hard on the farm, learning everything he could about growing. He studied horticulture just like his father, bringing new and innovative ways to produce different types of cannabis for different effects. He proudly explained the difference between indica that produces euphoric high versus sativa, a non-psychoactive compound, as well as the difference between indoor and outdoor strains. He discussed the process of creating hybrids with crossbreeding as drilling down to a specific type of plant that targets certain things to help people. He fascinated us with his research.

Alan's goal was to take over the family business one day and bring it into the next century with modern technics and science as his style of farming. Darry and Jill were so proud of his enthusiasm. His knack in transforming the business was brilliant. He introduced them to indoor agriculture, convincing them a grow house (greenhouse) was the future, and recommending hydroponics. He experimented with lights and air and researched the effects of C02 on plants.

Not long after, they built a sizeable greenhouse to control the temperature and lighting for optimum growth—studying the effects of certain fertilizers on the plants. They used timers to regulate the amount of water from the irrigation and lights to the plants each day. Their approach proved to be the way of future cannabis farmers.

Alan was amazing and became an integral part of the change taking place in California for legal recreational use as well as the medical use of marijuana. He belongs to a council that regulated growers—studying the background and prohibition history, up to the mid-seventies, when pot was dropped from a felony to a misdemeanor for carrying under an ounce. He was an integral part of the legalization set in motion and passed by vote. Acting as a spokesperson to lawmakers helped establish standards.

The future is excellent, and the Connors sat in the middle of big business. Who would ever think that smoking a little weed after school or growing a pot plant in your parent's back yard would have turned into this pioneering adventure? They created a growing family business that would be a part of the next generation.

Alan met Susie, a lovely girl in college he continued with in a relationship after he graduated. She ended up saying, "I do" years later. She always said she loved Alan from the beginning, and knew he was the one the first time she saw him in the library at school. Alan was quiet about his relationship, but we knew he felt the same way about Susie.

CHAPTER 8

My brother Mike and his family lived a peaceful life up in the hills of Norco, with his horses, the trails, and open spaces. Considering he was a member of the original crew of what became the S.W.A.T., a dangerous job he volunteered for when it all began, he saw a lot of things ordinary people couldn't imagine. Yet, he remained a good father and husband, not letting it affect his family. He never admitted he suffered from post-traumatic stress disorder. Back then, nobody knew much about PTSD.

Mike relied on his pride and joy, a big black stallion to keep him calm. The horse has four white socks and what appeared to be almost a white star on his face. Mike named him Captain. Captain was hard to handle at times; scars of abuse on his hide indicated he was savagely beaten before he came to live on my brother's ranch. Yet, somehow, the horse and Mike had a calming effect on one another.

The animal control found Captain roaming the hills alone when my brother got him. He was mean and disagreeable, and no one wanted him. They told people he would be suitable only for stud service.

Mike refused to allow that to happen. He took his time and slowly earned Captain's trust, feeding him by hand for months with small treats. One day, he told the horse they were going for a ride. I laughed at my brother, thinking this big animal understood his words, but that's what they did. They went for a long ride in the hills as individuals and came back many hours later as a team—partners with a special bond. Captain, although high-spirited, will let anyone ride him now, and not a horse for the inexperienced rider, but will eat only from Mike's hand.

We think horrible people fed and beat Captain, making him so untrusting of anyone with food. I can't imagine what this horse endured before my brother got him.

Mike's work life was stressful yet rewarding, so he purposely made his home life calm and spent every free moment with Jill, Mike Jr., and Sean. Both boys would follow in his footsteps and join the local Sheriff's department. They both attended the police academy, and Sean became a K-9 handler.

They all loved horses and went horseback riding together almost every day. The houses in their neighborhood were accommodating to people with horses. Small stables and great riding trails were found along with the usual sidewalks. Having so much in common with their neighbors, they always got together with parties and barbeques. We enjoyed coming to visit and joining them at these functions.

My kids always called the people of the neighborhood horse people. My brother's family and friends loved the reference and embraced it. Much care goes into owning these big animals. They need to be fed, and their owners must exercise and groom them daily.

The vet visited them regularly, and the farrier visited their home or the local stable. Since the horses walked on paved streets, many owners had their horses shod to protect their hooves from damage and wearing down too quickly.

Everyone seems to have the same devotion to the horse world. This group of people loved these animals and enjoyed getting out in the country, seeing it from atop their horse—so different a life for us.

Along with the horse people, they participated in football and baseball. Mike Sr. played on the adult softball team with the Sheriff's department, the boys for the YMCA athletics team. Jill was a stay at home mom, caring for horses, rabbits, the dog, and family and never missed any of her men's games while juggling some Saturdays between all three.

Jill's passion was horses. She and her family always owned them when she was growing up. Jill introduced the horse world to my brother, but the love never interrupted all the boy's game days. The kids of many of her riding friends and neighbors were on the teams, so they either carpooled or rode in a convoy of minivans or SUVs to the events. The weekends were crazy when the boys were young. I expect that's standard for most families.

When the boys were in high school, they received the awful news that Jill had breast cancer. That diagnosis devastated us all. How could this happen to someone so young and healthy? It wasn't fair, but cancer is not or ever will be fair, and doesn't discriminate for age or gender. When cancer attacks the individual, it attacks the family. Unless you've experienced this yourself, you can't imagine the pain and suffering of the entire family.

We rallied around her for support, and although she fought it with all her might for five years, she eventually tired of her quality of life and refused treatment when the oncologist prescribed chemo and radiation a third time.

They wouldn't guarantee the chemotherapy would eliminate the cancer, so Jill chose to live out her remaining days without the medicine. She didn't want to be sick for her son's social events, games, and proms. She died the year after Sean graduated from high school, two years after declining treatment. Mike Sr. and Mike Jr. felt devastated and sad, and knowing the end is coming doesn't lessen the pain. We thought Sean would never come out of the emotional black hole he sunk into.

Everyone handles grief differently. At first, Sean hated Jill for not getting the treatments. They argued and fought. In his mind, he thought he could force her to take the medication to help her survive. "She's abandoning her family," he said.

He continually ranted and threw tantrums, insisting the medicine would help if she would let it. Yet, for Jill, the side effects of treatment at the time was worse than the disease. She received a double mastectomy in the first year of her diagnosis, but that and the radiation wasn't enough to prevent the cancer from recurring. She tried to tell Sean there was no guarantee of life, even taking medicine. He withdrew from all of us. He said he hated us.

He wouldn't discuss his mother, and any attempt would throw him into a deep depression. He was angry at Ian for not helping find a cure for her at the Mayo Clinic. We couldn't make him understand that Ian was a heart surgeon, and breast cancer wasn't his field of expertise. For years Ian did a lot of research, and we helped Mike when looking for the best oncologist we could find.

In the end, the treatment for the cancer was too much for Jill to handle. She got down to 65 pounds at one point before choosing to quit chemotherapy. We adopted the holistic medicine approach. We called her with the new vitamins we found and offered advice we read from medical journals that might help, in hopes to keep her strong enough to fight the cancer.

Jill seemed as though she was becoming healthy again, and for a few beautiful years, her hair grew back, and she gained back the weight she lost. She spent time with her family, making the most of every moment. The perfect mom never missed an event while she was alive. She became bedridden and was gone quickly after that. I remember holding her hand one visit, and she quietly admitted she was scared. I remember listening to her speak of her fears; particularly of leaving the boys and Darryl alone. What if there was no heaven, and this was it? Her life just ceased.

I whispered in her ear, "how could this be it? God is bigger than this life. I believe God has a place in heaven for you, and I'll see you there one day." A tear rolled down my cheek as I rested my head on her pillow next hers and remained that way for a few minutes. I knew her time on earth was coming to an end and couldn't imagine what Jill might be feeling; yet knew the pain for us would remain; she'd pass to a greater place.

We stayed quiet for a bit, then she squeezed my hand and said with a smile, "I believe in God."

I said, "good, you know everything will be okay. He will be with you and make sure the boys and Darryl are good." I believe that with all my heart, but I sure hurt inside knowing how much we'll all miss her.

Mike Jr. displayed a strength no one expected. He helped care for Jill while going to school and helping my brother around the house. He tried to stay close to Sean, helping him through the struggle of Jill's passing. I worried he might need someone to lean on too.

He never showed much emotion or weakness, and cried only briefly at the funeral, before returning to the pillar of strength the family needed. I hugged him and let him know we were there if they needed us for anything. Both Mike, my brother, and Mike Jr. held it together, showing little emotion.

They handled their sadness and pain differently than most people, dealing with their grief by remaining strong and staying busy. At least I hoped they were but couldn't be sure. No matter how they dealt with it, their lives would go on. I hoped happiness would find its way back to them all.

CHAPTER 9

Kathy and Michael live a typical New York suburban family life. They own a big beautiful house and are raising four brilliant and loving children. Although Kathy never worked outside the home, she led a hectic life, driving the kids to school and practices after. Darin was a football player. He started when he was four or five if I remember, and they saw a football career in his future after only a few years playing the game. Darin was so serious about practice and strength training, and he could run.

David was Kathy's try-everything kid. He played t-ball, football, played hockey off and on, and loved all snow sports. He was into skiing, snowboarding, and snow sledding. He'd try anything fun, but never connected with any one sport. He's that all-around good kid, with a simple and unassuming attitude, never one to get ruffled about anything.

Daniel, the youngest son, loved the outdoors. He played with the older boys and learned his skills early to keep up. From snowmobile to motorcycle, Daniel was faster and better than the others. He competed in motocross at age 6, so that was another sport Kathy made sure to attend and encourage. I know she was anxious as well. Motocross races are dangerous. Watching your son fall and possibly get hit by another dirt bike is terrifying.

Brook, their only daughter, was a bright, charismatic child. As the youngest and only girl, she fought for her place among the boys. She's a typical girlie girl, with no interest in sports, not even watching her brothers. She took dance and tumbling lessons, and some cheerleading while she was young. These interests lasted only up to the age of ten, when her focus turned to fashion, music, and boys.

Her room, like all rooms in the house, was custom designed by Kathy's favorite interior designer, and posters of boy bands cover her walls. A built-in bookcase sitting against one short wall is home to every CD of her favorite music. She owns a spectacular collection. I used to pride myself on my music collection as a kid but can't hold a candle to her.

Brook probably attended more live concerts by the time she was seventeen than I have in my life. Michael took her to these shows in the beginning. Bless him, and I wonder if he wore earplugs. Brook dedicated all her free time to music, yet never wanted to play an instrument or take singing classes. I've heard her singing along in her room with these CDs, but she's never shown aspiration of becoming an artist in the music industry.

No matter her girlie and boy craziness. Brook eventually earned a law degree and passed the bar. The idea grabbed hold in high school, and she studied hard. Her determination earned her an acceptance to Penn State. After graduation and internship, she set her sights on becoming a partner in the law firm where her dad was now a partner.

Kathy stayed busy with a large household and servants. She planned extravagant parties and events for Michael and his office. Kathy made reservations and set up the banquet room with Michael's secretary when he entertained clients. Michael was a corporate lawyer, so his clients were wealthy and flaunted their self-importance. Despite these demands on her time, she kept the children in check and maintained her home.

This picture might appear perfect, but tiny fractures mar the paint. We all assumed everything was great. My sister never let on how much this life taxed her; that Michael's busy lifestyle wasn't at all what she wanted out of life. She loved Michael and the kids dearly but had no life of her own.

Kathy tried to tell me she suspected Michael of cheating on her, but she was too respectable to even voice the accusation. He worked long hours at the office, and always had a reason why he needed to go somewhere all day on Saturdays, missing the boy's games. She said the little things didn't add up, yet had no real proof of wrongdoing, only speculation. She didn't mention this was on her mind until it all blew up one day.

She's my sister, and I should've noticed something was wrong. We talked on the phone and saw each other on holidays. Why didn't I notice she was coming unraveled around the edges? She kept herself busy all the time, was the biggest cheerleader her family had, and was there for them, no matter what they did. They all loved her dearly, yet no one noticed she was unhappy. Perhaps she kept it so well camouflaged. She had me believing she was happy with their perfect family life.

We don't often recognize other people's trials. I thought my sister's life was perfect. She exuded strength and perfection, and never complained; it wasn't who she was. All you needed to do was look at her home and her family. They were all doing something constructive with their lives, everyone except Kathy, who lived for everyone else, making sure they were the best they could be.

I thought she was doing an excellent job of raising her family. They were wealthy and successful, what more could you want? Your children are healthy and well adjusted; each proficient at something Kathy helped mold. Even Michael, her husband.

She moved from her home in California when the children were just babies, relocating over three-thousand miles from our family. She's dedicated her life to them, yet no one ever asked if she was truly happy. We assumed this is what she wanted, yet we all know what assume means.

The trouble started with Kathy crying over little things, but no one thought she might be depressed. They felt she was being silly, overreacting to a situation that hadn't gone as planned, because she was a perfectionist. We are all to blame for not recognizing just because she never complained that nothing was ever wrong.

When we finally discussed it, she said she had everything, so if she complained, she'd sound petty and ungrateful. In my mind, I agreed. Not that she was an ungrateful person, but people would think that. After all, she had her health, where our brother's wife died of cancer. What could compare to your wife having cancer? What gives her a right to complain?

The reality is, it's not a fair comparison. Bad things happen to good people, and everyone's lives are different. How can we presume having money provides happiness? I thought maybe she just needed a break, that she and Michael should discuss a vacation with only the two of them. If he wasn't aware, she needed to tell him.

After we talked, I was sure she would tell Michael. They did eventually talk, and she asked him if there was someone else. He felt as if she'd slapped him in the face, from the shock, He never wanted a relationship with anyone else, thinking she was silly to suggest such a thing. He insisted there'd never been anyone in his life since the day he met her, and surely, she should know she was his everything, soulmate, and love of his life.

But Kathy didn't know that at the time. She felt unloved and unwanted; if she'd felt any different, maybe she wouldn't feel depressed. Knowing Kathy as I do, she's too proud; she never would've voiced it anyway. Mike, in her mind, would think her petty and needy. In the end, nobody could have done anything to change her feelings.

One day, for the first time in her life, Kathy suffered a panic attack. She was unable to catch her breath and didn't know what to do. She told us later nothing like that ever happened before. She was walking down the hall, felt anxious, and then blacked out.

The housekeeper heard Kathy's fall, ran to her, and tried to get her up. Kathy was unfocused and not responding coherently. The EMTs thought she'd suffered a heart attack and transported her to the emergency room. After several hours and several tests, the doctors said Kathy suffered a panic attack, and drinking too much diet soda wasn't helping. She hadn't been eating, and drinking the caffeine raised her blood pressure to an unsafe level.

If she continued, she might have a heart attack or stroke. Please don't tell me my sister might have died from drinking diet soda. We all drank them to avoid gaining weight from sugary soda.

The hospital staff talked to Michael about what happened physically and described Kathy's mental state. They told him she'd been suffering from depression for some time. She'd reached her breaking point, and it affected her health. We just witnessed the proverbial wake-up call.

Michael's phone call scared me, and I flew in the next morning. He said she was out of danger, but I didn't agree. He also told me he's the cause of the panic attack and felt sorry he didn't take her seriously.

As Kathy lay sedated in a hospital bed after her incident, I began to understand. I felt hurt that I didn't help her and promised her things would change. Her kids are almost grown and doing what they want with their lives. She created the best for all of them, and the sacrifice was extraordinary. Now it was her time. She needed to work on herself. We had to figure out what it was she wanted and needed.

Michael felt devastated. We all saw he loved Kathy so much, but busy with earning a living, her own husband didn't realize that sometimes he ignored the things she wanted or needed. He prided himself in providing for the family and giving her everything he thought she desired. As her husband, he blamed himself for her situation. The children all felt the same way. They all took the blame for not caring or being aware.

As they all gathered around her, promising to make things better, I felt for them, but no one should accept blame. Each family member was living life; and striving to be the best at something is all-consuming, and no one saw this coming. No one wanted them to quit striving for their ultimate goals, but Michael, Darin, David, Daniel, and Brook, each needed to figure out a way to pursue their goals more independently.

Kathy's situation wouldn't change overnight. Everyone needed to work to help her overcome this pain and helplessness. My living in Florida would make it hard to be there for her, and I'd need to find ways to encourage her to do things for herself.

Michael will be the most important person to introduce change. At the moment, we all felt helpless.

I stayed with Kathy the entire week she lay in the hospital, and a week later, she was able to return home. Once I knew she and the kids were okay, I flew back to Florida to my own family. I was happy to see Michael and the kids care for Kathy.

The truth was Michael and Kathy didn't need me in their marital business. I wasn't going to voice the obvious; that they must pay attention to each other. They need to talk more, but I know nothing ever happened, and there was no one else. Not once during my visit did Kathy repeat her suspicions of Michael's infidelity.

Michael and I discussed the situation, and he told me he's never been unfaithful. His reaction to me, even thinking he had, was all the proof I needed. He felt guilty Kathy would even think there could ever be someone else in his life.

Michael did admit he was selfish. He had become so focused on making a name for himself, he forgot Kathy was the center of it all. She's his world, and the fact she felt unimportant or cheated on, well, the pain showed in his face.

I knew Michael needed to focus on Kathy and not only on his career. They'd have plenty of time to talk it out. The entire family would need to talk, and each one needed to figure out a way to pitch in and improve their life as a family.

The kids all stepped up and did things on their own. While Kathy was still their center, and attended competitions and games, she allocated time to herself as well. They helped her with the house and preparing for big parties and entertaining. Michael assigned his staff to take care of clients instead of Kathy, which reduced the burden on his wife. His practice continued to thrive, and they could afford to hire the people to help Kathy.

Their life went on, and it took months of talking as a family before Kathy skimmed the surface of her mental illness. We found it difficult to vocalize the fact there is such a thing, but when we took the first step of saying the word, "depression," the healing began. Kathy discovered she wasn't the only one.

By speaking and treating it, she found many others suffered the same problems.

As the years passed, Kathy learned to cope with her condition. Darin, David, Daniel, and Brook were all great, and they all went on to follow their desired path in life. Darin, the oldest son, played football, and although never played pro football, received an excellent education, and eventually opened a sporting goods store. Later he added a successful online business where the items he offered could be ordered by customers and shipped directly to their home.

David, the second oldest son, expressed no interest in continuing with his education. He worked construction after graduating high school, and never looked back. He's always had a job making good money and is happy with his decision to work outside and build things with his hands.

Daniel's pro motorcycle career blossomed. He traveled year around and bought a beautiful truck and trailer to haul his motorcycles and gear to each competition. The four-wheel-drive Ford truck and trailer with his name and sponsor painted on the sides in black and red was an awesome sight. I was amazed to hear he tinkered around on his racing bikes and learned to quickly repair them himself when necessary. No one in our family is mechanically inclined, so tinkering was an understatement; he knew what he was doing.

The motocross career is synonymous with injuries. Daniel suffered broken bones, bruised ribs, and sustained a long list of cuts requiring stitches. Kathy and I talked about him all the time. She worried about him and whether all the injuries would affect his health.

When he came to Florida for motocross events, he always stayed with us. Daniel and Christian got along so well. They hung out as much as possible on these visits, and we attended some of the events.

To our eyes, Daniel never exhibited strange behavior. He always acted polite and had fun. The situation was yet another we should have seen yet didn't. Daniel, at one point in his career, suffered a broken collar bone and a fractured pelvis, but the whole family wrote it off as injuries accompanying his chosen career.

Daniel was laid up for weeks recovering. He was able to control the pain with prescribed pills, but we wondered, was he taking them only when needed? For the next ten years, he abused the drugs prescribed by his doctor, and at one point, was taking twenty pills a day. Later, people wondered how he survived with that much of the drug in his system? How did he avoid an overdose? Like many who abuse drugs, his body built an immunity.

No one spoke of this. We accepted the fact his pain was professionally maintained by a doctor's prescription. Christian said later he saw Daniel take pills during one of his stays at our house during a party. He didn't think anything of it because Daniel functioned normally. Kathy and Michael never questioned it because Daniel's orthopedic surgeon continued to refill the prescription for pain management. What they didn't know was Daniel could get them almost anywhere, and that's just what he did.

Daniel eventually started showing signs of an addict, but no one paid attention. They didn't know what to look for in his behavior. How could anyone know? He seemed to contract the flu a lot, and we later realized he was experiencing withdrawals on those days. No one understood how much work it took him to maintain his lifestyle in secret, taking small doses on days he was with family to hide his addiction.

He also competed less, and the times he signed up for an event, he wasn't as focused on winning, falling back and not showing his normal competitive drive. The excitement he felt at the beginning of his career was dissipating. The truck also got in strange accidents, unexplained dents and scratches began covering the fenders and bumpers that should have raised a question or two. He always insisted it wasn't his fault, and naturally, his family believed and defended him.

Everyone thought he was just tired. He suffered so many injuries over the years, the realization his career was coming to an end was inevitable. Although his wall of trophies indicated his accomplishments, extreme sports were too tough on his body.

He earned a lot of money, and his success in this motocross racing and trick riding was evident by his following in the racing world. The time to retire from racing had come, and he decided to move on.

Daniel found many different jobs. He's a popular guy, and everyone liked him. Since he owned a condo and lived alone, we were oblivious to the fact he either arrived late or left early from his job, sometimes failing to show up at all. He made excuses for why he couldn't work for that company, then easily found another job.

Daniel's behavior continued like this for a long time. He skipped days from work to pill chase. Then the condo fell into foreclosure, and he had to tell his father he needed money. His savings and investments were gone.

All the money earned and invested from motocross spent on what? Finally, once Daniel admitted pills were a problem, Kathy and Michael quickly convinced him to agree to rehab.

They quietly admitted him. A week later, Kathy called me to tell me what was going on. When I offered to come, she insisted the trip wasn't necessary.

They paid the back payments on the condo and cleaned it for Daniel when he was ready to come home. Neither brothers Daren or David made much of it and didn't discuss it. They accepted the problem and went on about their lives, both baffled they didn't notice the problem before now.

Brook was furious and couldn't believe what Daniel put them through. She didn't understand how he could do something like this to his parents. His addiction was our first experience with drug abuse, so no one knew what to say or how to act. The whole experience was foul to Brook, and she felt unforgiving about the cost of the condo, the rehab, and refused to talk about Daniel's getting sober. She considered it a blatant waste of her parents' money.

Brook felt angry her parents bailed him out and kept the condo for Daniel. She scolded them and said they should sell it and make him start over. They did want him to start over in his own place because moving back with them would only humiliate him.

They said, "He's our son, and we have to get him back on the right road. Letting his house go wouldn't benefit anyone, so no, we won't sell it, because it's not ours to sell." Helping him get back on his feet was the right thing to do.

Daniel came home, and for years, although fighting sobriety is an everyday challenge, lived a healthy life. He moved back into his condo and worked for several different companies over the years. Kathy and Michael, as devoted parents, made sure he had everything he needed to live and to fight whatever demons caused him to use drugs. They often paid his bills but never told Brook.

Present

CHAPTER 10

The Florida Connors—Ian, myself, Christian, Taylor, and Anna—are a happy family. We lead the typical Floridian lifestyle. We enjoy near-perfect weather most of the time. We're beach people and love it. The kids attend school each day and came home each afternoon. We enjoy the same activities as my sibling's families. Sports, trips, and holiday visits to the family.

Ian and I take pride in raising our children. We love supporting whatever they were into at the time.

With Christian, he spent his days with a basketball in his hand, with practice twice a week and Saturday games. He played for the Police Athletic League from age six until a junior in high school, when the coach took an interest in him. He stopped playing in the athletic league and played only for his school. From that day forward, colleges and he expressed a mutual interest for a possible career in basketball.

All boys his age playing basketball imagine a career in the NBA. Although it's a long shot, who am I to burst his bubble? Coach Burnum seems to think he's going places as well. We let him dream and practice to be the best he can be.

My girls, Taylor, and Anna, did almost everything together. They took dance; changed to tumbling, only to switch gears to soccer. By the time they were twelve, they decided tennis was their sport. I loved it, as I had played tennis when I was young and played in college. I enjoy hitting balls at the club with the girls. My girlfriend Jill teams up with me against these two tennis demons. Occasionally, they let us win.

Taylor and Anna are both intelligent girls. They were so quiet when they were young, people asked whether they spoke at all. I said my two little radar ears hear and speak fine. The fact people thought they didn't is hilarious, because they never shut up at home. But, when they were young, they were shy.

The twins spoke only to each other in public. Today my two girls are both in high school and talking non-stop on the phone or face to face to everyone. They grew out of their shyness in the sixth grade. Today they're class leaders at their school, and both excel in all their studies.

I was so proud when Taylor and Anna came home from school one day and told me they were both invited into the National Honor Society. Not only is it a huge accomplishment, but it will also be ideal on their records when college hunting starts their junior year. They will be sophomores this year, so have time before they start testing and applying to universities.

Taylor has no interest in organized sports. My daughter, Anna is the competitive one, who participates in team competitions at the Country Club. Taylor enjoys playing the game for recreation and exercise, but neither wanted to play on the high school team.

They both still surf often with their friends at the pier or at home. No surf competitions for either girl, those are something they enjoyed from the sidelines. Surfing is part of our lifestyle we enjoy and try to do together, but I don't push them into something they don't want to do. Ian and I agreed to give all our children freedom of choice to become whatever they want. We want them to choose without pressure from us, supporting whatever they're into at that moment.

Still, I'm surprised that, for as long as all three kids have been surfing, and their skill level, none wanted to compete, especially with the degree of competition they show with each other. I am their mother so in my eyes, they're the best at everything.

Both girls are into clothes and fashion, with Taylor the more fashionista. She seems to have an eye for putting things together. Her vision on different fabrics and colors is remarkable. I often ask her advice on special occasions when I want to impress.

The kids are great about attending the fundraisers for Mayo. They help bring awareness to cancer since they lost their aunt to it. They are helpful with the children in local hospitals. They volunteer their time on holidays and other significant events we host, with little or no coaxing from me. Most of our events take place at the hospital.

Halloween last year was so much fun. My girls dressed in funny costumes and went to the children's ward with candy and costumes for the kids. The nurses set up candy stations so the children could trick or treat throughout the children's floor. We spent hours playing, dancing, and singing with children who couldn't get out to enjoy Halloween with their families. The joy it brought to the parents watching their children engage in something other children take for granted was heartwarming.

I know. My girls sound like angels, and most of the time, they are. Typical siblings, they have those times when they fight and won't look at each other. They play pranks on each other too. We never know when something will happen. For instance, the time Taylor stayed home because she wasn't feeling well. Right before Anna was due back from school, she hid in Anna's closet, yet made it look as if she was in bed, sleeping. We quietly closed the door, not wanting to disturb her.

I went back downstairs, and Anna went into her room and turned on her music. She milled around in there for about fifteen minutes, singing and talking to herself. When she opened the closet to put away her jacket, and Taylor hollered, "hi there!" Anna slammed the door shut and screamed, Taylor still in the closet laughing away. Anna was so startled by the sneaky set up she wanted to kill Taylor that day. I needed to run in and referee that confrontation.

Anna was so mad at Taylor, she didn't speak to her all night. We all laugh about that now, but Anna was upset for a long time. I went into my room and laughed until my sides ached. I shouldn't have, but there's something so darn funny about scaring the life out of someone you love. I can't think of a time when I'd laughed harder.

We're horrible people, aren't we? The entire family finding joy in the simple act of fright. In this family, we all do it. We hide in the bushes or on the stairs, maybe behind the car in the garage. Our neighbors laugh at us when they see one of us preparing to launch out of the bushes to frighten one another. After the closet event, the girls made a new rule the very next day that they were not allowed in each other's room without an invitation.

Since that day, Anna spends her time finding little revenge tricks to get back at Taylor. Thankfully, they have a special bond. I suppose it's a twin thing. But there are times when I'm afraid they might hurt each other. Taylor was born first and likes to remind Anna she's older, even if only by two minutes.

My kids are all close. They unite like old western wagons when an outsider picks a fight with one of them, incurring the wrath of all siblings. Christian's first love in high school broke up with him in his senior year. I never saw two girls take such offense as Taylor and Anna. Christian wouldn't allow them to say anything to his ex-girlfriend about the breakup, so to get even, they never spoke another word to her. They'd see her at school, since she was a year behind Christian. The girls treated her as though she had the plague, avoiding conversation or greetings of any kind. That treatment towards her continues to this day. Talk about holding a grudge.

The rules don't apply to Christian, and I blame myself because early on I taught him to protect his sisters at all costs. And he always has. Christian will defend his little sisters no matter what. When Taylor and Anna had their first breakups, Christian was all about being the tough big brother, telling the boyfriend in question to watch out, Christian would be around. No talking behind the girl's back, no saying anything ugly about either girl, no gossip, period. Ex-boyfriends usually went away quietly. Since they're only fifteen, thank goodness there haven't been many.

The girl's first year of high school was uneventful. They quickly established status with their new peers. The fact Christian was their brother and a big basketball star at the school before they joined the freshman class helped. The School is also K-12, so they know most of the kids anyway. The transition from lower levels to high school is a significant step, no matter what school a child attend.

We loved the school and attended every game and event where parents were invited. Christian made sure to fill them in on what teachers to avoid and whose classes were the best. He made their transition from junior high to high school painless. Anna and Taylor seem to have no problem adjusting and love their school.

Christian's first year of college was exciting. Meeting new friends and playing on the team at North Carolina University was stellar. Making the team didn't guarantee a starter position on the basketball team in his first year, and although he felt let down, he got his share of court time.

Playing here was a significant change from high school ball. The level of athleticism among the players is unimaginable. All his practice and court time didn't compare to the degree expected at this school. He needed to work hard to be a part of this group.

He played well last season when his opportunities came to play in a game, and hopefully, he'll start this year in November. Christian is only six-foot, two inches tall. He gave Ian and me a lot of grief as a kid because we weren't tall enough, insisting his chance of being tall was slim to none. Ian is six feet, and I'm only five four. What can we say, it's in the genes and beyond our control? We tried to laugh and make fun, but Christian failed to find the humor.

Christian's lack of height never affected his ability to play the game well, and as a point guard, he needed a good scope of the game in play, knowing where everyone was on the court to help win. He did just that. We're not sure whether he learned this talent, or it came naturally. He and his high school team won the championship three consecutive years, and Christian was voted MVP his senior year.

We thoroughly enjoyed the excitement when scouts from different colleges came to see him play. They often watched entire games, taking notes, and watching each player on the team. One night during a playoff game, the man sitting a few seats down from us said, "take a look at that kid. Number twenty-four, wow, great point guard!"

I said, "that's my son!" a little louder than intended, but I couldn't help myself. Several people turned around and looked at me. Christian was a sophomore. The scout was from Oklahoma State, and was there to see someone else's kid play. He said he would probably get reprimanded, but his entire film was of Christian. He never said who he was there for; I was happy it was the beginning of Christian's scholarship chances.

During the summer, Christian stays with us most of the time. He'll return in August to practice with his team several weeks before school officially begins. His college life is busy. I hope he can unwind and enjoy this summer.

Anna has tennis matches scheduled at the beginning of the summer, and as the temperatures rise, the tournaments will come to an end. We enjoy attending the games, except they fill up an entire Saturday.

I must admit, I look forward to those few months not needing to drive my kids in different directions every day. Coming home and sitting out back during the sunset will be the highlight of the day. Everyone will have time to enjoy each other's company without the demanding schedules.

Our whole family is excited for Christian to come home tomorrow. We're planning a big barbeque with our neighbors, and some of the kids' friends will stop by.

We have chicken marinating in the refrigerator. Jeff and Susan from across the street, as well as their boys, will be there. We expect a good time for all.

I told the girls to invite some of their friends. We'll drag out the surfboards, kayaks, and paddleboards, and set up lawn chairs and folding chairs around the yard. I'm happy to be hosting a welcome home party. Everyone is excited. We haven't seen Christian in months. We thought he'd come home for Easter and spring break, but he had plans to spend the time with his classmates on Virginia Beach.

I assume all went well because we never received any phone calls, the ones parents dread. He's been a great kid, a model child all through school; level-headed, and earned excellent grades. Never got into trouble, never had detention at school. I didn't worry about him.

One time while meeting his friends at a local theater, another car collided head-on with his BMW. Although the other driver was found at fault, we received "the dreaded phone call," from the police, no less, and I drove right up there. Three teenagers were in each car; the kid driving the car that hit Christian's was acting goofy as kids often do.

The policeman said the teen must have hit the gas instead of the brake, causing his car to slam into my son's car. Unfortunately, they took one teenage girl to the hospital. I made all the boys get checked out to make sure there were no head injuries. It gave me a scare, and the car was totaled. Thank goodness none of the boys with my son were seriously injured.

The drive time from home to the mall is twenty minutes. At that time, my heart broke over and over. I felt awful with the anxiety of not knowing the extent of the accident. I imagined only the worst-case scenario when I heard "accident," and no, I couldn't talk to my son. I must say, the pain I felt until I saw him and his friends all standing on the curb looking remorseful was probably the worst I ever experienced.

The boys looked guilty too. I think they felt they did something wrong. Other than the music blaring in the car, they did nothing wrong in this situation. I felt so relieved, and I told each one to call their mom. As I hugged them all, I was reminded how life can change in an instant. The final story from witnesses saw the BMW drive slowly through the parking lot, looking for a parking space, when the Nissan flew out of a parking space. A girl was getting in the car. The passenger door of the Nissan hit her, knocking her to the ground. Witnesses said she luckily rolled out of the way as the vehicle hit Christian's car head-on.

They believed the other driver was impaired, but never told us whether it was alcohol or drugs.

Christian said when the other driver got out of his car to talk to Christian, his eyes looked crazy, and he slurred his words, so he believes the guy was on drugs. They detained him, and when the tow truck arrived for the BMW, the police cleared

Christian of any wrongdoing and allowed him to leave. How many cars does the average family go through when raising teenage drivers?

My girls go everywhere together, and if a friend or two joins them, a mom needs a bus. I opted for the Mercedes GLS with three-rows of seats. I've always been a sedan person but having two girls and their friends, I needed to switch up to the larger vehicle. I can pile them, their friends, and their stuff girls carry around with them comfortably in my SUV. They don't drive yet, so I drive them and pick them up most of the time. Eventually, both will get their licenses in the next school year, and although the thought terrifies me, I'll hold off the likely double worry until that time.

Time to plan the barbeque. I bought cases of soda, tons of chips and dips. I don't bake, so I went to the local bakery for cupcakes, cookies, and pies. I checked the speaker system to make sure all the rooms have music, and the outdoor patio is working as well. I programmed a great mix of tunes the whole family likes and set it to shuffle the songs. I hear a Marshall Tucker song playing on the sound system, "Can't you see? Can't you see? What that woman been doing to me," an Ian favorite.

Ian's choice of music won't last once the kids are all here. We all have such different tastes and genres, so I hit shuffle and let it pick something else. I must be getting old; I can't understand half the words the new music spews these days. I even sound old to myself, making such a statement.

Christian will arrive tomorrow evening around eight o'clock. I plan to have sub sandwiches tonight and relax. We can sit around and catch up with him before he runs off to meet his friends. The next day is Saturday, a busy day for the whole family. I wish the other part of our family, like aunts, uncles, and cousins, were here too. I could've planned a reunion, but that's a lot to handle, and planning for everyone to stay here is too much on Christian's first return home from school. I think it's best to do that another time. We'll see some of the family members off and on through the summer anyway.

The weather is warm, not humid yet, but those days are coming. One thing about living in Florida; it gets hot and stays hot for months. Our winters consist of only a few weeks of cold weather, and then it's hot again. With that heat and humidity, we also have the luxury of the beautiful green foliage surrounding us, a benefit of the tropical climate. We take the good with the bad.

The yard is blooming with colorful lilies, and Queens Wreath vines are spreading down by the street. The hedges in front of the house are a deep green, and the pentas growing in front of them are bright pink, white, and red. I love the new growth this time of year.

The flowers, the grass, and the ocean is a perfect combination of scents permeating the yard and the house. When I breathe in the aroma, it reminds me how fortunate we are to live in such a great place.

The house and its surroundings look perfect. Ian and I are looking forward to having our one and only son home. Our twins miss him as well. We have always been a close family. I'm happy the kids all get along so well.

Even when they were young, they all were awfully close. The idea of Christian going away to school was sad for the girls; in the beginning, he called them almost every day. When he got busy with basketball season and his studies, we made do with an occasional family facetime. Getting both girls, Ian, and I into one room at the same time was just as tricky.

The facetime phone calls were always fun. Christian would tell the girls everything about the campus and the kids that attended the school with him. I can tell he was sometimes stressed. So much went on at the school. His class and studies were hectic in themselves, then adding practices and games, not to mention travel days to other schools for games, it had to be overwhelming. He looked tired on some of these calls, but such is college life. I hope he comes through it okay.

We did make several trips to watch his home games and any games in Florida. We tried to visit with him to provide support, both mental and financial. On most occasions, those trips became more focused on his team than spending time with him.

Nothing compares to watching him play college ball so well. The atmosphere at the stadium was crazy, even a little bit intimidating. The excitement of the team, the fans roaring in the stands, the music blasting from enormous speakers, and cameras everywhere was something I never experienced. The arena holds over twenty-three thousand fans.

TV cameras sit everywhere, filming the game, the sidelines, and the fans. It took some time to get used to the loudness of it all. We did it for the love of the game. I couldn't believe how much the spectators were into the players. These people were not just parents, but ardent fans, screaming the names of each player when they scored or passed the ball. The students attended in large numbers to show their support.

I have a feeling as he gets more game time, we'll be travelling more. Christian was so disappointed when he would play only a few minutes each game. I reminded him he was lucky to be on this team, where they televise games. His presence offered an opportunity of a lifetime. He didn't agree with everything I said, but he's a kid, and basketball has been his life. It made him work harder and play harder and motivated him to play more. I saw the change in his game and can only hope his coach sees it too. I hope next season will be his season.

CHAPTER 11

Christian arrived home safely, and we all sat around talking about what went on while he was away. Taylor spoke about Christian's friends and how they look after Taylor and Anna. They're all great guys, and are there to help, provide what we need, and answer our questions.

Christian asked them where they ran into his friends. The girls were vague in their answers, but from what I gathered, they saw them at the mall and around town. The ones still here are in college too, so the social circles are crossing. These guys are all good guys, but the twins are fifteen, and Christian is almost twenty.

I don't see where they have much in common, and I voiced that. Anna said, "it's not like we all hang out. We talk when we see each other." She gets up and takes her dishes into the kitchen, looking bewildered. I want to make sure I'm in the loop, because the worst thing a parent can do is be ignorant of your child's day to day, no matter how innocent. The girls act as if we're crazy. "How do you live in a small beach town and not run into people you know?" Anna asks.

Taylor adds, "Yeah, exactly."

We might be making too much of them running into Christian's friends. Being a parent, I worry about the girls hanging out with older guys. These guys have been great ever since I've known them. It is obvious I was making too much of nothing.

We move on to the next subject. The twins want to know all about the girls Christian is meeting at college. What do they wear? What music is popular? Are they local or out of state students?

He smiled and said he'd met some cool girls. "I've been talking to different girls, but no one in particular. I get out and meet people when I can." He couldn't tell them how many students were out of state.

"Are they cheerleaders? What do you do for fun?" Taylor asks if Christian wants to be in a frat house.

He says, "not really. The dorm rooms in NCU are awesome accommodations for athletes, and no one on any team lives in the frat houses. That's just in the movies," he says, and laughs. Ian and I say something about Animal House, but none of the kids get it. The movie was before their time. I feel old in times like these.

Ian asks him how his classes are going. We talk about his teachers, and he says he's doing good. After grilling Christian for another hour, we all say good night. Laying in my bed, I'm sure I hear Christian's car start up and leave the driveway. Welcome home from the family, now it's time to see your friends.

Everyone except Christian rises early the next day. I didn't hear what time he got in, but his car is out there in one piece, so that's a good sign. We all grab a bite of food or coffee, our daily morning fix. I check my plans for the day. Ian sits out on the back patio, drinking his coffee, staring out to sea.

The housekeeper is sending over her cousin to help with food and preparation today, then she'll take off and leave us to our party. I'm grateful for the help. Carmen's family is always ready to help or fill in for her. We're so lucky to have them.

Christian and the girls all come into the family room around noon, conversing about who's showing up today. All Christian's old teammates from high school will be here. The neighbors are all coming along with some of my friends from our Country Club. Taylor and Anna have a handful of friends coming by sometime throughout the day. Taylor asks if Jamie is coming by. Christian has dated Jamie off and on since junior high school; off since they graduated.

He tells them, "I called her and let her know we would all be chillin' over here if she wanted to swing by." Anna and Taylor whisper back and forth about that news. They're less than thrilled, but I'm glad they don't say anything negative about Jamie. That would only set a bad mood for the party.

People started showing up around two o'clock. The rain finally stopped after on and off showers all morning. I hope it holds off, so we don't have to stay inside. Ian and Jeff, our neighbor, were manning the grill out back, where Ian put the chicken on around seven this morning. The smell of smoked chicken makes my mouth water.

Everyone is having fun, small groups of people and kids talking all over the house. I notice the boys disappearing up to Christian's room a lot, but they all appear to be having a great time being back together. Kids play in and out of the water all day. The sets are almost flat, perfect for paddle boarding. When it gets like that here, it looks as if we live on a lake instead of the ocean. I stand captivated by the beautiful green water and the calmness caused by the recent rain. A perfectly sunny day after the rain poured down out of a few standing clouds. No wind, only a stretch of the area receiving big fat raindrops, then the storm dissipates as quickly as it thundered in.

We arranged a nice mix of music to play. Some chosen by Ian, the rest by me, Taylor, and Anna. Green Day was playing at the moment, "Boulevard of Broken Dreams," "I walk alone." The clouds have completely cleared, and the day is turning out to be perfect.

By late afternoon, everyone is ready to eat. We set out a couple of folding tables on the deck. Once this crowd sat down to eat, all became amazingly quiet. The chicken quarters tasted fabulous, thanks to Jeff and Ian. We sat for a good two hours, eating, and talking. Enjoying people's company over food is the best. I try to speak to everyone and make sure they all get enough to eat.

After our meal, we all move off into small groups again. Many of the neighbors and guests began to leave. Jeff and Ian grabbed a to-go package we made of desserts and walked our elderly neighbors back to their house, bidding them a good evening.

When they return, our husbands took two comfortable spots on the back lawn closest to the beach, positioning the chairs to face the ocean. Both seemed to be enjoying the gentle evening breeze starting to blow. The two men stayed out drinking beer and talking sports into the night. I walked around the house with Susan picking up stray soda cans and beer bottles. Carmen and her family left a few hours ago.

The house was in good shape for the crowd. The kids all gathered upstairs in the game room, playing video games, and doing what they do. I told Susan to grab a bottle of wine and glasses, and I'd meet her on the deck.

As I patrolled the front of the house, I noticed the sky turning dark again, the wind blowing in storm clouds, and heard a soft rumbling in the distance. I made a quick patrol of the front. Christian and friends had retreated upstairs to the mother-in-law suite, where I heard rap music and detected a faint odor of weed. That song by Chamillionaire, "Tryin to catch me ridin dirty" playing, how funny or was it appropriate.

I've never had an issue with smoking weed, but somehow when it's your kid smoking it, the game changes, and it doesn't seem so acceptable. Also, these kids drove here, and although they're all over twenty years old, I still worry. I make a mental note to talk to Ian about this. I'd also like to check them before they leave to see if they're intoxicated. I did notice not one kid showed any sign of over-indulging so far. The last thing we need is for someone to get hurt driving home from our party.

I go back inside, making my way through the house to the back deck, where Susan waits with the glasses. She says with a smile, "to another successful gathering," while handing me a glass of rose'. We both laugh and sip our wine.

I've found a friend that enjoys a good rose'. Most of my friends like red. I don't think there's a white wine worth drinking, but that's my opinion. While I like a good red wine, I prefer rose'. I ordered this particular one, Clos Sainte Madeleine Cassis, from the local liquor store. It's not too expensive, and it's Susan's and my go-to drink.

Susan and I catch up on our summer plans with our families. The Jones' plan to do some traveling this year. We have no plans to leave town this summer. They're taking a family trip to Costa

Rica. She says they've been there before and enjoyed the trip immensely. The monkeys walk and hang out on the streets with tourist. This is something I have not experienced. I imagine the tropical country will be awesome.

We end up sitting with the guys and talk until almost midnight. We finally call it a night as the sky starts to rumble.

The music is still playing throughout the house. Black Eyed Peas is playing, "let's get it started, let's get it started in here." I say, "let's not," laughing as I reach to shut off the music.

We all laugh at my joke, and we walk to the front of the house. We walk Jeff and Susan down our driveway as the rain comes down again. We say goodnight as they cross the street to their house, we have a great time with them, no matter what we do. We talk daily with our neighbors, but oddly, we still find new things to talk about.

All the kids must have gone home; the only car in the driveway was Christian's. I see two heads up in the window talking and assume Jamie must have stayed. I hope everyone was sober enough to drive when they left.

I had fun seeing so many of Christian's, Anna's, and Taylor's friends at the party we hadn't seen in years. Some of the boys they hung out with growing up have become a successful band named Red Jumpsuit Apparatus. Their song, "Face Down," is doing great on the charts. Great guys, we always like seeing local kids do well and are happy they're all still friends.

Ian looks up at the window with the two shadows and smiles. "Christian has a guest?"

I tell him it's probably Jamie. I also tell him I suspect he and his friends are smoking weed. Ian doesn't show much concern, so I drop it, but I'm not sure letting it go is a good idea. I'm going to talk to Christian about it. Ian will need to be a part of the conversation, whether he likes it or not. I like things out in the open where our kids are concerned. I told them all if they wanted to drink alcohol or try something, the safest place would be at home. It looks as if Christian took me at my word. I'll need to remember that when we talk. I need them to feel comfortable coming to us with anything.

Sunday is tranquil around my house, with extra girls upstairs. I guess Taylor and Anna had friends spend the night. I wanted to check on Christian, but we gave him the in-law suite for privacy, and me barging in checking on him defeats that purpose, so I leave him alone.

Hurricane season is coming, and there's been no shortage of rain in the last few days. The dark and dreary morning makes me want to go back to bed. Dark low clouds circle out over the ocean, advancing ominously towards the shore. The waves have picked up since yesterday. Probably great for the adventurous souls who wait for these conditions to catch awesome sets one after another. It looks big enough to get barreled today.

Ian still has the *Times* delivered. "Old school," my girls say. He sits in the family room, drinking coffee and reading the latest issue.

"Do you think Jamie spent the night?" I ask.

"Naw, I took her home," Christian says.

His answer startles me. "I didn't know you were up. Did you have a good time yesterday?"

"Yes, it's good to hang out with my friends."

I notice he doesn't say anything else about Jamie, so I don't either. That privacy thing was lurking. When he was away at school, and I convinced him to visit us on his vacations, it was my idea to have his own space up there. Now I can't take it back just because I feel like changing the rules.

"I'm probably going to catch a movie and dinner this afternoon. I wanted to let you know I won't be here."

Sunday dinner is a big thing around our house. When the kids were little, the rule was, everyone at the table for Sunday dinner, and if you weren't, you'd better be sick.

Now here we are, with Christian breaking a rule. They grow up too fast and make their own schedule. I'm disappointed, but he is a man, and I can't control him and his day to day anymore. I look over at him to see if he'll say who's going to the movies.

He sees the question in my eyes, but I don't voice it. I try to avoid being too intrusive. He can read me. Funny, I'd have never expected that from my kid. He's always been able to sense things like that. When he's away at school, he calls and asks if I'm okay. I call it his sixth sense. He's always had it with Jamie too; always knowing when she's down, or something terrible has happened. He'll call, and she'd say my aunt or grandma is sick or whatever might have happened. I find it peculiar.

"I'm going out with Jamie. We're having dinner then see a movie."

"Okay." I return to what I was doing. Jamie's back in the picture.

Ian looks up from his paper. "See ya later, son."

Cristian makes a quick exit and returns to the in-law suite.

Taylor enters. "Christian getting back with Jamie?" Anna, her friend Beth, and another girl I don't know, come in behind. "Looks like it," Anna says, grabbing boxes of cereal from the pantry. The houseguests don't say anything, and they all sit at the breakfast bar to eat. They whisper to each other and giggle.

"Could be," I say. I thought the two would never get back together after a hard breakup in high school, when Jamie announced she was going to the University of North Florida here in town, and Christian should too. She made it very clear that if he was going, they were over.

They make a cute couple. Both good looking, Jamie has sandy blonde hair with soft brown eyes, encircled by the kind of eyelashes most people need to buy. She's small in stature, and always looked so much younger than her age. After they attended the senior prom together, that was the end of them as a couple. The night after prom, she informed him there would be no long-distance relationship.

I felt sad for them at the time. Christian was upset; it was all he talked about that whole summer. Going to college would keep his mind busy. I believed education with endless opportunities should be their priority. Christian shouldn't abandon his dreams because his girlfriend put her needs before his. The fact I'm his mother and biased had nothing to do with my view. That's ridiculous; of course, it did. I didn't admit that but did voice my opinion on several occasions.

No one wants to hear there are other fish in the sea; that college will be the best place to meet new people; girls, especially. No matter how often I said it, the pain of the breakup was there, and he didn't get any relief from my saying it. After one year away, here they are together.

The girls quickly dropped the subject of Christian and Jamie, moving on to their plans for the day, and I went about my daily tasks.

Ian didn't say much the entire day. He tinkered around with his Porsche out in the garage. He refuses to let anyone wash or detail his car. He moved the car quickly back in the garage for waxing because heaven forbid it should get rained on. He insists he must wash the car himself. He doesn't trust anyone to handle his prized possession.

The car is a 1990 911 Carrera Gamballa twin turbo. We live close to the Mayo Clinic, so Ian commutes very few miles. For some reason, that's important to him and his shiny car.

He found it online several years ago. We drove down to Palm Beach to look at it, give it a test drive, and after it was checked out mechanically, have it trailered up to our house. Between that and his Harley Davidson, he's set for toys.

The Harley is a black, chrome, and leather 1999 Dyna Glide with a twin-cam engine, the way a bike should look. Ian did a little custom work on the bike, but it's mostly in its original state. He alternates driving the Porsche and bike to work, depending on the weather. He hates to take either out in the rain. I laugh, but he hates water spots. I prefer the car to the bike in the rain for safety reasons. Ian buys his cars not on what is new but how good a certain model and year performs.

I prepared shrimp tacos for dinner, and we chatted about who was at the barbeque. The girls that stayed overnight were all great kids and hung out around the house before they quietly disappeared. Only one looked familiar. Anna mentioned how cute Steve got since he left high school. "He was kind of dorky looking when he was in high school." Taylor laughs. "Now, he's not. Steve goes to Central Florida. I talked to him a lot last night," she said, smiling. "He's going to be an engineer."

Taylor says, "No," dragging out the word.

Anna quickly blurts, "Shut up!"

Taylor laughs again, "You like Steve!" She forms a heart with her thumbs and index fingers.

"I do not. We were just talking." But the bright red hue her face turns tells us differently.

Ian finally interrupts. "He's over four years older than you, Anna. You should think about that since he's going to college in another city and will be around girls his age who are becoming women."

I agree with Ian. Steve is older, and the long-distance thing wasn't on the table for Christian, and probably won't work for Anna.

Anna's face is beet red since dad has joined the conversation. "We were just talking, Dad." She kicks Taylor under the table.

Taylor looking all innocent, says, "ouch, what?"

"Drop it, please," Anna pleads.

"So, what are your plans next week?" I ask, changing the subject. "I'll be working on the cancer foundation fundraiser with Bonnie over at Mayo. I have several meetings during the week. You two have nothing but time on your hands. I'd like to know what you'll be doing with it."

"I'm doing nothing," Taylor says. "I want to hang out, lay in the sun, and surf. Anna, on the other hand, will be dreaming of Steve."

"Shut up!" Anna says quickly, and gets up to rinse her plate.

"Okay, okay, enough about Anna and Steve," I say. I see a fight brewing even though Taylor is teasing.

Ian's not looking happy about this conversation, and I'll talk with him about it when we're alone. He's very protective of the girls, but he doesn't like playing the bad guy when it comes to the kids, so he makes me do the dirty work. He never says it, we all know that's how he is, and I'm the one usually dishing out punishments. Coming from him, they never last for long; he's a pushover.

All conversations in our house always end with, "Mom said." I must be the punisher, the rule regulator, and the last word on approving their actions. For now, this topic is over, and we'll continue at another time. Anna is looking more comfortable now that I have control of the conversation.

"Let's watch a movie," I suggest, and we all sort through the DVDs and check Netflix to see what movie will be a good fit for all of us. We all take showers and come back to settle in with our video and popcorn. I cherish this time because I know as soon as these girls get their driver's licenses, these peaceful little family nights will be history. Ian and I will be watching movies alone without the kids.

I bring out a big Hershey Bar and break off pieces for everyone. Chocolate is the best mediator when there's trouble in the house. Everyone joyfully takes some chocolate, and calm is restored for the night.

When the movie is over, we all go to our beds. When I ask Ian what he thinks about Christian smoking weed, he immediately takes the defensive.

"I'd be a hypocrite if I said anything to him about smoking weed, and so would you."

I agree, but I'm worried about other things. Ian doesn't believe weed leads to other things; people who do drugs are looking for an out or escape. If they don't struggle with addiction or psychological problems, they usually don't need to find a more potent high.

Ian has always been an advocate of marijuana for medical and recreational use. He knows a lot about the subject and has talked with other doctors at Mayo about the benefits of medicinal use. Many doctors in different departments agree, but that doesn't change the fact some people move on to other harmful drugs. No one can predict who that person will be.

"I want to make sure Christian isn't one of those people," I say. "I want to find out why he smokes weed, but I won't come down on him. I need to know he's acting responsibly to be sure he doesn't have a problem." I want Ian to talk to him as an adult about it. He finally agrees that he'll bring it up, and not make a scene. We snuggle and go to sleep. I feel as though I've gained a small victory.

CHAPTER 12

The following week comes and goes. We each have our places to be and go to them. I notice Christian is gone a lot at night. Of course, he's probably meeting up with his friends, catching up on lost time. Ian hasn't had the time to talk alone with Christian.

One day I notice Steve's lowered Honda leaving the driveway as I'm coming home. I ask the girls when I come in, was that Steve's car?

"It was, he was looking for Christian," Taylor says, then adds, "he sure lit up when Anna and I came out of the house to tell him our brother wasn't home, and it wasn't because of me or Christian. He definitely has the hots for Anna." Emphasis on definitely.

Anna's reply is "does not," as she gives Taylor the evil eye.

"It's okay for Anna to have a friendship with Steve; we've known him for over seven years, and he's a good guy. As long as Anna understands he's older, and he won't live here for the next three years, and long-distance relationships rarely ever work out." *I think out of sight, out of mind*, but keep that part to myself. Anna looks relieved. If she wants to start up a relationship with Steve, I want her to feel comfortable talking to me. Hiding it wouldn't be healthy for any of us. They've always been open to tell me everything in the past, and I'd hate for that to change.

The rest of the afternoon, Anna talked on the phone with one friend or another, and Taylor as well, was on her phone. I hope someone's out on the ocean today. The sun was shining, and the sky was clear; I hate to think such a day would be wasted on boy talk and iPhones.

"You girls didn't waste this day inside on the phone, did you?"

They said no; they surfed this morning and went for a ride to meet friends down by the boardwalk. "We hung out for a few hours and then came back right before you got here," Taylor said, without looking up from her phone.

I talked with them a bit about what they did, then went to check my emails. I missed a call from Ian. He had an emergency surgery added to his schedule and wouldn't be home for dinner. I decided not to cook, and instead would order Chinese takeout. I called Christian and asked if he would join us. He said no, he'd be home later. We'd save leftovers for him and Ian.

I let the girls take turns driving whenever we get the chance. Taylor has her turn at the wheel today. They both seem to be getting the knack of driving; we made it back to the house in one piece. I grabbed the handle above the door only once.

We set out our food on the table; one order of cashew chicken, one order of beef and broccoli, one order of honey chicken, a side of shrimp fried rice, and egg rolls; enough for ten people. We talk while we eat. I hear the latest gossip on everyone in the neighborhood.

"Shyanne Patterson, two doors down, is moving to her grandmother's in Tennessee because she got pregnant by a guy at school she no longer likes. Her parents are really upset and are sending her away," Anna says, spooning shrimp fried rice on to her plate, but never takes her eyes off me.

The look make me feel like there are questions that Anna is not asking. Maybe she wants to know if I would do the same to her or Taylor. Would I send them away if the situation arose? I hope they know I never could do that.

As though she read my mind, Taylor, between bites of her honey chicken, asks, "would you send us away if we got pregnant?"

"What?" I ask, eyebrows raised. Now I feel hurt that they would think it possible of their father and me. I look both of them in the eye, shaking my head no, as I chew my food before answering.

"Not that anyone is having sex, mom. I just want to know," Taylor says. "Would you react the same way? I think it's kind of harsh. I always thought the Patterson family was a close happy family and surprised they would ship off their daughter."

Anna nods in agreement and bites into an egg roll. Duck sauce drips down her chin.

"It's hard to say how I would react to something like that. I don't see your father or me sending anyone away. I think it's a family issue, and we'd deal with it as a family. I don't see how exiling one of my kids to be alone would help the situation. We don't know their story, though."

Taylor said, "I don't think she's keeping the baby."

"Oh," I said, "That didn't enter my mind, but that may be why Shyanne is leaving to have the baby and give it up for adoption. I still don't think I would ship anyone off. Also, giving up a grandchild would be too hard for me. Unsafe sex shouldn't be an option for any girl." How strange I never thought my daughters might be having sex. I'm getting old. Geez, I'm in my forties I don't feel old. I hate to think about these things. But what if they are having sex?

"Good to know," Anna says, then laughs. "Don't look so serious, mom. We tell you everything. You would be the first to know if either of us was doing it and got into trouble."

Anna's right. My kids tell me everything, at least they have in the past. Christian and I talked about sex not long after he and Ian had the "talk." He told me he loved Jamie and she was very special to him. I knew then he was telling me they'd been intimate. I told Ian the next day to buy a bunch of condoms and put them in Christian's drawer. "Safety first," I always say.

Taylor looks at me and laughs. "Speak for yourself. Just kidding mom, and we'd tell each other first, then you. I promise."

I know they're telling the truth. They even tell me things I don't want to hear. I'm glad we're that close.

"I hope so. I'll always try to be understanding and open-minded. I'm here for you anytime. I must say, I'm not ready to be a grandma in my forties. Nobody better get any crazy ideas." I point my fork at each of them in a stabbing motion. We laughed again and finished our meal. Taylor turned on the TV and we spent the rest of the evening talking and watching *The Bachelor*.

Ian came home late. I heated Chinese food for him and talked about his patient. "Sometimes, I wonder how I let my professor talk me into specializing in the coronary field. I feel as though I have no sympathy for some of my patients anymore. They don't take advice from the nutritionists. They eat all the things they shouldn't; drink and smoke cigarettes when warned about the danger and how they cause heart disease." He continues gripping a bar stool. "I look in the faces of the patient's family, knowing they expect me to fix their loved ones. All the while, this guy's killing himself with bad choices."

Ian continues ranting, "I warned this same guy years ago to quit smoking. I told him his cholesterol is too high and he was showing signs of atherosclerosis. He comes in this afternoon, nonresponsive from a heart attack. The emergency room team kick-started him and took him upstairs for me to clear his arteries. While we are doing that, I see he needs a valve replacement. I'll have him back in my operating room to do that once he's stable and can handle the surgery. If he keeps going, he'll need a heart replacement soon."

I rubbed Ian's shoulders as he sat down to eat.

"Why have all these surgeries and go through the trauma if you aren't going to help yourself?"

I don't answer his question because I know he isn't really asking me; he's thinking out loud. I bring up the fact the man's family wants him around and maybe this time, he'll take everyone's advice and start working toward a healthier life.

"Dropping one hundred fifty pounds is an excellent place to start," Ian said. His anger slowly ebbs, and he finishes his dinner. We drop the subject of his patients, and I fill him in on what's going on at home. I tell him I haven't seen Christian all day, but that doesn't seem to bother him as much as it does me.

"At his age, I didn't spend much time at home either," he said.

Random Summer Storms

He hasn't spoken to Christian about the weed, but it's only Monday; we still have the whole week. He goes upstairs to say "hi" to and hug the girls. That always calms him after a hard day, Daddy's girls to the end. I hear them up there, giggling and laughing.

Who knows what those three are talking about? I love hearing their laughter. All is right in the world when my family is home and happy. He stays up there for a good half hour, then comes down, smiling and in a better mood. I love the kids bringing him peace.

Finally, about mid-week, we have a Christian sighting, and we all enjoy dinner together. Ian grills Mahi-Mahi. I make rice and steam squash and zucchini; a mouth-watering meal we all enjoy. We all like fish, except Taylor, who eats just the rice and vegetables. What a shame to live on the ocean and not like seafood.

We have another rule, more of a tradition, in our family to ask each other how our day is. I work three to four ten-hour days at the station. Ian has a full load at the hospital with his on-call every third weekend. I want everyone to engage in conversation when we're together.

Christian says, "I've been hangin' with my homies. We go to the beach or shoot hoops. Nothing special."

Taylor and Anna hang around the house. They invite friends over almost every day. I'm happy their friends want to come here. I feel comfortable knowing where they are. I spend a lot of money on snacks and soft drinks, but it's worth it.

Christian also informs us he's going to take off after dinner. He and some of the guys are going to the mall then out. I wonder where "out" is.

Taylor asks if Jamie will be there. He says she'll be meeting up with them later. "You getting back together?" she asks Christian.

"Don't know, we're just hangin' out right now," he says with a shrug. By not saying much about her, I can sense he's working on getting back together. Christian would rather not speak than lie.

Anna's quiet. She took offense when they broke up, and is still chilly towards Jamie. "Right," is all she has to say. No one else adds to the conversation.

Christian is the first one done with his dinner and leaves the table. Not long after, we hear his car start, and he revs it a few times for his dad before leaving the yard. His way of saying, "bye, dad, my car is running great." I don't remember when they started it, but they both do it every time the other is around.

Ian smiles. They both consider themselves European car buffs through and through. When Christian was in high school, they spent every Sunday afternoon detailing their cars together. Father-son bonding with expensive cars.

Anna immediately starts up the conversation." I hope he's not taking back that . . .," she pauses, not saying "bitch," but we all know that's what she intended, and I frown at her.

"Well, she is," she says.

"Easy," I say. "One, we don't use that word in this house. Two, they both agreed it wasn't going to work with them both so far away from each other." I'm not sure if this could be a summer thing or a getting back together moment, but I do know there's bad feelings toward Jamie.

"She was horrible," Anna says. "Jamie called him names and said he was selfish for going away. How stupid is that? Choose her, or go play basketball for a D1 college. She's so full of herself." Anna rolls her eyes.

I understand why Anna feels this way, and I did too. D1 is the highest level of intercollegiate athletics in the United States. Not everyone will get such an opportunity, so why not take advantage?

Instead, I calmly say, "her feelings were hurt. She wanted them to be together. I do remember the arguments over his choosing basketball over her. I don't think she understood that he wasn't leaving her for good." At the time, I remember feeling she was selfish too. Why hold him back? I never let on my feelings of the relationship back then and am glad I didn't. By staying out of the whole thing, it would help them now if they remain together. How could she not see that bettering his future would be good for her future? Kids—go figure.

"I accept her getting back with Christian," Taylor says. "She was with him all through high school. She should have just stayed with him. Long-distance or not, it would be okay. She could see him as we do, going to his games and on holidays. I think she's realizing she made a mistake."

Taylor's attitude surprises me, I know she was upset with Jamie too. When it all happened a year ago, she acted very hateful towards Jamie. Now she seems to be over the whole situation.

"Great!" Anna says. "Way to have my back, Taylor."

"Come on, Anna," Taylor says. "They were cute together, always holding hands and telling each other secrets, and I'm sure he's never liked anyone else. I don't think he dates anyone at college because he never was over her. I didn't like what she did but seeing him so sad was worse. You heard the way he said he's talked to a few girls, but nothing special."

"How could he have a chance with anyone else? From what I see, she has him wrapped." Anna drapes her arms around Taylor and hangs on her. She makes these loud kissing noises next to Taylor's head.

Taylor unravels herself from her sister. "Give them a chance, Anna."

I'm not sure how I feel about them getting back together. Christian still has three years of school left to focus on, and I don't want him obsessed with thinking about the distance between them.

Ian interrupts to cut off the inevitable argument between the twins. "Well, I for one have had enough talk about Christian and his girlfriend issues. Do we have dessert?"

"I have Carmel-fudge gelato," I say, and everyone's happy again. Maybe just in my world, ice cream is the answer to world peace. But it works.

The summer days blend one to the next. Sherry comes to visit for a few days. She said she went to Miami for a week on business, so laid over in Jacksonville. She would be here only a few days. Most of her trips were like that. She hung with us during the day, and during the evening she and Christian headed out to the clubs at the beach.

Sherry's visits are always fun. One of us always plays "Oh Sherry our love holds on..." by Steve Perry. It's been done for years why stop now. We laugh and carry on the entire time, no matter how long she stays. I'm not surprised she fits in with Christian's crew. They seem to have a great time together. Everyone loves Sherry.

We talk for hours about her family and what everyone's been doing. Trevor talks to them only when they call him. He's still a merchant marine, so is on a boat for long periods of time. "My brother can make phone calls; he just doesn't, which hurts my mom. I used to try to visit him, but he never tries to visit us. I tell him the phone rings both ways, but he doesn't care." Renee has never gotten over Trevor, leaving home and walking completely out of their lives.

Alan is doing excellent. Darryl and Renee, well, they're always good. Renee started walking, and now she's all over town. She did a twenty-mile walk for cancer a few months back. Her next adventure is to join a group of ladies that hike into the mountains. "Besides the Trevor issue, they're all happy."

Sherry continues, "I'm happy for Trev. He's doing what he wants. I can't worry about whether he wants to admit he's part of our family or not. That's on him!" She's a hand talker, gesturing as she explains how it is. So entertaining and happy all the time.

"I agree, Shelly, but I feel bad for your mom," I say. "She always wanted a big family and for everyone to live on the property. Building houses on each corner of your acreage and having grandchildren grow up the way you all did."

"I don't know about all that. I'm not even sure where I want to end up. I do know things could be worse. The property is beautiful, and the mountains and rivers are peaceful. I'm not ready to settle down there. But one day, I will. Besides, I don't understand what his problem with weed is anyway. He got all crazy over it."

Random Summer Storms

I never talked to my girls about Darryl and Renee's "profession." They never seemed to care. But now suddenly, it's laid out before them. They look from Sherry to me and back again.

"What does weed have to do with it?" Taylor asked. Anna has the same curious look on her face.

Sherry looks at me. "They don't know?" She starts to laugh and doesn't stop until I finally speak.

"Uncle Darryl has a large marijuana growing farm. He grew for the government for many years. Now, since it's legal in California, he grows for himself. By the way, it's not legal here, if you get my drift." They don't appear happy, since they were never included in something this big in our family. I know they think if it's a family business, and everyone knows, why didn't they? "I wasn't keeping it from you, and the subject never comes up in everyday conversation." I don't want to think I'm deceitful, although that's practically my middle name.

"I kind of thought he was into weed," Taylor says. "He always smelled like it." She and Anna both start to laugh. Sherry joins in, and they continued laughing as we discussed her years of growing up on the farm. They talk of how common it is where Sherry grew up. Many families grew weed legally, some not.

She told them she first tried it when she was 16 years old. They both, to my relief, said neither tried pot or cigarettes yet. I noticed they said, "yet." That's a conversation for another time. Sherry explained it was nothing; everyone in her house smokes pot. "So, does, Chr..." she stopped mid-sentence, but it was too late. All three of us knew Sherry was about to say Christian. She apologized and said she shouldn't name names. That person can talk about it if they want to. She finished her beer and said she wanted to take a shower.

She left me there to explain all the things needed saying. No time like the present to clear the air, right? No, not tonight. I need to get some facts of my own before we have a family conversation about weed. "We'll all talk about this later." It's all I have to say, so I got up, straightened a few things, then went to my room.

Denise Ann Stock

    I figured this day would come. We should have discussed drugs and weed before they started high school. They were always such good kids and never spoke of it, so I kept putting it off. Besides, schools talk about not using drugs. What about that commercial with the eggs? "This is your brain, flash to two eggs frying in a pan. This is your brain on drugs." That was effective.

CHAPTER 13

That opened a whole can of worms. Sherry left the next day, taking Uber to the airport early in the morning. The minute the girls and I were alone, they wanted answers. They wouldn't let me sidestep the topic any longer. We talked about how Darryl went to horticulture school. We discussed how earthy and natural Renee is, and she and Darryl ran a marijuana growing business. I told them it was legitimate.

Both girls found this extremely funny. Then they were embarrassed. Does anyone know about Uncle Darryl? I told them no one asks, but I'm sure all their friends know. Trevor had a problem with it, that's why he moved away. The marijuana business is why he doesn't have a lot to do with any of us. "Your cousin still, to this day, doesn't like it." They did wonder why Trevor was never around for any holiday family stuff after he graduated high school.

"I understand how Trevor might not want to be a part of it, but what did we do that he never comes around us?" Taylor asks.

"Yeah, he has a lot of family he wrote off," Anna adds in an angry tone.

I explained a little of what happened back then, and how hurt Renee was over the whole thing. In the end, he made a decision, and it excluded all of us.

"That's pretty harsh," Anna says.

"So how did uncle Darryl and Aunt Renee get started?" Taylor asks.

I told the story of how they met, and then pooled their money to buy the land, and how Darryl landed a government contract and grew only for the government in the beginning.

They asked lots of questions about how long they'd been selling marijuana. Who buys it? Our neighbors would think we were druggies if they knew. They talked about it not working here in Florida; we're too snobby.

Laughing, I explained that many people are okay with it. They want to legalize it here one day. Until then, it's illegal, and jail time for a conviction is mandatory.

Both girls wanted to know if Grandpa knew about it.

I said no, he didn't have much interaction with Darryl and Renee, so there was no point in bringing it up.

"Grampa told me when we were twelve to stay away from drugs," Taylor says. "They make you do stupid things; for example, if you smoke marijuana, you might jump out of a twelve-story building. At the time, it scared me, and I remember telling Anna I would never try it."

I smile, thinking of my dad saying that, and what my mother told me when I was a teenager.

We went on to talk about what Uncle Mike, who is a Commander of the SWAT team in Riverside, thought of the growing farm. I said I never mentioned it to him either. They live in different parts of California, and I don't visit them at the same time.

They both looked at me.

"So, you just lied to Uncle Mike?" Taylor asks.

"No, not really, I just never said what they did, and he never asked," I added, defensively. They weren't buying it. Because honesty is a strong family value in this immediate family, and I've been dishonest with this topic all these years. To them, it was lying.

The excuse that if the paths never crossed, bringing up a vast disagreement wasn't cutting it. I knew they were on different sides of the spectrum, never to meet. The girls were right. I would need to come to terms with that. A lie is a lie. I have many things to come to terms with; maybe one day, we'll practice more honesty. The skeletons in the closet were rattling.

We talked about who smoked and who didn't. I said I tried it when I was younger, and never really cared about it one way or the other. So, when we moved here, I never gave it another thought. Besides, not being legal here, I couldn't afford to be tested positive. I'd lose my job. I never did it again, nor cared. I want them to understand there are consequences.

Taylor and Anna both told me they never tried it. Thank goodness, they're only fifteen. But my girls both know people who do. I, of course, wanted to ask who, but refrained, because I wanted them to open up to me. They need to feel comfortable telling me things and won't if I give them the third degree on their friends. I talked about driving while drinking or smoking, just in case those friends are driving them around in their cars. They both insisted no one drives while impaired. I think, "thank God."

With that came another honesty. What about Dad and Christian? I told them I don't know about Christian, but Dad is in the same boat as I am. He's a surgeon and can't have an illegal substance found in his system. Dr. Dad, as they lovingly call him, could lose his license to practice medicine, so, although he may have tried it as a college student, he no longer does it. That covered everyone.

I still had questions about who they know that smokes pot, and would like to know where they smoke weed. If their friends smoke, I assume Christian's friends do as well. Every question leads to another question, and I'm glad it came up. We all need to talk about it and bring the topic out in the open.

Anna and Taylor were open about the subject, and I felt positive about that. Nights went by where we didn't talk about marijuana usage. I knew it was coming, and wasn't sure how the girls felt about it. I want them to abstain for legalities, until they're old enough to handle a decision like that. They haven't consumed alcohol either, and I'm grateful for both. I remember the first time Christian drank. The guys were all just turning eighteen.

He and his friends went somewhere, and before the event, they bought and drank a bottle of bourbon and cokes. Christian never made it to the event. His friends brought him home and tucked his drunk ass into bed. I didn't even hear them bring him back to the house. The next day, he called them to find out what happened and where his car was. Those boys were on their way to drop his car off when he called. He had a terrible day that day.

Hangovers are an excellent cure for drinking. The boys wanted to avoid me, so they just dropped his car off in the driveway with the keys in it and left. I must admit, they took good care of him. Christian told me about that night, and was more embarrassed than anything. Completely losing your senses and self-control is a real eye-opener. Christian is a cool kid according to his peers and appearing stupid and drunk wasn't something he wanted any of his friends to see again.

Christian admits to light beer drinking, but no longer drinks hard alcohol. Now I think he smokes pot and can't help wondering if he smokes cigarettes. I hope not. We're about to find out.

A few weeks after Sherry's enlightening visit, we finally sit down at the dinner table. After our meal, as everyone is about to clear the table, I say we need to have a family talk. The kids give me that look, the one when they know you want to talk about something embarrassing or annoying.

Ian shoots me a look too, but his is more of a "what's up?" look. I mentioned to him we needed to talk, and he kept saying okay, but never started the conversation. I tell them to all sit back down. I start the conversation by saying it was great having Sherry here.

Going from that to while she was here, we discussed what her parents do for a living. Christian doesn't comment, and wears a poker face, but the girls seem interested.

I mentioned we talked about smoking weed. I say our conversation was that she has been smoking since she was 16. I filled Ian and Christian in on the conversation the girls and I had a few weeks back.

Taylor and Anna again state they're not pot smokers, nor do they drink or smoke cigarettes. They focus their attention on Dad.

"Why is everyone looking at me?" he asks. "I don't smoke anything either." He looks guilty, though.

"But you did?" Taylor asks, point-blank.

"I've never had a problem with anyone smoking weed," he says. "In California it's legal, here it's not. So, I'll recant my statement when we're here in Florida. I don't smoke anything."

Christian quickly catches on. "So, when we visit California, you do."

Both girls have a drop jaw moment.

"Yes," Ian says.

"OMG," Anna says. "Mom said you can't have it in your system."

Taylor doesn't comment.

"You understand it's legal there and not here?" Ian asks. "So, when I partake, I'm not breaking the law. That's true, I've never been tested at work. There's many factors; if you have excess body fat, it will hang on longer. And the amount of use is a factor as well. One joint smoked in California would probably stay in my system for only three days. So, by the time I'm back at work, it's cleared my system."

I see by Christian's facial expression he's calculating time and his size.

Taylor finally speaks up, "what about you, Christian? Mom said she tried it when she was your age. We all know dads tried it and still does. Where do you stand on the subject?"

Christian looks around the table then stands." Well, when mom was my age, it wasn't legal to smoke marijuana either. Legal or not, it's far better to smoke than to drink, in my opinion." He sounds like a lawyer making a case. He smiles as if he's just solved all problems.

"So, you do," Taylor says. The tone of her voice is almost funny.

"I studied it and tried it. It helps me when I'm stressing over my classes, my grades, and being on the basketball team." He stops talking to let it sink in for a minute before he continues.

"A lot of kids at school binge drink on the weekends. They party all weekend to cut loose from the stress and anxiety of classes and grades. I found that smoking in the evening after classes and studies helps me to relax, but don't feel the need to drink until I drop because of it." He watches us for our reactions.

We sit and reflect on everything just said. Those skeletons rattling in the closet are pushing open the doors and sticking their heads out.

"I appreciate your honesty, son," Ian says, "and don't want to be a hypocrite, but the fact is, you must be careful in your choices. Marijuana is illegal in North Carolina, and you could be kicked off your team and out of school. You need to make the right decision."

Christian fires back. "So, as a doctor, you'd prefer I take medication for anxiety than smoke weed?"

"No, I'm not saying that. I'm just warning you of the danger. You have a good point, and when election time comes around, you'd be wise to vote. Get this thing passed in all states for medicinal purposes, at least. I wanted you to think about the consequences of being kicked off the team for testing positive for marijuana."

"It looks like I need to make sure there's time between testing," Christian says. "Hopefully, I'll know when it's coming."

I'm not sure whether that's a dig at Ian for doing the same, or Christian being truthful.

Taylor quietly asks, "so, are you saying it's okay, dad?"

"Again, no, I'm not saying it's okay. It's still illegal, and there are consequences. There's also the fact everyone reacts differently to marijuana as well as alcohol. These substances aren't for everyone. Some people can have a couple of drinks and be fine, while others have a terrible reaction to a small amount. So, the choice is what's best for you and your health. Also, it's a choice right for your future. If you get caught, you can lose your scholarship. It's a lot to consider."

"The legal drinking age is twenty-one, so let's all keep that in mind when we consider trying something. Young people making these decisions scares me," I mumble, more to myself.

Anna voices her opinion. "I think Christian is right, dad. It's much better to smoke than take addicting pills."

"How do you know weed isn't addicting?" Taylor asks.

Anna points at me. "Look at mom. She hasn't smoked weed in how many years, mom?"

"About twenty-one since I found out Christian was coming," I answer, thinking back on when I did quit.

"I don't know, that's one case scenario," Taylor ponders.

Ian stands and takes his plate to the sink. "I think this was a good conversation. I don't want anyone smoking pot. Christian, I'd like to talk to you more if you aren't going anywhere."

Christian smiles. "Sure, Pops."

They put the dishes in the sink, then Christian follows Ian to the garage, where they had the sex talk years ago. The garage is the man's world. I mean the garage only. In this family, it's probably the only private place. The walls in the house have ears.

We clear the table and clean the kitchen. I ask the girls if they have anything else they wish to discuss. They both say no and go up to their room. I park myself in front of the TV and watch the World News. I'm always critical when watching other news shows. I never watch my own. I've already seen what's coming on; we talked about it and lived it for hours on end. I should give my support to the anchors by watching their segment but can't. We cover mostly local news. I can handle only so much.

Taylor comes down in her pajamas and snuggles next to me.

"Is something wrong, angel?" I put my arm around her.

She shakes her head no, but I can tell that there is.

"What is it? There's something."

"I'm worried about Christian. Maybe he should have stayed here and gone to school at UNF."

"Why do you think that? Going to the University of North Carolina is an awesome opportunity for him. I'd love for you to go away to college too."

"No way. I'm staying right here. I want to go to UNF and sleep in my own bed every night. If I want to try a drink, I want it to be here at my house with my friends, knowing you and dad are available. I don't want to try drugs, and I don't want to be pressured far away from home by strangers I just met."

"Well, okay, Taylor. I think that's awesome too. You do whatever you want. No one can make you do anything you're not comfortable with. You remember that wherever you are."

She snuggles closer without speaking. *God, I love this kid, thank you.* I'm so ecstatic at this moment, I can barely contain myself. My sweet daughter is saying all the things a mother wants to hear. I'm so blessed, I don't know what to do. Her worry about Christian does bother me, though. I wonder if she knows something I should know.

"Why are you worried about Christian? He's always been a smart kid. I think he'll make the right choices."

"You give him too much credit, mom. Yes, he's smart, but being out there without you and dad is different. Like Daniel, mom. Everyone said he had such a bright future with the celebrity status of the motocross world, then ended up in rehab. He doesn't even own a motorcycle, let alone ride one professionally."

"That's different, Taylor. Daniel was taking strong medication he couldn't handle. He's better now."

"Is he, mom? Do we know he's better? What's the difference between pot and pills? They're still getting high."

"That's a good point, sweetheart. I'll consider that when I talk to Christian." *How insightful is my daughter?*

"Keep an eye on him, mom. I don't want him to get swallowed up in basketball and school. It looks like it's harder than he thought. If he already needs help coping after one year, what will happen in his fourth year?"

"I will, Taylor." I hug her and kiss her forehead. Anna makes her presence known by clearing her throat.

"You're being a little dramatic, Taylor." Anna says, rolling her eyes.

"Hey, you all need to watch out for each other. If one of you needs help, the others should be there. You might think you're helping by covering for each other. If something bad is happening, you need to share that with me. We're a family, and whatever it is, we'll deal with it together. Do you both understand?"

"Okay, I understand," Anna says. She goes to the refrigerator and pulls out the orange juice, pours a glass and drinks it without another word. I thought she'd sit down with us, but she goes back upstairs. I find her behavior a little odd. Tonight, was tough on us all. Telling the truth is a good thing, but while baring the soul, it can cause others to worry. I can only hope if the time arises, they'll all come together with the truth. Secrets aren't good. I have many and wish sometimes I would have confided in my dad. Now he's gone and it's too late.

Shortly after Anna's appearance behind us, which I thought strange behavior for her, Ian comes back in from the garage, and says he's going to take a shower. Taylor and I watch *Entertainment Tonight*, then she goes up to her room. I watch TV by myself for another hour then decide to read for a while.

Ian is lying in bed, reading a book when I come in. As I change, I ask how it went with Christian. He tells me he thinks Christian is right. In his opinion, smoking weed for anxiety is far better than having a shrink put him on medication. I must agree.

"I give him credit; he's well versed on the subject," Ian says proudly. "I worry about him getting pulled over with it. He could also get kicked out of school."

I remind him of the problems of illegal possession.

He says Christian has it under control, and there's nothing to worry about, and he'll be fine.

I can see he's made up his mind and drop the subject.

I'll worry enough for both of us, because that's what I do. I can only pray Ian is right about Christian. I feel odd after talking with the girls. They've always held different opinions on many subjects. I felt a big divide separating them this evening. They're growing up with views and minds of their own. Maybe it's nothing. I need to learn to relax and trust my kids.

They're smart and have exercised good judgment so far. I'm a mother and can't help but worry, but I think that staying silent could be wrong as well. I don't want to be one of those parents that stick my head in the sand when it comes to facing difficult issues. I have before with family problems, and don't want to repeat that.

CHAPTER 14

The hot summer days slowly march on. The tropical weather here is beautiful. The only fault I find with it is when I wear work clothing, evening wear, or attend fundraising events. Maintaining makeup in the heat of summer is disastrous. I try to pick lightweight and airy clothing lightly applying my makeup, so it doesn't melt off my face before I get to my destination.

All other occasions are casual. Shorts, sundresses, and sandals. The breeze from the ocean helps, and it's always a few degrees cooler here at the beach than inland. Today I'm hosting an event with the cancer association far inland from my home, so it will be hot. I hope the fact it's on the St. Johns River will make it bearable. I'll balance business and social by having a crew from the station at the fundraiser catch the highlights for tomorrow's new broadcast. Heat or not, it's always a spectacular event for Jacksonville.

We'll be hosting the cancer awareness event in Metropolitan Park. Everyone always has fun, and it brings people together for a great cause. The event offers good food and fun games; and the grounds appear ready for a great day. The 5K run is happening simultaneously. We have tee shirts and balloons. We also like to do something extra special for the children battling cancer, and our Little Survivors group comes out to encourage the children receiving treatment that there is a rainbow at the end.

Children from the hospital will join us, and the foundation will grant them wishes. The Mayor of Jacksonville as well as football players from our local team participate. A hot air balloon will take people up. The balloon ride was one of our Little Survivors wishes while she was still undergoing treatment. She's doing well, and ready for that ride.

The day is fun from beginning to end. The crowd is huge and seeing all these people come together to support this cause always warms my heart. I spend the day making sure everything goes smoothly, which doesn't happen unless I make sure to drink lots of coffee. I try to speak to everyone. While I'm not on camera, everyone who watches our news channel on TV knows who I am. Hosting these events is my thing. I love it and host many every year.

A local tribute band is playing Lynyrd Skynyrd songs. *Gimme three steps, gimme three steps, mister, and you'll never see me no more*. The large crowd singing and clapping around the stage appears to be having a great time. I saw the original Lynyrd Skynyrd band play in California before their tragic plane crash in October of 1977. The crash took the lives of Ronnie Van Zandt, Steve and Cassie Gaines, the assistant manager, Walther McCreary, and the copilot, William Gray. The horrific loss was traumatic for the locals of Jacksonville.

Camera people are everywhere, shooting photos, and newscasters appear on camera and interview people walking the grounds. The segment we capture for this event will be a good one for tomorrow morning's news.

My day finally ends at 5:30 pm, and I feel fatigued from hours of standing on my feet. I get in my car and drive back to the beach. Turning into my driveway and hearing the crashing waves on the shore is a pleasure and a relief.

Anna is saying good-bye to a friend in a sporty Honda with racing stickers in the back window. Steve again smiles at me and flashes me a peace sign as he circles the driveway, providing me room to pass. His engine was making a throaty sound as he pulls the car around. I put the SUV in the garage and look for Anna, I plan to say hi to Steve but see only taillights as he leaves. Anna waits for me at the door.

"Steve?" I ask.

"Yes, we're going to see a movie tonight if that's okay?" she asks, lifting her chin a little in defiance, in case I oppose.

"I suppose it's okay. You two getting close?"

"Just friends hanging out." She gives me a side hug and opens the door. "You look tired."

"What are you going to see at the theater? "And yes, I'm exhausted; it was a long but successful day," I say, following her into the house. I hug her back and smile, since this is the first talk we've had in a while without the attitude.

"Not sure what we want to see yet," she says, then quickly goes upstairs, ending the conversation about Steve.

To my surprise, Ian's home, and he's standing in front of a plate of seasoned swordfish steaks. "I thought I'd grill some fish." He smiles as I walk over and kiss his cheek.

"You're wonderful," I say. "Fish is perfect. I can whip up rice and veggies." I take off my shoes and sit on a barstool.

"No, I have red garlic potatoes in a pot on the stove, and a salad cooling in the fridge." He smiles that lopsided grin I've loved my entire adult life. He still can surprise me and make my heart flutter.

I grab a glass of wine and follow him out on the deck, where he prepares the grill to cook the fish.

"How did it go?" he asks, scraping off the grill.

"It was momentous. Large turnout. I'm sure the contributions will double last years."

He pulls a chair out for me to sit while he goes back into the house. He comes back out with a drink and sits next to me. The horizon is beautiful, with orange and purple colors, and the ocean is dark and green where they meet. Ian suggests we take an evening dip in the ocean later this evening. Sounds lovely to me.

We chat a while about the event today, then I ask him about Steve.

Ian tells me he's seen more of him in the last couple of weeks than he has in a long time. "The reason being," he says, "is because Christian is back in town."

"I don't think he's here for Christian," I say. "I think he and Anna are getting close." I look at him for a reaction.

"Steve's a good kid, I've always liked him, although I wonder about the age difference and what they could have in common." He looks out at sea, thoughtful. "I don't like the idea of the girls dating, but if I had to choose for them, Christian's high school friends are almost family." He smiled at the good memories he had of the boys when they were in high school together.

"We do need to keep an eye on them. It could just be a summer thing. If they end up dating, he needs to be coming to the door and facing me."

He says, "no horn honking then leaving."

"Well funny, you should mention that, because Anna said they wanted to go to a movie tonight if it was okay."

"She's fifteen and dating?" He looks over at me and I shrug. "He needs to come to the door. No honk and run."

I nod in agreement.

Ian grills the swordfish, and I set the table before calling the kids to dinner. We all eat and talk about our day. If anyone is struggling with a problem or needs to discuss something now or in private, it will come up at the dinner table.

"So, you have a hot date with Steve tonight." Taylor looks at everyone to see if they know about Anna and Steve.

"It's not a hot date. We're just going to a movie," Anna says, turning red.

"Yeah, it sounds like a date," Christian says, smiling, although it more resembles a smirk.

Ian is just about to say something when Christian mentions, "I talked to Steve about taking Anna out. She's my sister, and there won't be any trouble." He looks at Anna as though he beat her at something, the big brother thing hard at work.

"Oh my gosh, could this be any worse?" Anna covers her face with her hands. "Does everyone have to get involved?"

"So, you get a boyfriend, and the whole family is in your relationship." Taylor giggles and then bursts into a fit of laughter. When she laughs hard like that, we can't help but join her.

"I don't have a boyfriend. I'm going to the movies with someone I've known since I was . . . like seven!" Her voice rises. "Can everyone butt out!"

"Okay, let's not start a shouting match at the table," I say. "Whatever this is, Steve is a good friend, and Anna will remember she's fifteen, not twenty-five. We'll conduct ourselves accordingly." Taylor is still laughing at her sister. I give her a look as I try not to giggle myself.

"I'll be keeping my eye on both of you girls when it comes to boys, and I'll have the last say," Ian says, looking at both girls with narrowed eyes.

I can tell by his tone he's serious. Christian and Taylor are still snickering behind their hands, and I let the conversation move on.

Around eight, Steve shows up at the door. We lead him into the family room, and he sits on the sectional at the farthest end from Ian. They talk while waiting for Anna. The conversation is comfortable; he's sat on this same couch many times. Ian and Steve talk about school and Steve's courses of study. Ian looks impressed.

All the guys Christian played basketball with are a great mix of kids from good families. We've never had any issues or problems with his friends.

Steve is a well-behaved kid. His parents are both career military. His conduct in our house all these years confirms he was brought up with good manners and respect. He's a good-looking kid, light-complexioned, a little on the skinny side. His hair is cut close to his head with a razor part cut into his hair. His mother is beautiful with very dark skin, and he looks exactly like his father, whose complexion is dark as well.

That was always a joke with the boys. When they were young, they spent the night at Steve's house, teasing him about being the mailman's kid, since he's so much lighter than his dad. His mom, however, said that's the Puerto Rican side of the family. His grandmother hails from Puerto Rico.

He was a little awkward in school. He stood over six feet tall in junior high, and I don't think he felt comfortable being taller than everyone else. His friendship with Christian began on the basketball court.

Steve has changed since high school, and now more comfortable with his height. He switched from wearing all baggy clothes to a more tailored stylish look. Since he's in college with kids from everywhere, he's probably not the tallest anymore.

When I join them in the family room, Steve stands and addresses me as Mrs. Connor. I give him a quick hug and join them on the couch. He was giving Ian the rundown of his first year in college. We talk about basketball; he tells us his parents were against college ball in favor of a real career. He's tall and an excellent ballplayer; we all thought he'd be a star. He always played power forward. Although his parents seem to have shut the idea down, he's happy with his choices and is enjoying school. "As much as anybody can," he says, laughing.

Anna comes into the room. "Hi Steve, I'm ready to go."

He stands, and we all hug and walk them to the door.

"We're going to the eight forty-five show and maybe get something to eat at Friday's later," Steve says, as they head out the door.

Ian looks at him and says, "Nothing good ever happens after midnight."

I laugh because my dad said the same thing to Ian when we first started dating.

"Understood, sir," Steve says.

Anna walks silently to Steve's car without comment. I'm sure she's probably embarrassed by her dad's comments. As we watch them leave, I notice he opens the door for her and then walks around to get in himself, points for Steve in my book. We stand on the porch and watch them back out the driveway and drive into the night. I don't know how I feel about one of our girls going off on a date alone. I know I need to let them grow up, but it's hard. All a the sudden, I am feeling emotional.

We slip into our bathing suits and go out for a dip in the ocean. The water is cool, not cold, and feels refreshing. Bobbing around in the waves, we can let the stresses of the day fall away. Ian swims down parallel with the shoreline and then back while

I float on my back, looking up at the stars; the perfect way to relax.

When it comes time to go to bed, we're both a little apprehensive, wondering what's happening with Anna. After a quick shower to remove the salt and sand. I join Ian, and we read, neither of us wanting to sleep until she's home.

At ten minutes after eleven, I hear the front door open, then the porch light goes off, and the door is locked.

I get up and creep out to see if it's Anna, but she says, heading for the stairs, "you can go to sleep now, Mom and Dad, I'm home." She skips up the stairs to her room where I hear Taylor's voice, "tell me;" and they begin talking about Anna's evening.

CHAPTER 15

The Fourth of July is drawing near. We always have a good time. This year Jeff and Susan, our neighbors, are hosting a family reunion, expecting at least thirty guests. I imagine it will be the best Fourth of July gathering yet.

We'll be cooking pork and beef ribs at our house, and they plan a colossal crab boil with blue crabs, potatoes, corn, and sausage. We'll hang out off and on all day, then shoot fireworks in the street together.

Ian's brother John will be here for the festivities this year. I'll put him to work preparing his specialties in the kitchen. I'm looking forward to a day with family and friends. Ian won't be on call this year on the Fourth of July, thank goodness, and it falls on a Friday. He'll be able to enjoy the day without being concerned about patients and possibly being called into the hospital. We're all looking forward to celebrating the holiday.

Everyone continues their day to day routines up to the 3rd. Ian makes sure all his patients are stable as he leaves for the long weekend. I look forward to his being home. I have no commitments, charitable or otherwise, for a couple of weeks. The weekend will be as my kids say, epic.

We've always had separate busy lives that keep us apart, so I'm looking forward to three whole days together without any commitments, and Ian not needing to answer the phone, only to jump in the car and head out.

John flies in on the 2nd, and one of us will pick him up. I made a list of items from the grocery store he and I need to make all our holiday goodies. The girls are baking their Fourth of July tradition, a sheet cake that looks like the American flag, with strawberries, blueberries, and white icing. They'll prepare it from a box mix, of course; baking a cake from scratch never works out for me.

Christian volunteers to drive to the airport to get Uncle John. We all hang out at the house and wait for his arrival. I prepare snack crackers with sliced salami, cheese, and a crudité platter. Ian oversees the martinis.

When they arrive, we all take the goodies out to the back patio where we can talk. Half of the terrace is a covered cement patio, crucial in the summer heat. The rest consists of wood decking out to the grassy area, open to the sun. Most summer days, the heat would be unbearable out there without the shade of the covered patio, and we couldn't enjoy the ocean view.

"Something about trying to breathe in this heat is like sucking air through a straw," John says, wiping his brow. He wonders if anyone ever gets used to this climate.

John brought each of the girls a pair of gold hoop earrings, and a gold BMW key chain; a bit much for the Fourth of July. I tell him every time it's not necessary to bring gifts each visit, but my words fall on deaf ears, because he gives me a look and continues handing out presents.

The evening passes quickly. Christian says he's meeting the guys in Jax Beach, and he leaves. The twins excuse themselves and go up to the game room. John feels tired and goes to the guest room, leaving Ian and me to our bedroom. I'm feeling relaxed from the martinis we drank.

Ian and I snuggle and fool around for a while, and I don't remember falling asleep. What I do remember is Mercedes nudging me to wake up. "Sorry, girl." We're all usually up by now, and someone would have let her out. She's dancing around my room.

"Poor thing," I say, and open the door out on to the back deck and let her go. What a patient pup, it's already 8:30. She's a forgiving soul, and runs out onto the grass to take care of business.

Ian is still sleeping, and I go out to the kitchen to make coffee and see who else is up. I'm the only one. Well, me and the king. I let our cat, Edward, out the family room door. He looks at me as though I stink, as he walks past me with his tail up.

"Sorry, sir, sometimes I like to sleep too," I say as he strolls past.

He stops and cocks one ear back, so I know he heard me. He continues around the side of the house without giving me so much as a glance. He's sure a sultry old boy.

"Who you talking to?" John asks, as he gets a cup out of the cabinet and pours coffee.

"Good morning, John. I was apologizing to Edward for not getting up and letting him out. He appears upset with me." I know I sound insane talking about my animals this way, but they're family members with demands.

"What did he say back?" John asks.

"Nothing, he acted as if I stink," I say, and sip my coffee.

"Well, he should not have acted like that, he has no manners." He looks at me, and we both start laughing. We both know Edward thinks everyone is below him. Crazy cat. Crazy people.

I'm feeling a little fuzzy from the Martinis. It's not my norm to drink more than two, and I indulged in four last night. I set out sweet rolls and sliced cantaloupe for everyone. I don't want to cook a big breakfast, and no one seems to want one.

John and I spend the afternoon prepping for our Fourth of July spread. We cut up vegetables and put spice on meats for marinades. We make everything we can today so tomorrow we can enjoy our guests and not spend the day in the kitchen. I bought rolls and lunch meat for sub sandwiches for dinner. Everyone can create their favorite, and we'll watch the movie "Independence Day" together tonight.

I'm enjoying everyone together, hanging out around the house. I feel as if we don't do it as much anymore as a family. Our lives are so busy.

Christian and John talk about the future of transportation. The idea of cars driving themselves doesn't seem futuristic to either one. We talk about electric vehicles and space travel, hopping from one topic to another.

We all hit the sack early to prepare for a busy day tomorrow. No drinks for me tonight; last night was a little too much. We'll have fun, and no one wants to retire early tomorrow, as fireworks don't start until nine, and we usually stay out until after midnight. We're all excited about the party; the one holiday all neighbors celebrate together.

I rise at my usual time walk around the house, making sure it looks clean and check all the food and snacks. Everything looks to be in order and ready for our big day. I walk out to the outdoor bar and check the keg of beer and lots of bottles for mixed drinks. I check the mixers and it appears we have plenty of everything. I can smell the meat slow cooking on the grill, which means Ian was up earlier and went back to bed. His ribs need to cook for eight hours to achieve the desired tenderness.

Everyone is waking up and coming down to the kitchen. John made a breakfast casserole yesterday that only needs reheated. I pop it in the oven and sit down with my coffee until it's hot and bubbly. After Ian, John, the kids, and I finish eating, we prepare for our day. The girls both wear flag print bikinis with matching shorts and tee shirts of the same colors.

I have a white pair of capri pants and a red white and blue top. John, Ian, and Christian don't seem to care about wearing the Fourth of July garb. Ian and Christian go out to the garage to arrange the fireworks for tonight.

John and I have everything ready to bring out when it's time to eat. Much of the food will need to be heated first. We listed what goes in first and how long each item cooks. Real chefs at work here; consummate professionals.

As noon rolls around, we all walk across the street to the Jones house. Their family reunion is in full swing. People are talking and laughing in all the main rooms. Jeff and Susan walk us around and introduce us to the family. They came from Chicago, Texas, Oklahoma, and some from Florida. Many we haven't met before and see several familiar faces in the crowd.

Trays of food wait to be heated. An aluminum tray of Mac and Cheese I'm sure weighs ten pounds, sits on the kitchen table. A huge pot with greens and ham hocks boils away on the stove. Susan's sister made four tomato pies, my all-time favorite. A secret family recipe.

My kids dart off in different directions with the cousins here visiting Thomas. We sit on the back patio with the adults. All the family members were friendly, and we readily join in with the various interesting conversations.

We sat over there most of the afternoon, until I finally got up. "I have dishes to heat up. I'll catch up with you all in a little bit."

The men blocked off the street and set up folding tables for us to bring the food out to the center. Our other neighbors brought tables and chairs as well.

Some of the guests came back to our house. Christian and his friends were already sitting around, waiting to eat. I set out snacks to tide them over until we set the food out. People were strolling in and out of the house and out to the street all afternoon.

Our house smelled fantastic from the various aromas. The side dishes and ribs were all finally ready at about five. I must say, the spread looks impressive. We ate for hours. We made a rule that anyone on the street can go up to our house and grab a plate. Most of the neighbors cook their own, and we all sit together and eat out in the street. Everyone shares dessert. It is always fun to go to our neighbor's house and forage for food we don't usually cook.

After we ate, the whole crowd pitched in and put away dishes, food, and folding tables; carting everything back to the home where it came. We rearranged the chairs, lining them up on both sides of the street to view the fireworks.

Darius and his cousin lit the fireworks from the Jones household, and Christian and Steve lit the fireworks from ours. Someone always says, "keeping up with the Jones's," a never-ending inside joke.

The fireworks show was incredible. We hooted and hollered for each one. I know those little cannonballs weren't legal fireworks; the sparkling bursts of color in the sky were awesome.

We all sat in awe, looking up at the display against the night sky. After the show was over and every firework sat smoking on the curb, we continued to talk about this year's assortment of fireworks as one of the best shows we've ever seen on the Fourth of July. We finally called it a night at almost midnight. I can't remember when we've enjoyed ourselves as much.

I called the girls to come home with us. They can hang out with the Jones family kids again tomorrow. As we went into the house, Christian and his friends took off in their cars, following each other down the street. A line of red taillights headed out of the neighborhood. At least they spent the whole day with us before going off to do what kids do.

I mention to Ian I don't recall Christian having such a nightlife before college.

He told me not to worry; it's what kids do at his age.

Sure, don't worry, he says. He may act as though he's cool with Christian's behavior, but I know he worries too.

I thought I was dreaming I heard music in the distance, and don't understand why it keeps starting and stopping. Music shouldn't stop abruptly without finishing the piece. Then I wake up and realize it wasn't a dream, and the music is the chime on my phone. I reach over and grab it.

"Hello?"

"Mom, I need you to come and get me." Christian was on the other end and didn't sound good.

I sat up in bed. "What?' I said, but that's not what I wanted to say. "Where are you? Are you okay?" Ian turned on the light on the nightstand.

"I'm okay, well, sort of okay, but need you to come to the hospital at Jax Beach. I'm okay, Mom, I just need you to come, please. They need my insurance to let me go."

"I'll be right there." I hung up and now am shaking.

"What's the matter?" Ian asks. "Who were you talking to?"

"Get dressed, Christian is at Baptist ER. He needs me to ride up there and get him. He said he's okay, but I don't believe him. He sounded funny." I grab a pair of jeans and slip on a shirt. Ian is getting dressed too. We run for the car, all the while trying to guess what happened.

"Maybe he was in a car accident, why would he need a ride? He drove his car," Ian says, as we speed down A1A to the hospital. Thank goodness it's not far. We pull into the emergency area and park, then run up to the automatic doors.

I rush to the information desk to find out where he is, but I see him up the hall, sitting on a gurney behind a partially closed curtain. "Ian, oh my God, he's right there." I wasn't expecting what I saw. Christian's face is swollen and bruised an ugly shade of purple. His face showed no contour; so swollen it was impossible to see where his nose began. Large tubes of blood-crusted gauze protruding from his nostrils.

"Christian?" Ian said, as he pulled the curtain open.

"Dad," is all he said. Ian rubbed Christian's shoulder and stood there, staring at him. Ian's experience as a doctor doesn't prepare him to see his son like that. I noticed Ian was physically shaken, and his voice trembled when he asked how his son was doing. He was examining Christian's injuries.

"Oh, Christian," I said through my tears.

"Don't cry, Mom, I'm okay." He tried to make light of it. "You should see the other guys." As he said this, the doctor entered the room.

I tried hugging Christian but felt awkward because I wasn't sure where else he might be injured besides his face. Ian turned to talk to the ER doctor, who was standing off to the side. He spoke about what was going on with Christian's face. He said the blow to his face was so hard, he's lucky it didn't drive the cartilage from his nose to his brain. Such injuries can be lethal. Ian quietly asks the doctor the right medical questions to access Christians condition for himself.

I didn't see any stitches. Christian looked like a balloon with eyes. I don't think I've ever seen so much swelling on one face.

"Christian is lucky," the doctor said. "His nose is broken, and there is substantial hematoma and facial bruising. The X-rays showed no cracks to his skull and signs of only a slight concussion. He'll be sore and not pretty to look at for a couple of weeks but will be as good as new in no time. We packed his nostrils but won't know if the nose will be crooked until the swelling goes down. We can refer you to someone to straighten it if necessary. He needs lots of rest. I want to keep him here, but he insists he'll rest at home. That will be okay if he lays down and stays there. I prefer he doesn't drive for the next day or two." He turned to Jamie.

For the first time, I notice Jamie is in the room with Christian. She's sitting quietly, looking terrified. Her pants were dirty with what appeared to be black skid marks, perhaps from the pavement.

"Jamie, are you alright?"

She stood and stepped into my arms. I hugged her, and she said yes, but her voice quivered.

I thought she looked a little traumatized and felt a slight tremor as I hugged her.

I wanted to know what happened, but the doctor was still in the room. I didn't want to freak out in front of him, and it took every ounce of willpower not to. I can't imagine what happened.

The doctor said the nurse would be in shortly to check on Christian. He saw no reason to keep him since we were here.

"Bed rest, young man," is all the doctor said as he left the room. Ian never mentioned he's a doctor. He's like that, but I see him looking over Christian's injured face just the same.

The nurse came back half an hour later with prescriptions and instructions to care for his wounds. She suggested we keep an eye on him because of the concussion, even though it was minor.

We discussed what happened. Christian and his friends were leaving a club at the beach. As they walked to their cars, a group of guys jumped them. Jamie got shoved to the ground; another girl was pushed against the car, and a massive brawl ensued, with two of the attacking group beating on Christian's friend.

Christian ran over and jumped in to help, and got a few punches in, and the last thing he remembers is someone coming up behind him and round housing him in the face.

"A chicken shit move," Christian says, shaking his head slowly.

As we prepare to leave the hospital, two police officers walk up and say, "Ian Connor."

Ian, my husband, of course, says, "yes," because we never use Christian's birth name, Ian.

They nod towards Christian and ask again if he's Ian Christian Connor. He says yes, but he goes by Christian. They want to question him about the fight in front of the Beach Club on 1st Street.

Ian steps in and says, "my son, as you can see, is injured, and the doctor said he needs bed rest. I'll be happy to bring him to the station for questioning after he's had time to rest. You are also welcomed to come to the house tomorrow if you need to question him. Tonight, unless there are charges, we're taking him home." He assumes the severe no-nonsense tone he uses at work.

The officer closest to Christian steps back and says, "Oh no, no charges, we just need to get some answers." The other officer states they would like to talk with him soon. He gives us a card with the name of one officer, then turn to leave.

Out in the parking lot, we notice Jamie drove Christian's car here. I tell her she may stay with us I can give her a ride home in the morning, or if she's okay to drive the vehicle, then bring it back tomorrow. Jamie says she'd like to go home.

We all hug and watch her drive away. I'm glad she had only scratches on her elbow. Getting into my SUV, I shudder, thinking about what happened tonight. "What kind of monster shoves a girl to the ground?"

Ian tells Christian we'll all talk about it in the morning. He wants to hear the whole story again before they speak to the police.

The ride home was quiet. We walked Christian up to his apartment suite to made sure he was going to be okay before we turned in for the night.

"I can't believe he was involved in a parking lot brawl," I say, shaking my head. "This is so unlike him. He's never been a fighter." I think back through his school years. I don't recall any black eyes or bruised knuckles from fighting. Well, there was the time he slugged the locker after a big loss to a rival basketball team, but that was nothing more than a temper tantrum.

"He may have won his fights," Ian says as he climbs into bed. I look over at the clock, and it's 4:15. We turn off the lights, but sleep doesn't come right away and there is considerable tossing and turning.

The following morning, we all rise a little later than usual. My pets are both in our room, jumping around and knocking things over in protest. Edward is sitting on my nightstand, flashing me the evil eye while knocking objects like my watch and phone to the floor.

"I'm up. I'm up," I say to the dog and the cat, opening the door to the back deck. They run out the door. I close the door behind the happy critters and walk into the kitchen. John is sitting and drinking coffee.

"Rough night, I take it," he says, and then sips the coffee.

Ian nods, but says nothing.

"Worse night I've had in an exceptionally long time. I need to go check on Christian." I pour myself coffee and get bottled water to take up to Christian's room.

"Is he okay? I heard you and Ian leave early this morning and woke up when you came back after four in the morning. It was dark, and I couldn't see who all was out there."

I tell him a short version of what happened. As I finish telling him, the girls come in and want to know what happened to Christian last night. It's posted all over Facebook that he and his friends had a bad fight with another group of guys.

They show me pictures; I'm mortified. The idea that everyone will see these images are horrible. With today's electronics, there are no secrets.

"Can we go see Christian? Is he at home or in the hospital?"

I let them know he's home in bed. They can go to his room after I check on him. Christian walks in just as I finish my sentence.

He resembles the elephant man with his swollen face. I notice he is hunched over a little too as he walks. His eyes are slits in his face now with the bruising darker and more prominent today. His balloon look with no features is quite scary. My son is completely unrecognizable.

"Oh my gosh, Christian." Taylor tears up with Anna following suit.

"You should be in a hospital," Anna whispers. They both go over and hug him. The twins are a little timid, not wanting to hurt him. He assures them he looks worse than he feels. I don't believe that, because I watched him wince when he tried to sit down, and I handed him the water I was taking up to him.

I ask him if he's hurting anywhere else besides his face. He says his elbow and hip are sore. He must have landed on the right side when he hit the ground. He also has a bump on his head. Ian walks over and asks him how he is doing. He can't eat, must have taken a punch to the jaw. He says he has no appetite, but we talk him into a chocolate protein shake. As he sits at the table drinking it, everyone is grilling him on what happened.

I picture in my mind one of them saying something to another in the bar and making them angry. The whole thing explodes into a slug out in the parking lot by the cars, all of them screaming obscenities, all covered in blood. What kind of thug would push a one-hundred pound girl to the ground? The thought of the whole situation sickens me.

I don't want to hear any more about the fight. I want nothing more than to shower and get dressed. Ian can get the details from Christian now for the police, while giving everyone else the details of last night's event. I suspect there's more than some guys picking a fight. When people drink, there's no telling what will set someone off.

Christian, John, Anna, and Taylor are still talking about it when I return. Ian is now looking at the paper in the family room. Based on his slow movements, I can see Christian looks fatigued.

I tell all of them we can talk more later, but Christian needs to go back to bed. Christian nods in agreement and heads for the in-law suite. It is obvious to me and I assume everyone else that Christian is hurt more that he is letting on.

CHAPTER 16

Facebook has its good points and can be useful, but it can also be horrible. Everyone saw the pictures of the fight on 1st Street. My sister called. I told her the entire story, of course, my brother, and Ian's brother checked in to see if Christian survived. Anyone who was a friend, or a friend of a friend commented on the story. The fiasco didn't die down for several weeks.

Christian was healing, his bruises turning that funky yellow color, and life returned to normal. All of Christian's friends that were there said the same thing. The fight was random, and the attackers were strangers. They must have done something in the club that pissed off one or more of them, and they wanted to fight when they were leaving. They said that stuff happens all the time.

I sure hope not. Handling another call like that would put me over the edge.

All the boys involved on both sides told the same story. So, a few misdemeanor batteries were charged to specific individuals that started the fight, and that was the end of that. Christian wasn't found guilty of anything, and we felt relieved, although didn't know at the time this would be the beginning of an investigation by the DEA. The police didn't share that detail about that night and neither Christian nor anyone else involved gave any more details.

We did not want him to get kicked out of school for this attack on him and his friends, and that part was a little vague too. Did these guys randomly attack Christian and his friends, or was it the other way around? Based on the charges, it was hard to tell. No matter how many times we asked about it, the answers stayed the same. I found out when people use the word random, it is usually anything but.

Jamie started hanging out around the house almost every day after the incident. I believe it brought them closer. Seeing someone you care about knocked unconscious right in front of you and not knowing if they'll wake up, changes your perspective. They became inseparable. She was at the house taking care of him every day. The girl was amazing with Christian, sweet, caring, and loving in every way.

We all accepted the fact she would be there, and even the twins slowly warmed back up to her, and they all hung out and entertained Christian as he recouped from his battle. Life started returning to normal, and we had one more in the house for meals.

John returned home a few days after the 4th. His visit wasn't as fun as usual. We hugged and said we would get together on the next holiday. All I want is to get through this summer before we start planning another holiday. Things happen, I know, but this was dreadful, and cast a shadow over our summer visit with Ian's brother.

The lazy summer passed, and we enjoyed the bright sunny days and brief afternoon showers. We surfed and built sandcastles out behind our house. The twins invited friends over every day. I saw them out in the water, teaching Jamie to surf, a huge inclusion into our family. They went about their business as if their brother was never knocked senseless by a thug.

Christian and Jamie hung out around the house a lot, and Steve was a regular. He and Anna hit it off and spent a lot of time together. Taylor had a boy come around also. She met him while surfing, and he worked at a local surf shop in Jax Beach. His name was Joel, the younger brother of one of Christian's friends. He seemed like a friendly kid who got along well with everyone at the house. I liked him; something about his character, he had an old Huntington beach surfer vibe about him that reminded me of our younger days. Odd, because he is only seventeen.

They were all great kids. Some days, when I arrived home from work, they'd all be hanging out in the game room or on the beach. One or more of the kids would fill me in on the sets during the great surf days, with information on wave height or days completely blown out. Today, Joel told me was, "a perfect day of epic waves, and they all were carving them for a couple of hours."

The housekeeper said, "they clean up after themselves. Good kids." If Carmen likes them and they haven't run her off, then I'm happy with them too.

A couple of times when I arrived home, I noticed cars and faces I didn't recognize. They were polite and drove expensive cars, Jags, and Mercedes, something I wouldn't question right away, because Christian drove a BMW. Steve drove a Honda he put over $10,000 in paint, exhaust, and installed a $5,000 stereo with booming speakers. So, I was used to seeing kids with expensive cars. Most kids that look like money are usually their parent's money.

Those kids came and went all summer as kids tend to do. Our weekends were quiet when the kids spent the night at someone else's home. No more summer camps, they were all too old for that. Some weekends the kids spent the night at our house. I never know how many would be staying. We had fun with a good group of kids.

Ian and I enjoyed those quiet weekends. We would rent a movie and pick up takeout from a local restaurant. We enjoyed early morning paddleboard sessions, with just the two of us. One morning we paddled up the coast just as the sun was rising. The sky was a beautiful pink and orange mix of clouds on the horizon. We were lucky to be out, the rain would show up by the afternoon. This time of year, it traditionally rains a short cloud burst every afternoon in July and August, before moving out to sea.

The ocean was calm this morning. The swell was almost non-existent, and water in the shallows was clear. We made our way up the coast so we can ride the current back home on this incredibly beautiful day. We'd been out for a good hour, and as we turned to paddle back toward the house, I saw the fin. I know sharks are out there; always have been.

The moment I saw it, my heart skipped a beat and sped up. I know not to panic; I've been in this predicament before. I continued to paddle and turn to Ian beside me.

"Ian, there's a shark ahead of us," I say, my voice shaking. Sharks typically feed at dawn and dusk, so the knowledge it's breakfast time for this big creature creeps into my mind. I also know these guys hunt in the shallows, sometimes in groups.

"He's looking for food," Ian says. "Don't make any quick jerks, keep gliding through the water. If he shows interest, head for shore. I think the shadow we cast is big enough to say predator not prey to him."

I lightly paddled a few times but kept moving in the same direction with Ian only a few feet beside me, ever watchful. The shark was a good size bull shark; I'd guess five or six feet. He darted around us just below the surface, and we continued toward home. He never broke the surface, swimming slightly below our boards.

He stayed with us for a while, appearing more curious than lethal. Then, as quickly as he appeared, he disappeared into the depths. My heart continued to pound until we got back in front of our house and made our way to shore.

Several species of shark frequent the shores. Black Tip, Hammer Heads, Lemon Shark, and of course, the Bull Shark, but they usually stay out past the shelf slope in murky waters. Lately, they've been hanging out in the shallow water close to shore. I'm uncomfortable with their change of pattern.

They say the three main killer sharks of humans are the Great White, the Tiger, and the Bull shark. I think about that when we're safe on the sand.

"Kinda spooky, huh?" Ian laughs.

"It definitely scared me." Although not enough to make me stay out of the water. "There's always that moment when you think you might become dinner. He was a big one, don't you think?" I ask, as we drag the boards up the sand to the house.

"Yes, I was thinking about six feet," Ian says.

We showered in the outside shower and toweled each other off before going into the house. Ian hugged me. "I was probably more scared than you, surfer girl." He kissed my forehead while rubbing my back. I laughed; I'm sure it isn't true.

"Right," I said. I smile and kiss Ian on the mouth. He took up paddle boarding only a year ago. He never surfed, but always loved swimming and body surfing. I enjoyed teaching him. He has excellent balance, and I must admit I got a kick out of watching him eat it a few times before he got the hang of the stand-up paddleboard.

He's still that handsome guy that whistled from the Huntington Beach Pier down to his friends in the seventies. Back then, I wanted to talk to him. I knew of him and saw him around but didn't have the chance to get to know him until that day, it was the beginning of us.

We spent a quiet day together enjoying each other in ways we usually can't when the house is full of kids and guests. I forget how easily he excites me and the reaction I get in return. Sex was never a problem with us throughout our marriage. I remember Ian talking one time with his father, and he said, "there are three things that will destroy a marriage; sex, finance, and in-laws."

We've always had the best of those three things and have been married for over twenty years. I love Ian today as much as I loved him then. That's not to say things have been perfect. We experience the same trials as most married couples.

The fact Ian's a doctor and handsome as hell makes him an exciting conquest for many single women. When I was pregnant with the twins, I attended several hospital gatherings where nurses blatantly showed their interest in him. One nurse offered to take care of him while I was pregnant. I remember thinking I'm as big as the broad side of a barn, but if she thought she could take him from me, give it your best shot. Ian told me every day I was a beautiful pregnant woman, and he was happy I was his. That crazy woman had no couth coming to me in that manner.

The nurses that are close friends of Ian and I, weren't happy with this situation, and the woman suddenly transferred to another local hospital. I never heard what happened, but when I met Ian for lunch one day, I asked about her. With a smile, he said she's no longer with the hospital. One of the nurses gave me a prescription sheet that said: "we take care of our own."

I love that group of women. They're dedicated to the hospital and loyal to each other. They all came to visit when the twins were born. I always remember their birthdays and bring treats to them when I come to visit Ian. Everyone loves a tasty treat; a small token of appreciation for all they do.

Several years later there was trouble in paradise. I don't know how it started, but Ian and I thought we'd outgrown one another or just grew apart. We discussed wanting different things in our lives. I don't really know what I wanted, but I knew Ian was bored, and neither of us was happy. We argued over little things. When he suggested perhaps, we needed to see other people, I turned on the mute button around him, and that was a slap in his face. I became numb to our whole relationship after that comment. I could no longer even say the words I love you. Neither of us ever liked fighting in front of our kids. They were young and didn't understand. The twins were about three. With our relationship falling apart, Ian moved out.

We separated for almost three months. Conversation was non-existent between us. Two people who could talk about anything for hours into the night found they had nothing to say to each other. Ian would come to get the kids and take them to the mall or out to eat. I never asked what they did or where they went. Sometimes they would spend the night with him. We had no rules; if he wanted to get them, he would call and say he was coming, and I'd have them ready.

The non-verbal passing of kids back and forth went on for several months. Out of the blue on one of these visits, Ian said he would like to talk. He asked me to meet him at the Island Grill on 1st Street. I assumed he wanted to ask for a divorce.

I prepared myself for our goodbye and what I would say. I felt nervous, and of course, I'd be hurt by it. I never gave this part of the separation much thought, but should have, because when it came down to it, I don't believe I'm ready to walk away and give Ian up to someone new.

I thought about the kids and how a divorce would be awful. They love us both and continuing to live in two households the rest of their lives would make everything difficult for them. I believed it's too late. He most surely wants to end our relationship.

Would we sell the house and buy two homes of our own? I really hadn't given this whole situation any thought. Well, today we'll talk about it and decide what to do.

I met him for a drink at this great little beach restaurant. I wondered why we hadn't eaten here more often, because after today, I'd probably never come back. The place would be a reminder of the end. Sitting out on the back deck, looking at the ocean with a soft breeze blowing on us, Ian said something profound and unexpected. I thought he was enjoying his freedom and was taken aback.

He looked down at his glass and then up at me and said, "so, we split and change all the things that aren't perfect about ourselves and correct all our faults for the next person we meet. It doesn't seem right. Why should we give up on each other, knowing we both made mistakes and have shortcomings? Why can't we change for each other and become the best we can be now, before it's no longer you and me . . . us?"

"I don't know, Ian," I said, still trying to come to terms with him not wanting to find someone new or more exciting, or whatever it was making him want to be with someone else. "I wasn't thinking about all that until you asked me to meet you here. The idea of trying to find someone new wasn't something I'd given much thought. I was sure you were already gone."

He told me he loved me and made me a promise to be all that I was looking for, and I promised to do the same. Despite our problems, we could do better. He reached for my hand, and I took his, and for the first time in a long time I wanted him, and he wanted me too. I hadn't stopped loving him, but during the last few months I tried to convince myself I had.

I remember looking into his eyes that day, wondering how I thought I could live without this man. At what moment did he realize he couldn't live without me? Maybe he knew before, or did it hit him today? We were prepared to give up on each other out of boredom. After everything we'd been through together. I smiled with tears sparkling in my eyes and said, "I never stopped loving you."

He said he knew and squeezed my hand.

Two days later, he moved back in the house, and since then, we've tried to be that person for each other, and are much happier. While we were separated, a man stalked me for several months; leaving weird messages on my phone and sending gifts to my office.

The man never revealed himself, but he knew my friends and the places I liked to meet them. I must have spoken with him somewhere on an occasion, though I don't recall him. I talk to anyone who speaks to me, including strangers.

Ian talked to him on the phone one time when he called and said he'd like to meet up with the man to speak to him. Ian said they could talk about the situation, and talk just "man to man," as if anyone would believe that. After subtle threats, he too disappeared from our lives.

No one has ever come between us. Marriage has its ups and downs. We fight and argue about everything as we both have dominant personalities, but in the end, it was never worth permanently leaving each other.

Regarding Ian's father's comment about the things that break a marriage, finances were never an issue, as Ian and I have both been successful in our careers.

We both benefitted from an inheritance from our parents we put in trust for our children. We also have the money we heisted from the Cartel back in the eighties that provided us with a start here in Florida. We never talk about the event to anyone, but the fact remains, we benefitted. Is stealing from criminals a crime anyway?

The last thing on Ian's father's list that kills marriages is in-laws, and we have great in-laws. I loved Ian's parents, and he mine. Our families are close, and we never fight among them for any reason. Our life is good, and we enjoy every minute of it. If we can keep our kids safe, happy, and raise them to become competent adults, we'll be more than satisfied. Ian and I know if we don't destroy us, nothing can.

We sit and reminisce about the good old days, discussing our jobs and how progress changes the way we work. I like knowing what new technology and research ideas are happening at the hospital, and Ian loves discussing it.

Out of the blue, Ian suggests I quit my job and stay home for the rest of the twin's high school years. I can always return after they graduate. With what happened to Christian he is worried. He believes this is the time in life when they need the most attention.

"I couldn't leave my job now and expect to get it back when the girls are out of high school," I say.

I don't think we have anything to worry about where they're concerned. Both twins would cry over a bad grade before I could punish them. They've proved time and time again they're levelheaded young women, and never gave me a reason to think otherwise.

I find it odd Ian would bring up my leaving a career I worked so hard to achieve, but he obviously believes there's a need for me to be home. I'll need to give it a lot of thought. I love my job, and not sure I'm ready to abandon my career. I worked hard for years to get where I am today. I believe I've raised three great kids while holding down a full-time job but would drop everything in a minute if I thought any of my kids needed me.

I express my views on my career and how important it is to me. Ian says he'll leave it up to me; it was just a thought. He smiles, takes my hand in his, signaling an end to the conversation. His facial expression suggests the topic is over, but I'll continue thinking about it.

I see no sign anything is going wrong. The girls are enjoying a great summer and there hasn't been any problems with either teen. I don't believe they need me while in school. Both have a busy curriculum with after school activities to keep them occupied. Soon they won't even need me to drive them around.

CHAPTER 17

One evening we're eating dinner while watching the World News. Ian, Christian, Taylor, Anna, and I engage in our usual how was your day conversation when the news anchor starts talking about American tourists on vacation attacked in Jamaica by some local men. We all get quiet while we listen to the story. The authorities believe the incident is drug related. Violence erupted, and some Americans got caught in the crossfire, narrowly escaping with their lives. What a scary situation.

We all watched for a few minutes, then returned to our dinner conversation. I didn't give it much thought after that, another rough day in other parts of the world. Sherry, my niece, showed up a few days later and stayed a week with us. She'd been traveling, and always stops in when she's on our side of the coast.

Shortly after Sherry arrives, she tells us she's one of the Americans that escaped the violence in Jamaica. She admits how scared she was with the whole ordeal. She mentioned she'd been on vacation in Jamaica several times with a guy she dates from L.A., who is Jamaican. She also says she and her girlfriends visited Jamaica several times without incident. She said she was interviewed on the news, but we missed that segment.

I found it odd she never mentioned why she was there alone this time. Christian and Sherry were buddy-buddy on this trip. I hope she confides in him what really happened. I think there's more than just a vacation to this story. Where are her friends? Would she go on vacation alone? We all know she travels for business, but she never said she was on a business trip, and she mentioned vacation.

We talk about the trip and her visit, but she sidesteps the questions with vague answers. Each of us asks questions and talk for days about her journey, since although it's no longer big news, it still gets airtime. Although she never elaborated, I wonder about the Jamaican from Los Angeles, and figure he probably fits into this story somewhere. How well does she know him? Where did she meet him? She says he's her boyfriend, he lives in town not far from the hotel she works at, but nothing else. She assures us it was a random act of violence, wrong place, wrong time. My senses perk up at the word "random."

Her visit with us isn't much different than normal. She hangs out with us during the day, lays out on the beach, and then Christian and his friends take her around town for fun in the evening. I start to think my imagination got the best of me. Her story was just what she said, she was in the wrong place at the wrong time. She told her story so convincing. I feel this is another moment where we should've read between the lines, but didn't. We stuck our head in the sand and believed her story. If I had a brain, I would have noticed there are no coincidences.

The week of Sherry's week of visit passed quickly. I spoke with Renee a few times on the phone and let her know Sherry seemed fine. Renee said when they talked on the telephone, Sherry spoke as if everything was okay, but Renee never mentioned she didn't believe Sherry's story either. She just wanted Sherry home safe. Renee's a very private person, and I think she wanted this handled by her and Darryl.

At the end of the week, Sherry returned to California. I asked Christian if she said anything more to him. He said no. For the first time in my life, I felt Christian might be lying to me. I felt sad, but he's an adult and has his own life. Still, the fact he wasn't straight with me cut to my heart. Was he covering up for her? Maybe, I felt sure she told him something in confidence he didn't want to repeat. The investigative side of my job in the early years won't allow me to drop this.

The whole situation didn't sit right. Renee and I spoke a few times after about Sherry. I asked Renee how well she knew the Jamaican guy? She met him briefly a few times, I was told

Random Summer Storms

Sherry was casually dating him. Sherry and her friends talked fondly of him. Sherry and the man never had any problems, so Renee wasn't concerned. She now says she believed Sherry's story, so who am I to question another family's friends and what they do? I let it go.

Ian and Darryl talked many times about football and checked in with each other as always. No one seemed to care Sherry was in another country where violence erupted, and it was on the world news. No one remembers a scenario similar to this over twenty years ago. They all were willing to let it go, so I'm sure no one cared that I wouldn't. They brushed the whole thing off.

I need to get a grip and stop finding the worst in everything I hear. Okay, I'll stop digging, but I have a bad feeling, just the same. I focused my attention on my immediate family. My kids all had full calendars, places to go in the evening; birthday parties, the movies, the mall, or just hanging out.

My girls had a calendar—funny thought for two fifteen-year old girls. They did some things together, but now had boyfriends, and many days they made plans independently. They were growing up. I established boundaries for them. Curfews for date nights, each knowing I would wait up for them. They'd call if they were running late. Anna and Taylor followed the rules; and everything worked well.

Christian and his friends came and went daily. He was twenty and had no curfew. They attended concerts and clubs all summer. Christian spent some days here at the house. Jamie was a constant in his life. Ever since the club fight, I rarely saw Christian without her. I met her parents when they were in high school. I hadn't seen them since. Christian and Jamie got along well these days; I never heard them argue as they did in high school. I felt they'd matured.

Ian and I enjoy all of Christian's friends, all great kids with exciting goals and ideas for their future. They knew they were always welcome in our home.

We enjoyed their company, and the boys often sat and talked with us. On some of those nights, they came by and hung out for a good hour or two before leaving for the clubs or wherever.

Several of them are twenty-one, and would drink a beer at the house. Discussing everything from sports to politics, they had become adults.

I've smelled weed on a couple of them, but don't worry, since all the boys can hold an intelligent conversation, and none show signs of intoxication. I recall the summer I was twenty and all the things I did. Most of my actions were harmless, but I tried a lot of new things, many illegal. I can only hope they're all being more responsible and don't make the same bad decisions as I did.

I know they all drink beer after they leave us. Not all smoke pot, but it's obvious some do. It makes me wonder where and from whom they get the weed. I think of Dewey and Chase and the operation of weed distribution they ran for years. They both retired from selling weed in their thirties. We all bought our supply from them in our early years. Odd I would think of them in this instant.

My friends and I did the same things. Is it a rite of passage or a road to disaster? At some point, I must let them choose for themselves, but it's hard. I sit there thinking about my summer as the boys all walk out the front door to whatever awaits.

Thinking of Dewey and Chase brings a smile to my face. Dewey, unfortunately, died a few years ago from lung complications after being admitted to the hospital. We flew out for the funeral and to make sure Chase was okay. They'd been together for many years.

Dewey was one of Ian's oldest friends growing up together in the same neighborhood since they were in elementary school. Ian and I learned about Dewey and Chase's relationship in our early twenties. Chase had a successful stereo business when he and Dewey crossed paths not long after they moved into a great house in Laguna together. They shared a close bond and lived together until Dewey died.

I can't hear the song, "Fortunate Son," by John Fogerty without thinking of Dewey. I find it strange how you hear a song when you're with someone, and forever it's in your memory. You think of that person every time you hear it. Dewey and I were riding in Ian's van down Pacific Coast Highway when the song came on the radio, and it's been stuck to him ever since.

I go to sleep thinking of the things that happen when I was Christian's age. I wake the next morning to a beautiful sunny day.

I walk out the back door and look at the ocean, the bright sun reflecting off the glassy waves, then walk to the front of the house and see Christian's BMW sitting in the driveway. I walk upstairs, and both my girls are asleep in their beds.

My world is good today, and I prepare to go into the office. Ian is on his way out when I get out of the shower. Just another day in the Connor house. No worries today. I focus on my day in the office.

While Ian and I are at work, my kids enjoy summer fun. Life is much more manageable since they're now old enough to take care of themselves. All the kids were good growing up, and we didn't have many after school problems. We had a few incidents now and then when I needed to rush home because one of them got hurt. Carmen, the housekeeper, is in the house, but she's only the housekeeper, and we can't expect her to take care of them. After all, she's not a babysitter.

When they were young, they attended daycare. As the kids got older, they would come home from school and do homework until I arrived from work. I usually get home around one or two in the afternoon so most of the time they're supervised.

On rare occasions, accidents happen before I get there, typical with all families. Christian stepped on a nail on a piece of wood on the beach. I arrived there within minutes to drive him to the emergency room.

I recall the horrible time when Taylor and Anna went surfing and were horsing around on the same wave. The nose of Taylor's surfboard shot up and hit Anna in the face. When I walked into the house, Anna was sitting on the floor, holding a wet towel over a hole just under her lip that went through to her teeth. Back to the emergency room we went.

We lead a typical family life. Today I can't help but wonder what the kids are all doing. Is Christian spending all his time sleeping, and smoking weed? Is Anna spending all her time with Steve? And how close are they? Taylor seems to be okay, but I don't really know for sure. She doesn't talk much about Joel, who hangs out sometimes. What's she doing with her summer? Should I be worried about my kids? Ian might be right in wanting me home, but perhaps I'm just obsessing.

The more I think about it, the more I think this could be a good time for me to be home with my kids. I hate to quit my job, but I guess I'll talk to Andrew, my boss. Maybe I'll suggest taking a leave of absence to spend time with my family. I have vacation time to use if necessary, and combined with leave, I could save my position and return.

I schedule time with Andrew so we can talk and see if it would be possible for me to leave and come back to my same position. My day is full as I work through my packages for the news broadcast, coordinating who will be assigned what story. I'm the one to ensure we're on budget as well as to arrange a smooth order of stories to the show.

Having a good script for each newscaster created to their personality helps pull the show together. The timeline is essential too. We must keep all the stories within the designated time allotted.

The day passed quickly without talking to Andrew. I jump in my car when I get a text telling me Andrew is sorry, sad face emoji, let's talk first thing tomorrow before we get into production. My days are like that sometimes.

The next day, I drink my morning coffee, and the next thing I know, it's three-thirty. No lunch, no breaks, and the day is over.

My work is interesting and, most of the time, exciting. The people I work with are a fantastic group; hard-working and fun people. We work together great. I push them sometimes, as that is part of my job. I work closely with the news director to provide ideas for him to make television worthy. We're all dedicated and make it work.

When I return home, I see Steve's car parked behind Christian's, with Jamie's car facing out of the driveway. I hear music playing from Christian's room as I get out of my car. The curtain opens, and Christian hollers, "Hi, Mom!" and Jamie waves at me. Yellow Card-Ocean Avenue, "let your waves crash down on me and take me away."

"Hi, kids."

I go into the house, and Carmen is preparing to leave. We exchange pleasantries, then she's out the door. She never really says much about what the kids did during the day. I hope that means things were right around the house. I slip off my office clothes and into shorts and top. I walk out on the back deck to see what's happening with the rest of my family.

The first person I see is Steve stretched out on a lounger, all six feet five of him. I stand beside him. "Hi, Mrs. C," he says.

"Hey, Steve. Not surfing today?" I ask, looking out to see Taylor and Anna riding waves.

"No, I'm not a water guy. I have to admit the idea of swimming where you can't see beneath you bothers me." He laughs.

"I hear you. I think God intended it that way, so if you're dinner, you don't see it coming." I look over at Steve, who wears a bizarre look on his face; there is fear in those eyes. I quickly add, "I'm just kidding; the sharks don't like us. I think most bites are accidental or curious. They're looking for fish or seal. You're more likely to be hit by lightning than bit by a shark," I say, hoping to make my statement sound less ominous.

"I don't go out in the streets during a thunderstorm, either" he says, looking out to sea.

I pat him on the shoulder and go inside. I don't think I made him feel any better. I ask if he's staying for dinner as I walk towards the French doors.

"No, thank you, ma'am, we're all going for chicken wings, if it's okay with you." I smile at the politeness of these kids.

"That's fine. If you'd like a drink, you know, there are sodas and water in the outdoor fridge by the grill there." I point and go into the house. I hear him say thank you as I head for the kitchen. He knows where all that stuff is, I don't know why I pointed it out. A habit, I guess.

Steve leaves shortly after our conversation. While I sat on the patio, the band Yellow Card was still playing on the stereo.

I find myself still singing "Ocean Avenue" in my mind. "If I could find you now, things could get better." Last summer, Christian and his friends hung out with the guys from Yellow Card for a while. They held a concert at the Veterans Memorial, ending their tour here. I'm not sure how the kids met them, but they hail from Jacksonville.

I'm humming along when the girls come in and tell me about their day. "The waves were a little flat today; should've taken out the paddleboard," Anna says, more to herself than anyone. They ask about going for chicken wings later. I said Steve told me and that would be fine. I ask them about Christian and Jamie. They say the two were out back with them most of the day, hanging out in lounge chairs. "Christian doesn't surf much when Jamie's here, but they did lay in the sun most of the day with us." Everyone seems to be getting along well.

I don't even want to think about Christian and Jamie lying upstairs in bed all day and was glad to hear that wasn't the case. Now I need to try to get that vision out of my head. Mom's don't want to think about their kid's in intimate relationships; it's too much to comprehend.

Ian rolls in around six. I tell him everyone is going out, and we'll have the house to ourselves again. We talk about his day. He performed two bypasses and consulted on an upcoming double valve replacement surgery.

"We've been successful with these surgeries, but there's always a percentage that doesn't survive," he says, with a shrug.

His attitude sounds cold and robotic, although I understand it's a hard part of his job and he must detach himself when having these conversations with the patient and family.

While he unwinds, I tell him I'm going up to Beach Side Seafood to buy fresh sea scallops to sear for dinner. On my way back, I shuffle my pandora, and the Beach Boys start singing, "California Girls." "Well, the east coast girls are hip, I really dig those styles they wear."

I sing along and recall how I used to relate to this song. I'm a California girl, originally, but the east coast beach right here in my area is awesome. We see as many tan and beautiful people here as any other beach, including California. Two of them, Taylor, and Anna, were born and raised in Florida. The east coast from Atlantic beach down as far as Miami is different from the west coast, but the beach life is the same.

The locals are loyal to the beaches, just like the Californians where I grew up. The beach offers a laid-back atmosphere where people are casual and friendly.

Bicycles and pedestrians gather on the beach and throughout the streets of town every day. White sand and green water up and down the shore offer mostly small waves, but surfers flock to them daily. A boardwalk with local surf shops and cafes faces the ocean. Regardless of the beach location, the lifestyle is definitely the same.

I'm happy our move from California didn't take us up to New York, Arizona, or Minnesota, to the other Mayo Clinics. I'm a beach girl through and through, and my life would be incomplete living away from the ocean.

I pull back into the driveway with my fresh scallops. My Pandora shuffles again to the kid's mix with EMO music. Taking Back Sunday starts belting out, "I just want to bring you down!" as I pull into the garage. I sit and listen to the end of the song. I must be old school; I thought this was alternative music. The girls, however, explained it's a style of emotional or confessional lyrics known as emocore. Not too far removed from my eighty's punk favorites.

Whatever you want to call it, the sound and lyrics change, but the idea is still the same. The music is self-expression, and I'm into it. Music has always changed my moods or deepened my feelings.

Well, I don't have time to hang out in the garage and ponder whether a song is punk, emo, or alternative; it's time to get the scallops cooking.

Ian and I share a quiet evening watching TV and talking about the kids. We discuss the fact we've never had any concerns, and they've all been good kids. We end our day feeling we have nothing to worry about; they're all okay. At

Denise Ann Stock

about eleven, I hear a car pull in the driveway. The girls talk out there for a few minutes, then come in and go upstairs. Another uneventful night; typical in any family with teenage girls. The twins are home, and I can sleep now.

CHAPTER 18

I finally get the opportunity to talk with Andrew, my boss, the Executive Producer. I tell him my plans, and we talk about how we can work out something so I can be home. When he calls me a few days later, suggesting I work remotely from home, I can hardly contain myself. I can put together the items I usually collect and continue to construct the newscast as always. The arrangement is perfect since most of my work is done on the computer when I'm in the office.

Andrew explains that he'd like me to come in once every couple of weeks. I'd participate in meetings and be available for breaking events, even if that means coming in every day for that particular story until the event finalizes, standard procedure for any catastrophic news story. He asks me to sign a contract, which guarantees my continued employment and salary. The arrangement would be a trial basis, of course, to see if we still can present a top-notch broadcast. I'm confident in my ability to produce.

Keeping my job and salary is critical because the Connor family would need a strict spending budget if I don't get paid. We can live off Ian's generous salary, but we've never followed a budget. We lived very comfortably, without imposing strict spending limits. I can't wait to tell Ian and the kids about the arrangement.

The plan is to finish out the week. Jason, our technician, will configure a computer for me with everything I'll need to work remotely. He'll have it delivered to my home on Friday, then will come over to test it to make sure our internet connection is strong enough to handle the workload. I'll be set to go. I'm excited and pleasantly surprised how easy we agreed on the arrangement.

That evening I break the news, and Ian is delighted, although the kids don't react as I expected, and frankly, I'm shocked at their reaction.

"Why, mom, are you sick?" Taylor says, before spooning gumbo into her mouth.

"No, I'm not sick. I thought it would be good to be home with you all. Your father and I are always gone. I felt like I should be here for your high school years. Don't you think that's awesome?"

"Now, when we're grown and don't need a babysitter, we stopped going to daycare because we were able to take care of ourselves at twelve," Anna adds, with that " miss thing" teenage attitude, typical when she opposes something.

"I'm not staying home to babysit you. I'll be here if you want to go somewhere, or we want to do something together. I get to work from home. I thought you'd be happy for me, for us."

"That's cool," Christian says, and both girls glare at him.

"We're just wondering why now, mom? We have three years of high school left, and then we're off to college," Anna says. "We may leave the state like Christian did."

"I'm not leaving," Taylor interjects.

Anna flashes Taylor the evil eye. "Okay, so you're a baby, and staying here. My point is, we're too old for a babysitter now."

"I'm not here to babysit," I say. "Did you ever think of my feelings or why I might want to work from home? No, I'm sure you didn't. I have the opportunity to enjoy the beach every day and spend more time with my family. Why begrudge me that?"

I'm acting overly dramatic, but my twins' reaction upsets me, and I expected a warmer welcome. I guess them not being excited hurt my feelings just a little, but no matter, I'm their mother, and they'll live with my decisions.

The table gets quiet, and I look over at Ian. He's probably thinking the same thing about their reaction. Yes, maybe I'm staying home to make sure my kids don't get into trouble, but why would they care if I'm here in the house? I let them have

Random Summer Storms

whoever they want over, and always given them the freedom to come and go. I asked them only to call me at work if they were leaving the house and let me know how long they would be gone. I had rules for them when I wasn't here too.

I didn't say anything. I just started eating my food slowly, waiting for a reaction, but not before I gave everyone "the look," the one when I'm not happy, or the same one I gave them when they were younger in public that means, stop what you're doing right now.

I wondered if anyone would say anything, it got so quiet. Finally, Taylor says, "I'm glad you're staying home, mom," then comes around the table and hugs me. She takes her plate to the sink and starts rinsing it.

"Me too. Good for you, mom." Christian says, getting up too, and it didn't affect him anyway. That left Anna, who never has any problems, so I'm confused with her attitude about my news.

Finally, Anna voiced her opinion. "Mom, I'm happy. I just thought you were doing this because you felt you must watch us now. We're older and know how to take care of ourselves. If you're happy, I'm happy." She gets up and takes her plate to the sink. I feel guilty because I want to keep an eye on them, so I wasn't being entirely truthful. I also would enjoy hanging out with them for the rest of the summer. Them not wanting me to is what made me upset.

We've reached that place in life where Mom doesn't fit into their daily plans. It happened with Christian when he was fifteen, and I knew it would happen with the girls. Like it or not, we're there.

I let the conversation die; no need to comment further. Besides, the plan is already in motion. Whether the kids like it or not, I'm staying at home. The house gets quiet with everyone in their rooms doing whatever it is they do alone. After cleaning up in the kitchen, I go into the sitting room and find Ian reading a medical journal. He doesn't look up when I come in, so I leave him with his magazine.

I wander around the house, feeling blue. I don't like the emotional gap between Anna and me. I'm open and willing to listen whenever my kids need to talk. Anna seems withdrawn and opposed to my being in the house during the day. Of course, my mom's mind tells me I should figure out why she doesn't want me here.

She's not talking, and I need to know why, so I grab my phone and look up music on my Pandora. When the girls were little, they each had a music playlist on my phone. I never took it off when they got their phones. Anna loves Justin Timberlake.

I quietly go up the stairs, looking at Anna's list to pick a song. Our family likes music. I check on Taylor; she's on her phone talking to someone. I hear the muffled sound of laughter and animated conversation.

I continue past Taylor's bedroom to Anna's room. The door is closed. I tap lightly.

"Come in," Anna says. I open the door just a crack and reach my hand in with the phone. Justin Timberlake is singing the chorus "Cry Me A River, Cry Me A River...." I don't hear anything but the song. After a few moments, the door pops open, and Anna is standing there, smiling.

"Mom, what are you doing?" She laughs. "I love Justin!" She steps aside to let me into her room. I do a little dance as I enter, making her smile. I'm corny sometimes.

"I know," I say, then laugh, and we both sing, "you told me you love me. Why did you leave me all alone?" The two of us continue singing in our high voice. "Cry me a river." As the song ends, we laugh and hug each other.

"I didn't want you to go to bed with this tension between us. I want you to know I trust you. You can still do what you do all summer, I'll be here if you need me. I'm not here to snoop on you. Maybe we can all go to the mall and shop or surf together. I promise I won't babysit you or your friends."

Anna hugs me, "I love you, Mom, and I want to do stuff with you too. I wanted you to know you didn't have to do this for us. We'll be fine. I thought maybe it had something to do with Steve and me."

She looks me in the eye and says, "I like him, and he likes me, but we both know he's here only for a couple of months and then goes back to school. His parents weren't too thrilled with us dating either, so when you said you were staying home, I took offense. We're both taking a lot of heat from certain people." Anna looks down at her hands.

"I didn't know, sweetheart," I say, taking her hand," I think Steve is a good guy, and you know we like him and always have. I'm sorry, Anna, is it the age thing?" I feel bad why anyone would have a problem with them being together.

"It's the black and white thing, Mom. Don't worry, we can handle it. We're staying out of trouble. I don't know about Taylor though; she's always getting into trouble!" Anna saw Taylor standing just outside the door listening. I look up and see her too. She was caught eves dropping.

"What?" Taylor asks, laughing as she runs and jumps on the bed behind Anna, acting as if she's strangling her. We all laugh and hug and roll around on the bed. Both girls sing along with the next song on the playlist, NSYNC's, "bye bye bye," bouncing on Anna's bed in a mock dance.

"That's an old school song," Taylor says.

I hug them both and tell them good night. I shut off pandora and head back to my room.

I feel better about Anna and me, but I wonder why Steve's parents aren't happy with him seeing Anna. Of course, they probably want him to concentrate on school, not girls, and she is younger, but Anna mentioned the black and white thing, so Steve's parents might not want him dating a white girl. Anna's the perfect girlfriend, smart, beautiful, and doesn't do drugs or alcohol. Color was the last thing I expected to be an issue.

She's showing me she wants to be independent. Anna was very mature in her discussion with me. I need to continue to trust her and let both Taylor and her grow. I can only pray they make the right decisions.

I go downstairs and find Ian still reading his magazine. I start rubbing his shoulders as I update him on what went on upstairs. I look out the window, and Christian is driving off into the night.

He's always made decisions I'm proud of, so why do I feel as though he's going off the track? Before this summer ends, I'll find out what's making me feel unsure about my son. I hope I'm just being overprotective. All my kids are growing up and need space, and it's probably me resisting them growing up. This situation is emotionally difficult, and I trust them, but wonder whether I'm trusting them too much.

Waves washing onshore is the only sound of the night. I walk out on the back patio and sit with a glass of wine. The moon is full and bright, so I don't turn on any lights. I can't see the stars twinkle because of the brightness of the beautiful moon reflecting off the dark black ocean. I feel peaceful and soothed, truly blessed to live in this piece of Heaven on earth. We have nesting turtles, so we're not allowed to have back porch lights on during certain times of the year. The sea turtles, loggerhead, green as well as leatherback, lay their eggs from the end of April into May. A non-profit group comes out and posts markers on the nest to keep people away.

Usually, the turtles will hatch on a full moon closer to October, and all the baby turtles will make their way to the sea. The same turtles come every year to lay their eggs. The bright lights on the houses confuse the baby turtles, and they go the wrong way, sometimes dying on the dunes.

I sit out there and listen to the sound of the waves in the dark. It helps me relax and feel at peace; my haven where I can unwind. We're lucky enough to have over one hundred feet of beachfront property.

The houses along the beach all sit on at least one acre of land, and we enjoy plenty of privacy. We rest on the border of Ponte Vedra Beach and Jacksonville Beach. The beach is mostly private, with only a few municipal beach accesses between the homes on our street. If you're unfamiliar with the area, you won't know where to go, so you see mostly people who live here walking the beach, with fewer walking at night.

I sit and enjoy the ocean with the moon's reflection for a good hour before I go in and get ready for bed. I snuggle in with my book, and Ian joins me. We love to open the windows, but it's not cool enough. July always brings hot and muggy weather.

I spend the rest of the week organizing at the office so I can start my new adventure of working remotely from home. An announcement to my co-workers is scheduled for Thursday. They're all happy for me, and I tell them I'm available at home. The computer is ready, and they'll deliver it and set it up on Friday. I'll meet them at the house to make sure I have what I need as far as space and cabinets.

Everything else is life as usual, although there is a little commotion at my house as the electrician and technician set everything up in my office. I called into our internet carrier a few days before to get it up to speed. Another perk is that the station I work for will be paying the internet bill for my house as I work from home. The kids will also love the increase in speed from our internet, enhancing their enjoyment when they're on their phones, iPads, and gaming on their X-box.

Monday, I log on and start my new daily routine, and its business as usual. My inbox is overflowing. I make a few calls to co-workers to make sure we're on the same page concerning topics for our next airing. Some items are better face to face, but between the phone and computer, I'm accomplishing my tasks. I get up and walk out back several times during the day to stretch and get away from the computer. The convenience of taking my breaks right on the oceanfront is awesome.

I wish I could set my workstation on the back patio. The elements of sand and wind would destroy it, but it would be awesome. I snap a picture of the view and send it to my boss, Andrew, showing off my new office digs. He sends me a text that he's envious and to enjoy.

I'm fortunate to work for a company so understanding. They must appreciate and value my work, or they wouldn't have allowed this set up and let me go and found another producer.

My first couple of days pass quickly, performing my job in a completely different way than normal. Once I found a rhythm, it became easy to keep up with all my normal daily tasks.

The kids came and went as usual. They were enjoying a fun-filled summer, and I stayed out of their way. I notice the same faces on most days, but my job demands my time, and I don't have the luxury to watch anyone's activities, so I stay to myself.

Taylor and Joel are surfing and hanging out around town. Joel is an exceptional surfer. Anna and Steve are watching TV or playing video games and cruising around town as well. Although it's my house, I try not to make my presence known, trying to convince them I'm not watching and keeping tabs. They must notice I don't call them as much to see what they're doing since now I can see them. That should win points.

Christian and Jamie still hang out together almost every day. They'd come down for microwave popcorn and sodas and take movies back up to the in-law suite. I'm sure Jamie sometimes spent the night, but she'd leave early to avoid interrogation. I wonder what her mom thinks on the nights she doesn't go home. I guess they're okay with Jamie and Christian and don't mind.

On some nights, Christian's other friends come by and pick him up. On those "guy nights," we didn't see Jamie. They hit the club scene a lot for guys not old enough to drink. I believe the clubs were eighteen and up. Some of these guys were over twenty-one. I'd find out later they were washing off the X's indicating they were underage so they couldn't order alcohol. After removing the X's, they could be served until, of course, a bouncer or someone working the club found out, resulting in an unceremonious eviction from the club. I can't say much; we used fake ID's when we were under twenty-one.

I never knew what time he was rolling in at night, but I'm sure it wasn't before midnight. I approached the subject a few times, and Christian gave me an abbreviated version of hanging with the guys. He's too old for curfew.

The twins were on their best behavior. They went out together a couple of times a week. Some nights they'd go out with the boyfriends only once or twice a week. They and their girlfriends would alternate staying at one another's house.

I remember when they were younger, both were too scared to sleep at anyone else's home. I'd take them and their pajama bags and drop them off, knowing by seven-thirty or so I'd get the call to come to get them. They finally outgrew that at twelve years old. Funny what comes to mind when I think back to their younger days.

The girls love it when I buy all the ingredients to make a homemade pizza. I bought premade pizza dough and rolled it into personal size pizzas, and each girl could put whatever she wanted on hers. We chopped vegetables, set out pepperoni, ham, and sausage. Ian's a big fan too. All the overnight guests would then head back upstairs for movies or video games.

All my kids used to love to do the dance video, but I think they outgrew that. I enjoyed watching. I talked about it recently, and both girls freaked, mortified I brought up the idea. What? It was fun. I learned to stay downstairs now because mom's suggesting what's fun apparently isn't fun. Who knew? I find bringing this stuff up to see their reaction is humorous, their mortified faces are priceless.

Since I started working from home the summer involved nothing unusual. I enjoyed sitting and talking with Ian about what the kids did each day, and everything was ordinary. I worked; they did what kids do. I think I was wrong, and maybe they didn't need to be watched, but I enjoy working from home. No suits, I can work in my pajamas if I choose, although I don't because with three kids, I never know who's coming in that door at any given time, not to mention spur of the moment family visits.

I also take the opportunity to drive to the Mayo and surprise my husband with lunch. He occasionally gets a few minutes. I call the scheduling nurse, usually Peggy, and check for an open spot on the calendar for a moment with the surgeon (the kids call him doctor dad and I call him my surgeon). She recognizes my voice immediately.

I run up to his office with sushi or hot pastrami sandwiches, one of his favorites. We find a quiet place to eat our lunch and enjoy a few moments of peace. I treasure these moments, even if they're few and far between. The one today is cut short when he receives a page.

Ian's days are busy, with no two days alike. He makes morning rounds every day, not knowing what awaits. Someone might have been admitted last night and is scheduled for surgery today. He meets with other surgeons, radiologists, and specialists to discuss one patient's diagnosis, and treatments for others. They speak of progress and future prognosis; each doctor wanting the best outcome for each patient. Discussion and treatment continue throughout the day before he makes final rounds and finally comes home.

CHAPTER 19

August has arrived, which brings the hottest part of summer. We've held several barbeques with the neighbors, but it's so hot, we seek shelter in the house. Even living on the beach with a breeze blowing almost all the time, the tropical weather here is humid and gets uncomfortable. We had big ceiling fans installed out on the back covered patio, but it still gets warm even with an offshore breeze. After the sun sets, it becomes tolerable. The weather channel reports ninety-eight degrees, but it feels like one-hundred and eight.

What does that mean? In my opinion, this weather is hot as hell, period. They say, "feels like," which combines the temperature and humidity to give the heat index. So scientific. I'm working on a story about how heat affects our senior citizens. I got the idea from Ian as his patients at the hospital sometimes struggle with the temperatures and their health. People over sixty-five years old are susceptible to heat stress and struggle to adapt to the change in weather. Ian told me heat stroke landed many a patient in the hospital.

I get up from reading through the research pieces I received, needing a break from looking at the computer screen. I feel stiff and achy and rub my eyes as I walk into the family room.

Carmen is cleaning closets. Ian, Christian, and the girls are all gone, so it's the perfect opportunity to clean out the closets and get rid of old junk. I'm working in my office, and Carmen lets me know she's finished upstairs and is going out to clean the in-law suite. We walk to the door talking, and Carmen goes up while I return to my home office to work on the next show.

She's up there for only fifteen minutes before she comes back down. Her face is white as a ghost. She says she didn't sign up for this, and then rattles off a sentence in Spanish. I speak minimal Spanish, but when she crossed herself, I knew it was terrible. She was too terrified to go back up to the suite. I don't know what to think about this, so I grab my phone and walk up there. I want my phone with me in case I need to call 9-1-1.

I'm frightened by what I might find, but my initial look is a neat and clean suite. Christian is good about that. Nothing scary or upsetting in the sitting area or small kitchenette. Maybe there's a snake in here. We sometimes find the critters in the planters.

Forests abound all throughout Florida. Pine trees and wild brush grow everywhere. Lots of creatures, such as snakes, lizards, possum, rats, and who knows what else live, but I'm not finding any. Thank goodness; any of these would be awful in the house.

I go into the bedroom and the dust skirting is pulled up, the vacuum is lying on the floor, and Christian's closet is open. I see a nine-millimeter Glock on the top shelf. I grew up in a house with guns and am comfortable around them, so pick it up. I check the slide, and although there's nothing in the chamber, the magazine is full.

Christian is old enough to buy a gun, but I wasn't aware he was interested. Ian owns a handgun and a couple of shotguns. We've always been open with the kids about our firearms. They always knew Ian owned them, but they were off limits. I find it strange he bought a gun without telling Ian.

Does Ian know, but didn't tell me? Either way, I feel uncomfortable. I set the handgun back where I found it. As I sit on the bed, I remember the dust skirt, so squat down on the floor and look under the bed. I see a rifle, and assume Carmen hit it with the vacuum cleaner.

I lay on my stomach and pull it out slowly. When I see it's an AR-15, I feel as if I might vomit. I never held one, and it looks ominous coming from under my son's bed. I've heard it's nothing more than an ArmaLite hunting rifle, not an assault rifle, though it looks assaulting to me. The fact I found it under my son's bed scares the hell out of me.

Random Summer Storms

I've never had a problem with owning guns. and am a Second Amendment advocate. Now for some reason, I want to know the rules, and how a young man can buy a rifle and handgun at such a young age.

Both guns are clean and oiled. They haven't been fired lately or handled much from what I can see. As I said, I owned many guns in my life, and these two-look new and show little use.

Neither Christian nor Ian are hunters. So why is the rifle here? I check it as well, and it's not loaded. I start to search the room for bullets or other guns but find no ammunition. I didn't find shells for the Glock in my search, either. So, there are two legal weapons in my son's room, and I don't understand why we've never discussed them. The suite is not completely separate from our home and bringing something like this into it is something we should have discussed. I removed the magazine from the Glock and set that, as well as the AR-15, on the dresser. I didn't find a magazine for the AR-15 and wonder if one exists.

I need to talk to Carmen and call Ian. I also need Christian to come home and tell me why he has these guns in my house. I can't help but think something awful caused him to have them. You see on the news all the time where a student shoots up a school. Please don't let that be my kid. I feel the hair on the back of my neck rise. This can't be happening. Once again, I feel as though I haven't been paying attention.

But what signs are there for this? What child-raising book prepares a parent for this moment? Hell, I don't even know what this moment is. The reason is probably rational, and I should stop thinking the worst, but the college shootings keep flashing in my mind, and I want to cry.

I go down to talk to Carmen about her find, but she's already left for the day. I try calling her, but she doesn't answer, and I can't blame her for reacting that way. I feel scared too. As frightened as she is, I don't know if she'll come back. I'll give her some time and call her again later.

I call Ian and got his voicemail, of course, and left him a message to call me immediately. I then call Christian and am told to leave a message. I don't want to think the worst, but this is the worst. Then again, what if he wanted to buy guns simply because he's old enough to own them. He's an adult who can buy what he wants, but even at twenty, I still consider him my child.

I don't like this at all. A college student goes out and buys an AR-15 and a handgun. If we lived out in the country where people hunt for food or sport, maybe this would be okay. Here at the beach, it's a recipe for disaster. Here at the beach, Ian owning a gun never warranted a second thought. But we don't hunt here, and to my knowledge, weapons aren't permitted on the beach.

Ian's the first to return my call. I tell him what I found in Christian's room. He says he's discussed guns with Christian, and Christian said he was going to buy one someday. He doesn't have that kind of money now. How did he buy them?

I see this as a problem. Ian says he doesn't have any more surgeries or appointments today, so he'll come home now. He said if Christian calls, tell him we need to talk to him, but stay calm.

I tell him I'll try, but I'm freaked out. After we hang up, I pace around my house. I can't calm down until we talk about those guns. Why does Christian have them? About twenty minutes after I called Christian, he calls back. I tell him I want to speak to him but not on the phone.

"I'm heading home right now, mom. I'm about five minutes out." He pauses and then asks, "everything okay?"

I assure him it is, but we need to discuss something.

Ian pulls into the driveway shortly after our conversation. I open the door and wait for him to get out of his car. He walks up to me and gives me a reassuring hug, but by the look on his face and how I felt, I don't think either of us are reassured. We go in and sit down to wait for Christian.

When Christian arrives, he comes into the house before going up to his room. He looks at us and smiles. "What's up?" The smile dies on his face when he realizes we're upset about something. His dad coming home this early is a sign something's wrong.

He walks in the room slowly, looking from me to Ian. "Is everything okay? Did something happen?"

Ian gestures to a chair. "Sit down, son. We want to talk about something."

I speak up immediately. I know Ian planned it differently, but I can't hold back. "Carmen found guns in your room today when she was cleaning," I blurt out.

"Why is she cleaning?" he asks. "I told you I'd take care of the room. I don't need her to pick up after me."

"Who cares what she was doing in there?" I ask. "Why are the guns in there?"

"I'm old enough to own a gun," he says, his jaw set. "Dad and I talked about it."

"That's true," Ian agrees, "but you need to realize this is our house, and anything that happens on this property reflects on the property owner, your mother and me. Stashing a gun in your room is important enough to tell us, not to mention how you purchased it and how it's to be properly stored. What would have happened if Carmen accidentally discharged the rifle by hitting it with the vacuum?"

Christian tells us it wasn't loaded, and the safety was engaged on the pistol. Christian is angry and insists he's not an idiot. We argue back and forth about the safety and storage of guns, but it's irrelevant. He's avoiding the real question of why he has them in the first place. I need to know now.

"Okay, so you wanted to buy a gun," I say. "Why? You wanted to buy a rifle. Again, I must ask why, and of all rifles, why that style? When you talked to your dad about the purchase, did you tell him when you were buying them? Those guns aren't cheap, so where did you get that kind of money?" I would think he'd enjoy doing that with his father.

He answers too quickly. "I bought them to intimidate, to show I mean business." The look on his face suggested that perhaps he spoke too soon.

"I don't understand, Christian," Ian says. "Why do you need to intimidate anyone?" He directs the question point blank, leaving Christian no room to lie. I can sense Ian is starting to get agitated with our son's answers.

"Intruders," Christian says.

I can sense he's thinking hard to give the right answers, and isn't being completely honest. Our son is holding something back. Is the intimidation for here or at school? I hope he doesn't think he can take them to school. Surely, he's smart enough to know that would never be allowed.

"You're going back to school, Christian. You can't take those with you. Guns are forbidden on campus. Besides, we have guns to protect this house. Why would you need more? What aren't you telling us?" My tone comes out as a plea.

He looks up at the ceiling and inhales a few breaths before he starts.

I'm totally unprepared for what he says, but I should've seen it; should've known things didn't always add up. You know what they say, be careful what you ask for, because you might not like the answer. If you can't handle the answer, stick your head in the sand and don't ask the question. But the question has been asked and it's too late to stick our head in the sand.

My job in the beginning as a journalist was to find a story and dig up all the information that I can. I was known for my tenacity. When it concerns my son, it has a whole different feel. I fear the story he's about to tell. Please, Lord, don't let him be a psycho who wants to shoot up a college because he's being bullied or hates Mondays. I would never forgive myself if I ignored him reaching out for something he's going through. So, like it or not, Ian and I are about to be enlightened.

CHAPTER 20

When Christian stands up and paces the quiet room, we fear the worst. He stops in front of us saying he'll start from the beginning, asking us not to get angry.

Unfortunately, we're already upset, but we need to hear him out to help him address and solve the problem. So, we agree to remain calm while he tells us the story. I'm not sure I want to hear what he has to say.

It all started shortly after the first few months of college. At school, other kids were always talking about buying weed. Christian admitted he tried it a few times the summer he graduated from high school. Most kids smoke it, so no big deal, right? He found it calmed him in the evenings when he tried to sleep at night after the stress of class exams and working out with his team. He had a lot to handle, with learning all the plays while maintaining good grades. Marijuana helped him cope.

The problem was, no one knew where to buy weed. When he came home during Christmas break last year, he talked to a friend who told him, "I can get you all you want." So, Christian took back several ounces to his classmates. Although it was a hit, it lasted only two days, so he called his friend and told him he needed more. Christian drove down on the weekend and bought a couple of pounds.

Once the other kids had a supplier, they came. Christian explained how they had a tight-knit circle of friends to whom they sold their product. Pretty soon, Christian and a friend of his from school were driving with five to ten pounds of the best weed with funny names those students saw every weekend.

Christian and a friend of a friend from high school were both making big bucks on this deal as well; with unknown friend supplying said weed.

I immediately imagine which friend it might be.

Suddenly, Christian was involved in a big business. Someone was regularly driving or flying hundreds of pounds of weed in from California. Christian went into detail about the plants they're growing are nothing like me or dad had in our day. They assigned names like Grape Ape, Purple Kush, White Widow, and Sour Diesel. The hybrid supreme product college students expected.

Christian and his friend would supply it, and everyone wanted it. They get three hundred and fifty dollars an ounce, while Christian and his friend made one hundred dollars an ounce. With that kind of money, they could afford the gas, and still have plenty left to spend. Kids would buy it then take it off-campus and sell to locals. Once the word spread, everyone wanted some, and they never ran into any problems. They sold mostly to students and off-campus people in business at the college.

I guess they never thought about getting pulled over or an outsider stealing from them, but with those guns, maybe they had. So, my son has been dealing marijuana with his friend since last Christmas. Karma is slapping Ian and me in the face. I feel those skeletons jumping out of the closet in droves.

Okay, so Christian says he and his friend are getting pounds of weed from another friend, who's getting larger shipments of marijuana from a friend in California, but he won't say who these friends are. I wasn't surprised he didn't divulge the name. He said there were no problems nor any competition.

It sounds like a neat arrangement, but things are always good until they're not.

So now we hear the story and how it began. Why, with all these friendly weed sales, does Christian now need a gun and rifle for protection? Who needs to be intimidated? That's where the whole story takes a turn, but I remain quiet, as promised.

The story continues as Christian tells us a friend who lives in California comes to town at the beginning of the summer. This friend is the unknown who wants to get in on the action. He promises better prices with the same frequency of shipments, except they'll go straight to Christian and his college friend. They no longer need the guy they were getting the marijuana from in the beginning.

At this point, things start to unravel. Happy weed dealers are no longer happy. This original distributor and his friends are the people who attacked Christian at the club, a fight we now know started when Christian and said friend told the original distributor they wanted to use the new source. Same product; better prices. Christian was open to letting the original supplier in on his deal.

The original guys didn't like losing this business. They mentioned something about control, refused to let it go, and said the deals needed to stay the way they were. The original distributor had an agreement with his supplier he wasn't going to walk away from so easily. At this point, maybe the distributor should have said they were dealing with dangerous people.

Christian never named anyone at the bar, but that night, they argued. Threats were made, leading to the fight in the parking lot. Friends became enemies.

To make matters worse, shortly after that fight, the original distributor was pulled over by the police and arrested after leaving a party with a bag of pills and a couple of pounds of marijuana in his car. Christian tells us he'd planned to purchase the pot that night after they left the club.

The original distributor forgot about it because of the club altercation. Christian went to the hospital after, so he never got the weed from Brian, whom we now know was Christian's distributor. It sat in his trunk for a few days. Everyone forgot about it.

That caused another problem between Brian and Christian because he got pulled over, and said he got charged for something not "technically" his, but Christian's.

Christian explains, "how is it my fault? I wasn't even there that night, and Brian was drinking too much at a party. All his friends told him not to drive, but Brian didn't like people telling him what to do. They all said Brian was yelling at everyone that he was fine; he could drive, and he would go straight home. He lived only a few blocks away."

The cops say it was a random check; and he was swerving in traffic. Bad luck all the way around. Christian feels guilty about that. I couldn't help noticing it was random again.

The cops and the DEA jumped all over the rest of his crew after that night. No one is talking, but we know they're questioning everyone who hung out with the distributor. He's now in jail, sentenced to serve ten years. At the beginning of Christian's story, he wasn't naming names, but now he's coming clean. I guess it's okay, since we may never see this distributor again. I wonder what these kids are thinking; and I know my parents probably thought the same thing of us when we were young.

So, we're talking about the same Brian that drove that beautiful Jaguar we saw in the driveway at the beginning of summer? Yes, Christian says, the very same guy.

Ian said we wouldn't interrupt, so Christian continues his story while Ian and I are bursting with questions we must hold back. He also tells us another friend of his, Mike and a kid he doesn't know, also went to jail recently because the DEA kicked in their door, and confiscated cocaine and several pounds of marijuana from their apartment. They're all connected in the business of buying and selling from Brian.

They had no idea anyone was watching them. "So, Brian gets busted, and sure enough, right after the guys picked up product and went back to their apartment, they got rousted. They were breaking up a pound on their coffee table when the cops pounded on the door, and the next thing you know, ten cops are tearing apart their place. Mike and his buddy are cuffed and sent to jail. Christian tells us they started getting threats right after that. Mike tells people it was us who turned over on them."

"They think we turned them in because we found a new source, but that's not true. We were all friends, and none of us would talk. Brian's cousin doesn't believe us. His cousin also blames me for the several pounds in the trunk Brian got caught with and says I should admit it was mine and go to jail instead of Brian. Mike and Brian's cousin threatened us and said he was coming for us ten deep."

Christian's face is intense while he's relating the story. I clearly see he's shaken up as he talks.

"They threatened to come, and we'd never see them coming," Christian says. He says another friend gave him the AR-15.

I'm concerned because the guys know where we live. Why would anyone Christian hangs out with have that gun in the first place?

Christian said he, too, was questioned by the DEA, although they didn't seem to know anything about him and his college dealing.

I don't believe that for a minute. I think the DEA is closing in on the whole operation, and everything is about to go off.

The DEA guy said they knew where Christian lived, and who he hung out with. They dropped a few names like Jamie, Chris, Brian, and other friends he gave by their full names. The agent in charge said he knew Ian's dad was a doctor and his mom worked for the news station.

So, what we gather from this story is, the group of friends was selling weed at all levels, and now the cops and DEA are watching them. Brian got caught, and so did some of his buddies. Before the big bust, Christian was bailing out on them for new suppliers. Now Brian is blaming Christian and his friends for the bust.

Christian finishes up the story by telling us he obtained the AR-15 only after finding out some of Brian's cousins were coming for him last night. We are wondering what Christian thought he would do with a rifle without ammo. He said he'd planned to buy some today.

We asked Christian what he thought would happen to his family, unaware he might be murdered in his sleep. Good Lord, what a nightmare. I am concerned that he couldn't come to us and angry that he didn't. I wish he would have told the police and asked for protection.

By this time, Ian's heard enough and wants questions answered. He adjusts his seat to face Christian. "Your first year of college, you were selling weed, without thinking what it might do to this family?"

"It started small then blew up," Christian says. "We just wanted a little weed to get through finals."

"You were driving pounds of the stuff across state lines, and never worried it's a federal offense. You never thought about the possibility of prison?" I ask, shaking my head.

"No, we never drank. We were careful, and it was always me and…." He stammers, not wanting to divulge his friend's name.

"Too late for secrets now, son. They're coming for you, and we need to know who to protect."

"I know you don't want to name names, but we need to know what we're up against. Who's coming? Who's in danger? Should we call the cops on these guys and have them picked up?" I ask Christian, as I look to Ian for answers.

"It's Pete," Christian says. "He went back to school to wait for it to blow over. He doesn't fight, but said he'd come back if I need him. He's a good guy. There's no need to tell anyone about him, and I don't want to call the cops. I think giving names with make it worse, and they'll keep coming."

"All the more reason to tell us everyone that's involved," Ian says. "We need to get a handle on this."

"Well, Brian's in jail and about to be bonded out before his trial. His cousin Tim is the one who said he's coming for us, along with whoever else they had in their crew. I don't know all of them, but Brian had a few cousins that will do whatever he tells them.

Mike and his roommate are still in jail. They have priors and were on probation, so we won't see them for ten years or more unless they snitch out Brian. That's what I don't get. Mike is Brian and his cousin's biggest problem. Why they want us is crazy. All we wanted was to get the weed cheaper, and we'd let him in on that deal too."

"This is all so extreme," Ian says. "Why haven't you guys talked to each other? Maybe we can work something out, let his lawyer take care of everything else. Violence won't keep anyone from going to jail, only guarantee a longer sentence if they come here and threaten us."

Christian stands up. "This isn't your fight, Dad! I was hoping to talk it out, but I plan on being ready if I can't. When Brian gets out, I planned to talk to him. I think he'd be okay if we talked and he understands I haven't said a word to the DEA. I can handle it."

"Son, you made it my fight when you brought those people to our home. I'm telling you this; if they want a fight, they picked the wrong house. I'll be ready for them. Those little punks won't get away with threatening anyone in this family." Ian stands up and bows his shoulders. I know that stance. It's fight time.

"I never wanted this to happen," Christian says. "I never thought something like this would happen; we were all friends." He finally breaks down. He sits down on the couch, and Ian sits down next to him, and tears slide down his face. His dad pats him on the back.

"We'll get through this together, son. When it's over, there will be some changes." Ian continues to rub Christian's back, then squeezes the back of his neck like he always did before a game. "We got this. I won't let you face them alone."

I'm scared to death and don't know what to do, but my motherly instinct says to grab a gun and protect my family. If it comes to that, I will.

We talk into the night. I'm grateful the girls are staying with their friends and going to the Red Bull Night Riders surfing competition. It allows us some time to figure out our course of action.

Personally, I'd like Christian to go back to school and forget he ever sold weed. He needs to tell all his friends the shop is closed for good, then put the word out to Brian and his friends that it's over, and they're all leaving town. It worked for Ian and me.

We know that's a band-aid approach, and it won't go away on its own, and we'll need to face it head-on. We need more information, so we continue drilling Christian.

We talk about the DEA and what they know. Somehow, they knew Brian was the head guy, but Christian says that's not true. Christian met another guy while they were all out one night. Big guy with dark hair named Luis. Brian was real protective of keeping Luis's identity secret. Luis was a nice guy, not a thug like those other Dope Boys, and for some reason, he liked Christian a lot. He treated him good, buying all his drinks and inviting him to go out with them every time I saw him. We talked about cars for hours one night. "I took his car for a spin. It was a big BMW 7 series, fully loaded."

"He's the one I wanted to get together with my new connection. I thought it would be good for all of us, but Brian and his crew took offense. Anyway, I never got to tell him about my connection getting weed at a better price. I was never brought around Luis or saw him out after that first night. I hoped to talk to him about our connection and see what he thought."

"Do you think that talking to these guys will help?" I ask. "I mean, let them know you don't want a fight, and we don't either. Maybe we could sit down and talk it out."

"That's an option, but if they want a fight, we'll give them one," Ian says.

I know he means it. He hasn't been in an altercation in a long time, but never has backed down when challenged to a fight. He looks at Christian. "Call these guys tomorrow. Tell them you want to meet and talk. I'll go with you, or we can meet here."

We all hug and go to bed. We haven't been setting the security alarm, we did tonight. Ian tells Christian to keep the gun by his nightstand just in case, and Ian will be armed as well. I doubt anyone will sleep after our discussion.

When we're alone in our room, I watch Ian set his loaded handgun on the nightstand, then pull out the Mossberg, check the condition of it, and look on the shelf for ammunition. His father used the gun on the Trinity the night we were attacked by the Columbians back in the eighties. History is repeating itself. I think again of that horrific night, then turn to Ian.

"Do you think they'll be bold enough to come to our house and attack?" I ask. "These kids today, who knows what they will do," I say, when Ian doesn't answer right away.

He fluffs up his pillow and lays down. The crease in his forehead tells me he's still trying to figure this whole thing out. Sleep won't come easy tonight.

"Yep," is all he says.

I let it go. I'm sure Ian will come up with something. That's who he is. I can't help but lay here and blame ourselves for this outcome. We never talked about weed before this summer. I fall asleep, dreaming about being attacked on a boat, reliving the Trinity nightmare, but this time my kids were in the dream.

CHAPTER 21

Christian calls Brian's cousin and tells him he wants to meet. They cuss and swear a while before settling into a civil conversation. We hear a one-sided conversation for a few minutes, and Christian finds out Brian's lawyer will post bail on Monday. They set up a meeting for then, and agree to a truce, if only temporary. I don't trust them, but what choice do we have? They agree to talk in a public place, and Ian and I will be there.

We plan where we're going and how we're going to sit. Each of us plans a line of escape just in case. We have no way of knowing how they'll react or how they want the meeting to play out.

We all feel nervous for the rest of the weekend. When the girls are home, we don't mention anything about the meeting. We try to keep it light and enjoy the rest of the weekend. I hate deception, but don't want the girls involved. Keeping them unaware of the situation is our only way to protect them. I feel as if I've been here before and recall it didn't work out as planned then.

We cook hamburgers on the grill on Sunday. Jamie joins us for dinner. For a moment, it feels like a regular day, with the girls in the kitchen, cutting up lettuce, tomatoes, and onions; the guys out back, cooking the burgers on the grill. I prepare baked beans with Mac n Cheese in the oven. It smells terrific. I've felt queasy and scared every day. I haven't been able to enjoy a meal all week.

As we sit down to dinner, we talk about the Night Rider Competition. The talent it takes to do the tricks they do in the dark is amazing. Many people go out to watch, and only the surfers understand the difficulty in pulling off the tricks, not knowing where the wave top ends, where the air begins, or how fast the sets come in. Spotlights help some. Anyone who's night surfed knows it's different. Performing tricks in the dark is the crazy amazing part, and only the most accomplished and experienced surfers can pull it off.

The girls and all their friends attended. "It was so awesome!" Anna talks about her friends competing that night. Taylor explains how the competitors get towed by a jet ski up and down the surf line. The sheer strength of the guys standing on a surfboard and hanging on to a pull rope for fifteen minutes to find the best wave for the most tricks is incredible. "These guys were doing three-sixties and flips; you had to be there." They told us all about it through dinner.

We all relax and watch TV together in the family room that evening. Christian takes Jamie home and returns an hour later. I admit I was worried the entire time he was gone; fearing someone might attack him on the drive to Jamie's. He came back, grabbed an apple, and headed up to his place.

Tonight, is yet another sleepless night for Ian and me. We both toss and turn all night long. By four, I can't flop around anymore, and get up. I brew coffee and check my email for the day's work. I want to accomplish as much as I can early, so I can go with Ian and Christian to Chili's for the meeting. Ian doesn't want me to go, but no way I'm staying home. Besides, Ian would look less conspicuous at another table with his wife than alone.

At noon we head out to the restaurant. I feel doom is imminent. Ian is looking as though he's dead set on the prospect of a fight, which gives me no comfort.

When we pull into the parking lot, Christian points to a car and tells us Brian and his dude are already here. We let him go in first; wait ten minutes; then go in.

They're sitting at the bar and don't notice us come in. We choose a table with a view of the bar, order soft drinks and look at the menu. They talk for quite a while. We order appetizers, but only pick at them.

We can't hear the conversation. The jabbing hand gestures, and facial expressions indicate it's not a friendly conversation.

We get up and walk out to the parking lot to wait for Christian. He stays inside another twenty-five minutes. The waiting rattles my nerves.

We stand off to the side as they finally walk out the front door of the restaurant. I'm sure Brian and his sidekick don't see us. Brian's friend shoves Christian and says, "this ain't over, punk." Brian tells him to chill out, but it's too late, and he takes a cheap shot at Christian.

Ian jumps out from between the cars and shoves the guy. "It's over, Bro."

"What the fuck, old man," he says, then throws a punch at Ian, who blocks the blow. "You don't want to go there, my friend. I'll knock you into next week." He throws up his hands and set his feet to kick the guy in the head.

Christian, ready to kick ass as well, steps in front of Ian and shoves the guy, then raises his fists. "You and me, player."

I had no doubt they meant business, but I was surprised Brian was the one to stop the whole thing.

"Okay, okay, not here. Tim, back off," Brian says, in a low voice.

Christian is in Tim's face, and Ian is bowed up and ready to fight. More shoving ensues, then other people start coming out of the restaurant.

"Come on, Brian is right," I say, making it seem as if Brian and I are allies. "We don't want to make a scene." Brian nods my way, and for the time being, it appears he and I are working together to control an ugly situation.

I try convincing Ian and Christian to get in the car. "Christian and Ian, do as I ask."

Tim mumbles, "take you all the way out next time, bro." He draws out the sarcastic B-R-O. At that point, we all now know he's the one who hit Christian from behind.

Christian throws a fist at Tim's face, but Brian yanks Tim by the arm, and the blow hits air.

"We're cool, Christian," Brian says. "I got nothing against you as long as you be straight with me. We leave it here." He reaches out for a bro handshake half-hug guys do. Then Brian pats Tim on the arm, "let's go." Tim would rather fight than walk away. His anger is evident in his face and pumped-up chest.

But he does what Brian says and backs down. They walk over to the Jaguar and drive away, leaving my two guys standing there. Tim punches the dash as they pass us, and is talking very animated to Brian. He had it in for Christian. Walking away was not how he wanted to get back at Christian and his old man.

We get in our car and I ask, "do you think it's over?"

They both say, "no."

"I don't think Brian is the problem," Christian says. "I believe Tim is acting like a thug wannabe. We used to be so cool and were friends, homeys, but he sure switched fast. Tim is going to be trouble wherever I go. That's cool. I'll be ready for him."

Neither I nor Ian comment, but we're both worried.

Ian turns in his seat to face Christian. "I want you to return that rifle to whoever gave it to you. You don't know anything about where it came from or how your friend obtained it. I also want you to get a lockbox for the pistol and leave it here when you go back to school. Do you have a permit to carry a concealed weapon?"

Christian says no, but he'll get one.

"Until you do, it stays in the house in a lockbox," Ian says. "I don't want to find out you're carrying it around in the car. We know the DEA is watching. That's all we need is for you to get locked up for a concealed weapons charge. The situation looks out of control. Brian might not have an issue with you, but Tim's a loose cannon and can still be a problem."

We return to the house, and things settle down. The rest of the day is business as usual. We tell Christian he shouldn't go out alone for a while. He admits he's talked to all his friends and they agree and will be watching for anything weird or out of the ordinary. His friends will all let him know if anything is going down or be with him when it does. If anything is happening, someone will let Christian know.

Christian gives the rifle back to the guy who let him borrow it, who previously got it from Brian. How ironic is that? He traded it for stereo equipment. That rifle had a lousy history. We found out someone used it to shoot up a strip club. These guys were obviously criminals, much older than Brian and Christian's group. He tells us the shooting was no more than a warning, an intimidation, and no one was killed. We'll never know the target for the warning, but the message is clear.

"Great, a gun in our house was used in a felony," I say. "I hope you realize what your actions have caused this household." But as I say it, I think back on another time when Ian and my actions brought hell down on our family. What were we thinking when we were stealing from a drug cartel? Christian's situation is no different. We're on the wrong side of scary people, and the consequences are always the same.

Later that evening, as we lie in bed, I tell Ian this reminds me of a time when we put his parents and our families in a dangerous situation. I want him to be easier on Christian, but he needs to know these kinds of people aren't playing around. We don't know who we're dealing with from top to bottom. What if those kids are low on the food chain? What if a bigger and more dangerous group is behind the business dealings? What would they have against Christian?

I hoped the threat was gone once Christian and Brian talked and made peace. Within a few days, Brian and Christian spoke on the phone, and Brian said not to worry, he wouldn't come for Christian. They were trying to determine the identity of an informant, and Christian was not at the top of the "rat" list anymore. He was a part of the group under surveillance by the DEA. Brian told him, "watch his back man, someone is turning over on anyone and everyone to keep from going to jail themselves. They'll give up you, me, whoever to save their own sorry ass."

This is a new threat. We all talked about Christian not purchasing anything, and telling his person not to ship anything here, or he'd be facing prison time too. We never noticed any suspicious cars on our street. Our neighborhood watch would see right away. Christian said he never noticed anyone following him. I reminded him the DEA knew where he lived and the names of his friends, and they were watching.

The DEA was another problem. We wanted Christian to tell us where he gets the weed, but he wouldn't say.

"The less you know about that, the better," he says. "If the DEA is watching, you'll get involved, and I want to fix this myself."

Christian said there could be fallout from that, and he didn't want us to know anything that might inform on his connection. He tried to keep that person out of it and warn them what was happening. He could be right about the less we knew the better. I remember a time I felt the same way.

One night during dinner, the twins asked what was going on. They heard things around town. Except for Steve, they don't hang with Christian's friends. Christian assured Steve wasn't involved. He smoked occasionally but refused to get involved with selling. The girls' friends had older brothers that bought weed in the same circles, and there was talk about some getting shook down by the cops.

"This all comes back to Christian, from what we hear," Anna says, then looks at Ian. "It's not just Christian. We also heard dad is involved, and there was a fight in a Chili's parking lot with some of Christian's friends."

"Me, that's great." I know Ian's worried about this affecting his position at Mayo. "That isn't exactly true," he says. "We had an altercation, no fight."

Taylor sets her fork down. "But you were there. Mom, were you there? Why did you guys go to Chili's without inviting Anna and me?"

Anna nods. "You know we love Chili's."

"We wanted Christian to talk to Brian," I say. "We went just in case. It wasn't a fun outing."

"In case of what?" Anna asks. "You're all covering up something. What happened to, we're a family, and always stick together, no matter what?"

It looks as if it's going to be a long night. We'll need to tell the girls what we've been doing, and then explain what happened at Chilis. I'll tell them, but first, I want to find out how much they knew, and needed to hear what they found out on their own. I asked what kind of gossip was going around town about Christian.

In the end, we all needed to come clean to keep everyone safe. We would all share everything we know to find a solution to this catastrophe. I only hope the knowledge doesn't cause harm to anyone in my family.

CHAPTER 22

First, the girls mention that when Sherry was here, they heard her talking to someone, telling him the trip to Jamaica was a failure. It sounded as though she was talking to her boyfriend, who they believed was Winston. It sounded like an argument. Sherry told Winston she'd be home in a couple of days, and they could talk about the details then. She said she was caught up in some shit and lucky to get out alive, then added, "no thanks to you!" Whatever that meant.

"We couldn't hear what Winston said but could tell he wasn't happy by what Sherry said to him," Taylor says. "We heard only her part of the phone conversation. Sherry told him to shut up during the call, and that avoiding prison or not getting killed was the most important part of the trip. She hung up, threw her phone on the bed, then dropped the F-bomb." Taylor pauses and looks around the table.

"We ducked back in our rooms and acted like we didn't hear anything," Taylor continues. "The whole conversation was strange. We were left wondering what it was all about. Sherry never said anything to us when we went downstairs."

"I acted normal, and talked about the family," Anna adds. "We told her what we'd been up to and were glad she was here."

Taylor asked her if she felt okay after everything that happened before she got back to the United States. She said she was okay. Sherry didn't talk to us anymore about her trip to Jamaica. The conversation was about us and what we'd been doing. Sherry is always fun, and the girls love spending time with her. At the time, they didn't think anything about the phone call or what was said, but they knew she was upset, and rightfully so. Anyone would be. They had no reason to believe she was doing anything illegal.

"Then when we were out the other night, some guy said they know our cousin, that she gets good Ganja," Anna says. "We don't even know what Ganja is." Anna throws up her hands and shrugs.

Taylor says she thinks it all has to do with weed. "But it was strange because we didn't know the guy." She looks at Ian and Christian. "He was kinda creepy coming up to us like that. But that isn't what bothered us. Our problem is that you guys just told us about Christian." Both girls are looking at Ian, Christian, and myself. I feel incredibly guilty and wonder if Ian and Christian feel the same.

"You tell us Christian smokes weed, and Sherry's parents have a marijuana farm in California," Taylor says.

"Suddenly, everything has to do with weed, including weirdos coming up and trying to talk to us on the beach." Taylor says. "So, do they call weed Ganja in California?" She makes this face I'm familiar with; the one when I say maybe, when she knows I mean "NO."

I think it strange that a guy would say that out of the blue. I mention that Jamaican's call marijuana Ganja. "That's peculiar. She just got back from Jamaica." We all talk about that for a minute. Why would they use Jamaican terms? I wonder if Sherry's boyfriend or whoever she was talking to is Jamaican. No, probably not.

The fact the guy used a different word when referring to weed was probably no big deal. I expect lots of people use the phrase.

Christian confirms Sherry's boyfriend is Jamaican, and she does, in fact, buy pot from him. She never had a lot on her when they were together. "Who was the guy who said she gets good Ganja?" he asks.

"I don't know him, but he knew me, Christian, and Sherry," Taylor tells Christian. "The fact she doesn't live here and comes here a couple of times a year made it weird."

"Sherry may have shared some with the guy at a club or something," Christian says, thinking back. "Do you remember what he looked like?"

How would some random guy connect my girls with a woman at a club? Unless maybe he heard them talking about Sherry and recognized the name. That made sense to me. I don't like the fact a random guy said this to my daughter. "Where were you when this guy said this to you?"

"We all were hanging out at the pier, a small beach party," Anna says. "A few people were drinking beer, but most of us were just hanging out, riding skateboards and the usual stuff. It was over by ten, and we all went home after. That dude was a little older than the rest of us. He was with two other people his age, but not a part of our group. We didn't know him or talk to him." Taylor describes him as a tall skinny guy with brown hair cut close to his head. No one she remembers seeing before. Not a local beach guy either.

How casual people are about drugs. How odd this guy would say something like that to someone, especially two fifteen-year-olds. What would possess him to reveal to a couple of kids he gets marijuana, or got it from a person they know? I don't like it. I don't like the fact no one knew him. He shows up out of the blue to hang out with a group of kids. I wonder if he was DEA. I don't like a lot of things I'm hearing.

I also don't like the fact my niece is hanging out with a Jamaican guy who could be getting weed from his country, and having Sherry bring it back. She's our niece, and we love her, what if something happens to her? We stand by and say nothing. I don't know for sure that's what's happening, but it feels wrong, and my instincts are usually right. That incident in Jamaica wasn't a coincidence. I don't believe it was a wrong place, wrong time event.

I'm sure of it. The big question is, how does this guy on the beach know Sherry is related to the twins? I need to find out. Everything points to the DEA undercover guys checking into Christian and Brian's crew. I don't like the notion the DEA might use our daughters to get information. They're minors, and the DEA will force me to seek legal action. I hope it won't come to that, but we need to get to the bottom of this.

I'm full of questions, but not for the girls. They don't know anything, and don't need us grilling them about a casual night with friends. I knew it wasn't necessary but reminded them not to talk to strangers. They responded with exaggerated eye rolls. Do the girls need protection too?

We continue the discussion, only providing them a short version of what's happening with Brian and Christian, only that they're trying to work out a beef.

I also don't want to involve these kids. I have bigger plans for their lives. I never dreamed we'd be discussing this with my kid, but Christian made bad choices and put himself into this horrible place in his life. We must figure a way out of this mess.

Bad decisions or not, he's my son, and I'll do whatever's necessary. Ian feels the same way. He's not a fight or flight kind of guy and will always fight to the end. Although he's never served in the military, he possesses the mentality of a Marine. I sometimes wish he'd walk away.

We all go to our rooms after the hour's long conversation. We didn't tell them their brother is selling weed at college, not that Brian was going to prison soon. We felt no need to say the DEA was watching the house. I never mentioned the fact I thought the guy they met was a DEA agent. I just have a feeling he is. I feel bad keeping things from my girls, but don't want them to have any part in this situation. My family's safety is the desired result.

Ian and I continue talking. "What do you think is going on with Sherry?" I ask. "There's more there than is being said. I also wonder if she lives on a grow farm, else why would she have Jamaican weed?"

Ian doesn't think that's unusual. "She can't take weed from Darryl. Everything involved in growing marijuana on that farm is regulated by the state. They come and inspect the plants and the number of them growing. He must account for all of it at any given moment. He'd lose the business if they found he was illegally selling it on the street. I know he and Kevin would never take that chance.

They've worked too hard and fought too long to legalize marijuana. Kevin was presenting bills in front of the legislature, winning over the government, and people. Making it a business for the family, only to throw it away for a few extra bucks doesn't make sense."

He's right, of course. "She probably went out on her own. She hasn't lived at home on the farm for years. She has her own suppliers and does everything separately from Darryl and Renee. That's probably where the Jamaican comes in. I'm speculating, but that's what I think.

Sherry's never given me any reason to believe any of these things. So much of what's happened points to her." I feel bad coming to this conclusion. "If she's in this deep, she needs protection too."

"When it comes to a perfect product, Darryl, and Kevin, with their technology and education, would be hard to compete with. Growing her own would be difficult and costly. The illegal growers get popped all the time in Humboldt, so it would make sense to go outside of the area to compete. She could get busted. I don't want that to happen. We can tell them what's happening, and then she can separate herself from it. I wonder how she met the Jamaican."

"I wonder too."

Another night of lost sleep. I toss and turn, sleeping off and on for short periods, and so does Ian. Everything that happened this summer is running through my mind. I worry about Christian. I wonder if he'll get out of this without jail time. What do they have on him anyway? Maybe nothing. Possibly association with Brian is the only link.

It seems if they got the primary source of marijuana traffic, this would go away. Christian isn't the primary source. Or is he? I hope not.

He said he met the big guy Luis, and said he was going with someone else. It appears Christian is closer to the top than I imagined, but there isn't an importer. As I mull it over, I realize this weed grows here in the United States. They're shipping across state lines. So, they believe Christian is one of the primary connections, and whatever the DEA expects to get from him could take down some or all the high-level traffickers in this area of marijuana sales. The problem is, how do Jamaica and Sherry fit into the equation? I doze off, only to wake up with the same thoughts rattling around in my head. What does Sherry have to do with this? How are Christian and Sherry connected in the setup? Besides the obvious, they're cousins.

I sit straight up. Good Lord. Is Sherry the new connection where Christian will get the weed cheaper? Could they be bringing in Ganja from Jamaica to here, then from here to California, or wherever Sherry goes? So much for getting any sleep now.

I see it's almost five in the morning, anyway, so will make coffee and start my workday if I can focus on the program. Ian gets up shortly after, and tells me he didn't fall asleep until after two a.m. I pour him coffee while he heads for the shower. A little later he comes out, toweling himself off.

"I'll call my brother today in between patients and talk about Sherry."

I can't help but notice, for a guy in his late forties, Ian's in great shape. He's still slim and muscular, and living on the beach, his skin is dark. What a handsome hunk I married. Okay, back to reality.

I take my eyes off Ian and focus on the situation at hand. I feel good focusing on something else, even if only for a second.

"See what he knows," I say. "I had a thought last night. What if Sherry is Christian's new connection? I get this awful feeling the girl is. It's the timing of her visits, and all that's happened this summer leads me to believe it's true. That trip to Jamaica only strengthens my belief. That trip is key, and we could have lost Sherry with what happened there. What a horrible thought."

As Ian leaves for work, I kiss him good-bye as always, but I let the kiss linger longer than my usual morning peck.

Ian reciprocates and smiles, wrapping his arms around me. He doesn't say anything; just smiles, winks, and walks to the garage. He's riding his Harley to work today. He always wears a jumpsuit over his clothes. He quickly zips into it and fires up the bike, revs it a few times for effect, then roars out of the driveway.

I stand there and daydream for a while. Ian owned a Suzuki when we were young, and we rode around town wearing our bathing suits. Everything was close by, and we never thought about what might happen if we got in an accident with only our bathing suits to protect us. We had no cool zip-up suits. No helmet, either.

The neighboring homes are all quiet, only the sound of Ian and his bike. I still hear it as he speeds out of the neighborhood and hits A1A. The loud rumble of the motor probably woke up the Smith's. As the sound fades, I stand and gaze around my quiet neighborhood.

Any other morning this would be a lovely day. My kids are all sleeping safely in their beds. I hear the sound of the surf. Mercedes, consistent with her daily morning ritual, ran down to the end of the driveway as Ian left. Like a sentry, Mercedes trots back toward me with her tail flying like a flag. Her job done for the morning; she comes into the house with me.

Edward, the king of the household, sits on the back of the couch in the family room, looking at us commoners with disdain. He then walks to the back door and looks at me, the signal to hurry and open the door for him. To my surprise, he actually lets me scratch him behind the ear before I open the door. Did I hear him purr?

The cat normally bats my hand if he doesn't want to be touched. Being the king, I allow him his way. Today he takes pity on me, by rubbing my shin and utters a soft meow. Petting him and rubbing on me is the most contact he's allowed in a long time. I wonder if he senses my worry.

I turn on my computer and let all the programs load while I finish my coffee and eat a piece of toast. My inbox is full. I work for several hours before the kids go into the kitchen for breakfast and start their summer day. Taylor gets to the kitchen first.

I walk in behind her. "Would you like me to make you some eggs or French toast?"

"No, thank you," she says, then Anna comes in a moment later. "Did I hear French toast?" she asks, smiling. "You haven't made it in a long time."

"French toast it is. I'll make some bacon too." I rub Anna's back as she passes me and takes a seat at the breakfast bar.

The twins sits side by side, looking exactly alike. They have brown hair from their father's side, with white blonde streaks from their time in the ocean and sun. Their eyes are pale blue. I can tell them apart from their eyebrows. Anna has one curved eyebrow a little off from the other. Taylor has a small beauty mark by her mouth, just like mine.

They're spectacular looking girls even with mussed up hair in tee shirts and pajama shorts. I say this because they're mine, mother bias, but both are beautiful girls. Petite and toned from surfing and tennis. They look so much like my mother at times. I smile at mom's memory, then plate the French toast as I admire their beauty. When Christian walks in, it's only ten-thirty. "Do I smell French toast and bacon? Awesome!"

He sits next to Anna.

She laughs. "He surfaces."

Christian's not normally an early riser. For us, ten-thirty isn't early, but for a Christian sighting during summer vacation, it is. He gives her a friendly little nudge with his shoulder as he sits.

"I smelled the bacon, and I didn't want you two to grub it all," he says, stealing a piece of bacon before I set the plates down.

I put a plate in front of each of them. Taylor's plate has two slices of bacon, but she picks at them. She's never been a morning eater. I'm glad she at least drinks her orange juice, while the other two eat like starving dogs. We talk casually about our plans for today.

"How is working from home going?' Christian asks.

"Good, I've been able to get a lot done. I need to go in for a couple hours meeting today. I was thinking of getting some fresh fish for dinner on my way home. Will any of you be here for dinner?"

"Catfish nuggets! Please, please, please," Anna begs.

"I was thinking of something healthy and grilled," I say. I act as though I'm giving it some thought. "Sure, catfish nuggets, grits, and a vegetable."

Random Summer Storms

"Yes," Christian says. Taylor says she'll be home for that too, the one-child that has never liked fish but will eat catfish nuggets. She loves grits and would eat them every day if I made them with lots of butter and salt.

All the kids hang out around the house today. Both girls have boyfriends over, and Jamie is coming by to lay in the sun. After the meeting at the office today, I'll call them on my way home to see how much fish I need to buy.

I haven't been to the office in over two weeks. The meeting was informative, and I'm glad I went in. We're making some changes to production. The big bosses discuss the new setup and how pleasantly surprised everything is running smoothly with me at home. Mr. Marshall (Ted) had his doubts in the beginning. Knowing he's accepted the "work from home" project makes me happy. Job still intact.

I prefer to call him Mr. Marshall in the company of others, my way to show respect for his position as my boss. I always want my team to show him respect when he's in the building.

Ted tells me it isn't necessary, but I continue to call him Mr. Marshall anyway. The same way he always says "yes, ma'am," to my female coworkers and me.

Ted is originally from the south, and this is a southern attitude. His family were wealthy plantation owners. He's a no-nonsense boss and can at times be very direct and often blunt. He runs a multi-billion-dollar business, and this station is only a small portion of it. It's his baby, and he's hands-on, where most men at his business level probably wouldn't come to these meetings or be involved with this small production.

He's invited Ian and me to dinner at his Florida home on several occasions. His wife Beth is a beautiful woman about ten years younger than him. I call him Ted at these times. The two are a handsome couple, and we always enjoy visiting with them.

Their home is an over the top, thirty-six thousand square foot summer home. They live in New York most of the time. They have a place in the Trump tower, in addition to homes in Los Angeles, California, Vail, Colorado, and an Island in the Caribbean.

Beth is wife number three and jokes about it now and then. She says she's the last wife Ted will ever have, dead or alive. She sneers, then laughs. I hope so; they seem incredibly happy together. Anyway, back to the topic at hand.

The meeting went very well. I record all my notes down on my iPad and send them to the desktop at home. Making the rounds, I talk to my coworkers and tell them I miss them but working from home is a pleasure because I don't have any of these clowns disturbing me all day. They know I'm joking, and we laugh together.

Back in my car, I call the house. Carmen hasn't returned since the gun incident. I've tried to call her, but she never calls me back. I sent her a final check and a note of apology, but still no response.

I tell her Christian bought the guns legally, and there's no reason to worry—a little lie. I'd love to have her back. I sent her a few week's severance pay and hoped to hear from her again someday.

She's been with us for eight years. We helped her become legal. The whole family was there the day she received her certificate of citizenship. The Lopez family all came back to our house, and we made a huge feast to celebrate. Everyone had a good time, and we've been like family ever since. Until I hear from her again, I hired Handy Housekeepers to come in and clean twice a week. It's not the same without her.

No one ever answers the house phone, so I eventually stopped calling, but the security system is attached, so I keep it. I could probably have it set to my iPhone, but that's technologically too much. Maybe one day. I send a text to all the kids' phones and ask if we're having guests for dinner. I get a text message back from all them, asking who would be staying. Five so far for dinner. I want to be sure and buy enough fish.

My next call goes to Ian to see what time he's coming home, and if he talked to Darryl about Sherry. I must leave a message, of course. Ian's never available on the spot when he's at work. I'll wait to hear from him. I go to our local fish store, and they have some beautiful catfish fillets I can cut into nuggets.

Smoked salmon they smoke themselves, is available. I love it, and it's one of Ian's favorites.

I stop at the grocery store for things we need at home, but as usual, I pile a shopping cart full of items I don't need. Food never goes to waste in our house. We always have an extra hungry mouth.

Riding in my car, I listen to Tonic, "Open up your eyes, just let me go." Ian's and my interest in music are so different. He always listens to older rock and roll. We'd never find Tonic on his playlist. Funny how opposites attract.

Steve helps me unload the groceries. What a good kid. Everyone else is busy, sitting on mats down on the beach. No one notices me lugging bags of groceries into the house. I don't mind today. I take comfort in knowing nothing terrible happened, and they're all here and accounted for. However, small a feat that is, I'm grateful. I stand at the window and watch Taylor take a wave nice break right. She rides it only for a short time. It looks to me that sets are rolling in too close together with not enough time in between to get in a good ride.

I go to my office after putting away the groceries to get more work done. Ian finally calls me back around four to tell me he talked to Darryl. Darryl told him Sherry's been dating a Rastafarian for the last year. Winston seems like a nice enough guy. He's religious and mellow. Darryl says he's mentioned him before to Ian.

Ian says they talked about weed sales. Darryl wouldn't be surprised if Winston had some side business going on. No, Sherry isn't a part of it.

I asked him if the job at the Holiday Inn is in fact a travel job. I pointed out the fact that within two years, she rose from clerk, to assistant manager, to international travel manager at that one location. It seems abnormal.

Ian says Darryl told him Holiday Inn went global right before Sherry started working there, and mentioned Darryl took offense to the question. Of course, he would; we're talking about his daughter possibly trafficking marijuana from Jamaica.

Darryl seems to think Sherry's smart and exceptional at her job. Ian goes on to say. "I asked him about Jamaica. He told me

Winston's family still lives there. She gets to stay free at their home."

I would think she gets to stay free at any Holiday Inn globally. Darryl says she doesn't go there for business. I don't agree but keep that to myself. She may not be going for the Holiday Inn, but she's going for business.

My question is, why does she visit his family without him? Do they ever come to the states and visit Sherry? It seems to me they're awful chummy. How many times has she been to Jamaica in the last year? Three or four? Ian says he had to stop drilling Darryl because he was getting pissed off. He told him about the guy coming up to the girls at the beach, and the comments he made. There might be reason to beware.

If she's bringing weed to Florida for personal use, she needs to be more cautious. If she's trafficking it here, a bigger problem might arise. Ian expresses his concern about the DEA, and lets Darryl know we wouldn't be talking about any of this if we weren't worried and didn't care about Sherry.

Darryl said he'd speak to her. He also stated that if things were so bad, Ian needed to watch his own family.

Ian pointed out this is no small problem for any of us. If the kids are transporting marijuana over state lines together, it could quickly come back to the guy with the marijuana farm. Darryl agreed, but wasn't happy, and then disconnected the call.

The conversation didn't go well, but the message is out there. We can only hope everyone concerned heeds the warning.

"You're trying to help Darryl and Sherry, you're his brother, why would he get mad?"

Ian defends Darryl. "It was a lot to take in at one time." Having the kids put his business in danger is something else entirely. We both agree he'll do something. He needs to because his business and lifestyle is at stake.

So, with that lousy conversation between brothers done, Ian informs me he'll be late. He has a patient that has been in distress off and on all day. He'll stay until the said patient is stable. It could be a late night for him. I'm used to this. I tell him I'll see him when I see him. We hang up with, "I love you."

I like to soak my fish in buttermilk before I batter and fry. I cut the fillets up into one and half-inch squares, then place them in a Pyrex baking dish and pour the buttermilk over the top. I put them in the refrigerator for one hour.

The kids are all still down by the water, running in and out of the waves. Everything appears as it should; another beautiful day living at the beach. The surf turned choppy since this morning's breaks. Fun in the sun and splashing in the water took the place of surfing and paddle boarding. An awesome sight for a mom.

I pull out the fryer and take out everything I'll need to make the dinner. The Cure Love song comes on the speakers in the kitchen and family room. "I will always love you... whenever I'm alone with you, you make me feel like free again." I hear the kids coming in from the outside shower. Joel is picking up his things and heading for the door with Taylor in tow. "Good tune," he says, pointing at the ceiling as they pass.

"Oh, you like the Cure?"

"Yeah," he says, nodding to the music.

"You can't stay for dinner?" I asked Joel.

He tells me no, and then thanks me for letting him hang out.

"I gotta work. Goodbye," he says, and smiles back at me. Joel holds the door for Taylor as they go out front to say goodbye away from the rest of us. Nice, I think to myself. A kid with a job.

The others ask if they can help with anything. I say no, and they watch TV while I prepare dinner. Fried fish smells so good when it's cooking, but afterwards, the whole downstairs smells like stale fish. The smell is good enough to bring Edward into the kitchen. He rubs around my legs until I give him a little taste. Mercedes barks at the unfairness. She has a delicate stomach and can't eat anything fried. The smallest bite could end up in disaster for the wood floor.

Taylor and Christian set the table while Anna takes out condiments. Jamie and Steve sit at the table. We sit down to one of the yummiest batches of fried catfish I've made in a long time. They all thoroughly enjoyed the dinner. I get compliments from each one.

Everyone helps to clear the dishes and put everything away. They all settle in upstairs, playing video games and talking. I turn on the TV for background noise, but don't pay it any attention.

Ian comes in right as I finish the cleanup and sit down. He leans down to give me a hello kiss. The fish is all gone, so he makes a sandwich and tells me about his patient and his day.

"It was difficult," he says, "but I'm home now, and that's all that matters." He slowly begins to relax with his feet up on the coffee table while eating.

I hear the kids come down the stairs a few hours later, and assume the guests are going home. They say they're going to the Dairy Queen and asked if I would like something.

I say no, thank you, and tell Christian to take my car; they'll all be able to ride together more comfortably. As they pull out of the driveway, Ian stands and watches them go.

The car was gone from the house for only a few minutes when my phone buzzes. Taylor sent a text telling me the cops pulled them over and asked them to get out of the car so they can search inside. Can you come? Please hurry. She ended the text with a sad face. I read this aloud to Ian.

"Let's go," he says.

We jump up and run to his car, and we're on the highway in minutes. The lights from the police cars are flashing ahead of us; the kids didn't get very far. We stay back a respectful distance and watch. Four officers from two patrol cars are patting down Christian and Steve, while the other four are seated on the curb. Jamie's purse sits on the hood of the patrol car.

I say a prayer no one was carrying anything illegal. Praying for them to have nothing illegal was crazy, but necessary these days. After the police search the boys, they tell them to sit on the curb, then search my car. A media badge sits on the dash. I rarely go to the scene of a story; I use it to park when I can't find a regular spot. I know I'm cheating, but it's one of the great perks of my job. The officer shows it to the other one then puts it back.

It looks like an unsuccessful search as they don't find anything. One of the cops tells the boys to stand up, and he searches Steve again. That makes three times since we got here, and it really pisses me off, so I jump from the car and stomp toward the scene.

Ian's at my heels, warning me not to approach them in a hostile manner. I'm not listening as I barge right up to the scene. "You've watched COPs; you know what can happen," he warns, as I press forward. I suspect Ian's picturing me startling one of them and being thrown to the ground.

The cops finally notice us for the first time, and one tells me to stand back. I know better, but these are kids getting ice cream, I say to the officer who searched the boys. "Clearly, the boy isn't carrying anything. He's wearing jersey shorts, boxers, and a jersey tank. If you search him one more time, I'll report you."

"Ma'am, you need to step back from the scene," the policeman calmly says to me, then stretches an arm out to block my way. The other cop says, "how do you know what he's wearing and if he has anything on him or not? That's our job to find out."

"I know because he spent the day at my house. They're driving my car to get ice cream."

They searched Christian only once, and no one searched the girls. Steve is the only black kid standing here; the only one they searched three times. "This teenage boy is a passenger in my family car. You patted him down three times while we watched you from our car. I won't stand for you to touch him one more time!"

"Why did you pull them over, officer?" Ian asks.

The officer doesn't answer right away, so Taylor speaks up.

"Christian and Steve were in the front seat. Anna and I were in the back. I noticed the police car first when he pulled alongside us. The policeman looks over at Steve, then waits for us to get ahead, pulls in behind us, and immediately hits his lights. The other cop car pulls up as soon as we were on the side of the road."

"So, you saw an African American kid in an expensive car, and you wanted to find out? What?" Ian asks the officers.

"We had probable cause," the tall one says.

"You haven't answered my question. Why'd you pull the car over? Taillight, lane change, or speeding? But you didn't you said probable cause." Ian is looking at the officer with narrowed eyes.

"Maybe I can help. I'll call out a crew from the news station and give them a story tonight for the morning news. Jax Beach police officers pull over kids for going to get ice cream, with an African American teen in the front seat. They weren't speeding; the car's in good condition; no taillights out. Nothing illegal found, but all teenagers detained and searched for good measure. Or, should I say, probable cause." I know they saw my Media parking pass and figured I wasn't bluffing. Just in case, I pull my cell phone out for effect.

"The kids are free to go," they mumble.

Ian tells them to be safe as they depart. The kids all snicker as they get back in the car. I ask them to get their ice cream and come back home carefully. Ian and I walk back to Ian's Porsche in silence. I wonder if that was as random as the police were making it. Or did it have something to do with Christian and his summer troubles?

The kids return home within half an hour, and all go upstairs to the game room. Before going up the stairs, Steve walks over and thanks us for tonight. "I appreciate what you did, Mr. and Mrs. C."

We tell him it was nothing. I stand and hug him.

"Just the same," he says, "they had me pegged for something."

Ian stands. "It wasn't right, and we need to change that. Always be respectful like you were, Steve. Unfortunately, they can sometimes be easily provoked." They do the handshake shoulder hug.

Steve smiles. "You had my back, Mrs. C, I thought you were going to do something crazy the way you were coming for that big cop. I think you scared him."

We all laugh, then he goes upstairs to hang with the rest of the kids. I hear him say something about me being a "momma bear," then we laugh more.

"Just what were you going to do?" Ian asks me.

"I wanted to intimidate him, the way he was trying to intimidate those kids." My son's words echoed in my head.

Ian puts his arm around me and says in my ear. "I love you, mamma bear."

I tell him I love him too. "I don't want my kids to think it's okay to cross a police officer. I also don't want them harassed for no reason."

CHAPTER 23

The time is nearing for Christian to return to college. Since the talk with Darryl and the meet with Brian, it's been quiet. Someone must have said something to the cops or DEA because we heard Brian was serving ten years. Christian was upset about it. He claims Brian was an alright guy and didn't deserve this. I know he doesn't want to hear it, but this is the price you pay for dealing drugs.

"You have to know in the back of your mind that one day you might get caught. The thing is, he didn't just have marijuana. He was dealing several different kinds of pills, Xanax, and Ecstasy. Kids get hooked on that stuff. Your cousin fights his addiction to prescription pills every day."

Ian and I talk several times with Christian about getting away from this. I think he understands this isn't the life he wants to lead. His wakeup call is calling right now. Sever all ties to the weed business and make a clean break.

I hope Sherry learns a lesson from all of this too. Although there was no proof, she did anything wrong or was involved in anything illegal, I hope she does the right thing. Her wakeup call was the trip to Jamaica. The experience was dangerous, and no one knows what really happened on that trip, or what she was doing there, other than her story she was visiting Winston's family. I have a feeling she wasn't an innocent bystander in the wrong place at the wrong time. She was in more danger than she and the news reported.

This scenario was too much like another World News story many years ago; and not what it appeared. Maybe that's why I'm so skeptical about her version of what happened. I'm relieved it ended the way it did.

The summer is ending, and we're getting the kids ready to go back to school. I'm shopping a lot with my girls, and they love that part of back to school. We buy notebooks, pens, and all the school supplies. They all need new clothes to start a new school year. Christian's not opposed to new clothes to take back to college, so he tags along with us on our last big outing together before he leaves. After shopping all morning, we go to Campeche Bay for Mexican food. We finish up our shopping at the mall in the early evening.

We started our back to school shopping early this year, since Christian is going back in a week. He starts team practice before school officially begins. He'll need to get back and settled into his dorm before the rigorous schedule and life at school begins. I hope this year is good for him, and he leaves every aspect of this crazy summer behind. Well, except for Jamie, she's been good for him, and has become a big part of the family.

We all eat a quiet dinner together, then Christian goes up to his room to talk to Jaime on his phone. The girls go upstairs and do what they do. Ian and I get comfortable on our bed and read. Lights out early at the Connor house. I'm blessed at the end of another beautiful day.

Shortly after two in the morning, I hear the girls in our room.

"Dad, dad, wake up." The two girls are both standing on his side of the bed. Ian and I sit up simultaneously.

"What's the matter?" he asks, and the girls both shoosh him. "There are some men out on the driveway creeping around the house," they whisper. "Burglars."

Ian leans over and grabs his pistol from the lockbox in the nightstand. He gets up and tells us to stay inside. I start to argue, but he silences me with a hand up. "Keep the girls safe! If that means running down the beach to the safety of a neighbor's house, you do it. By then, you'll know whether to call the cops or not."

He goes downstairs and slowly walks toward the front of the house. He doesn't want to run out shooting, because it could be Christian's friends coming to visit him or going home. He slowly opens the door, Ian doesn't turn on the lights. He sees three men. They don't appear to be armed, but one never knows. All three are creeping slowly around the cars and appear to be casing the house.

"Can I help you?" he asks to their backs, staying in the shadows to remain invisible.

They jump and turn around.

Ian doesn't recognize them, but one says," it's payback time for you and your little bitch son." He jumps towards Ian, but Ian anticipates the move, steps forward, and punches the guy in the face, and they immediately start fighting. As if on cue, Christian runs down the stairs and jumps on another one.

They're all out there punching and bouncing off the car. I tell the girls to call 9-1-1. Mercedes is barking up a storm behind me as I sneak out on the front porch. I wonder why Ian hasn't fired the handgun, even as a warning. He's in full contact fight mode. All of them are kicking and punching each other and bodies are slamming against the side of Christian's car, only to bounce back and hit harder. I hear grunts of pain, but the lights aren't lit, so I can't see who's hurt, and who's getting the upper hand. They're all shadows in the night.

I need to help, so I head back into the house, but can't stand there and do nothing. I run back into our room, grab the Mossberg shotgun, unbox a handful of shells from the top of the shelf, and load the gun as I return to the front yard. My hands are shaking so badly, I can barely slide the shells in place.

When I get back, they're all beating each other senseless. Who are these guys and why are they here? Payback for what? Brian, DEA, who the hell knows? The fighting continues, and everyone is bloody. They continue pounding each other and staggering around the driveway in between hits to the face and body. Every time I hear a punch connect, I cringe. I still don't hear sirens. Where are the cops? Are they not coming because of the other night? No, that's silly.

I decide I can't wait for them, stepping off the front porch. I pump and fire the Mossberg into the air, and everyone stops fighting. Ian had a gun, but I wonder why he never used it. At that moment, the motion sensor light over the garage comes on, when Christian stepped in front of it. I'm sure that was intentional. I can see the gun in Ian's pocket, and again wonder why he didn't discharge it.

The blast from the Mossberg commands everyone's attention, thank goodness. I recognize one guy as Brian's friend from Chili's. The shotgun pellets rain down on everyone and hit Christian's car as well. It also startles these guys into running.

At first, Christian goes after them, then Ian calls him off. He says the cops will get them, so let them go. At that moment, one of them starts firing rounds into Christian's BMW. The thought that one of them also had a gun during this altercation is horrifying.

I hear my girls screaming in the house as well as the dog going crazy, and duck down on the porch as Ian and Christian both hit the pavement. One of the assailants says " let's go, let's go." Finally, we hear sirens. Ian and Christian remain behind Christian's car. The shooting stops, then all three guys run for their vehicle, a dark blue Honda sedan parked down the street in front of Mr. and Mrs. Smith's house. Please, let the cops get them before they get away. They were shooting at us in our neighborhood. Or were they just shooting at the car? I feel as though they were dumb kids, because if they wanted to kill someone, they would've fired during the fighting. They didn't; they just meant to show how tough they are, acting like real punks, but we were more than they expected. I'm just not sure at this point.

I set down the Mossberg, leaning it against the wall by the front door and tell Ian I'm going to check on the girls. Ian and Christian will wait out front in case they return, and Ian is now holding his gun.

After one last look around, I run into the house to check on Taylor and Anna. They're crying and hiding on the floor by the couch. I do my best to soothe them.

Our driveway lights up in blue as the police skid onto the pavers. Ian and Christian are kneeling. Ian tells the cops his wife and daughters are in the house, and the attackers are in the blue Honda that just drove away. The officer calls it in, then take the handgun Ian set on the ground in front of him. Ian and Christian are allowed to get up, and two officers announce to the girls and me they're coming into the house.

I tell them we're in the living room on the floor. I put my hands in the air as the policeman introducing himself as officer

Ryan walks in, asking if we're armed. I tell him the Mossberg is loaded and leaning on the wall on the front porch. One officer goes out to retrieve it, while the other comes cautiously into the living room. Once the police feel there's no threat, they talk to us about what happened here tonight.

I see the rescue vehicle in the driveway. I tell them I must see my husband and son, and we all go out together. Ian was gravely injured, but never said a word on a night similar to this. We almost lost him. I wanted to make sure that wasn't the case tonight.

We all walked out to see the EMT's and make sure Ian and Christian were okay. The girls hug their brother and dad with relief on their faces. I was thankful the guys sustained only cuts, scrapes, and bruises. Christian's face has just healed from the last fight. Now his eye is swollen shut again blood running from his nose, and he has a fat lip. His knuckles are all bloody and swollen as well.

Ian has a bruise and swelling on one side of his face where his cheekbone was cut and appears to be favoring his ribs on the right side. His knuckles are bruised identical to Christian's.

After they bandage up our two men, we go into the living room to talk about our attackers and why they might have come here. Taylor and Anna told the policemen how they were both still up snap chatting with friends all night. Girls seem to do this a lot. They heard noises coming from the front of the house. Usually, it's just Christian and his friends coming and going, but tonight was different. These guys were squatting down as they walked around, creeping in the dark, looking in windows. Taylor believed them to be burglars. The girls felt scared and woke their dad up to check it out.

Ian starts his part of the story. He grabbed his gun and went out to see what they were doing. When he got out there and confronted them, they attacked him. He didn't use the weapon because they were kids. He said he wanted to scare them and send them packing. "I wasn't sure why they were on the property. I confronted them when I realized they weren't friends of our kids."

When he asked them what they were doing, they started swinging. Christian came down and jumped into the fight. They were hoping to keep them here until the police came. Christian says the fight just kept going. Their three good-sized attackers weren't going down easily. They kept coming at Christian and his father. "That's when my mom came out on the porch."

I took over, describing what happened. "When I realized the fighting wasn't going to stop, I fired a warning shot in the air. As the pellets rained down on them, they started to run. They took off down the driveway toward their car parked on the road."

Officer Ryan asked why we thought they were on the property, and whether we knew them. We said no. Although Christian said one kind of looked familiar, he wasn't sure.

"After they ran off, we thought it was over until one of the guys, the tall one I think," Christian says, trying to recapture what happened, "turned back around and started shooting. It looked to me he only wanted to damage my car. I don't know how many times he fired."

The cops asked, "why did you think that."

Christian told him he didn't think they were shooting at him and his dad. He could tell the guy was shooting at the vehicle, because Ian and Christian were standing in the middle of the driveway.

"It looked as though the guy was aiming at my car like he wanted to damage it. He could have easily shot one of us. We dropped to the pavement but were still out in the open. Maybe he was a terrible shot; it looked like he had it in for my car." Christian is looking at the ground, shaking his head.

Ryan says, "that's very strange," and jotted notes on his pad. "You say you know these guys?"

"No, I don't know them," Christian says. "I thought one looked familiar, but I, for sure, don't know them."

I think Mr. police officer was trying to trap Christian. I wonder why they don't believe this is just a random burglary.

"They ran down the driveway and jumped into a car they had on the street," I say. As I tell my story, the radio makes a sound, and the officer walks towards the door to talk in private.

He returns a few minutes later and says they have the car and the three suspects we described. He tells the other officer that one of the suspects stashed a recently fired gun under the seat.

Well, that's a relief; at least they have the guys.

A detective and a team were out front of the house collecting evidence, putting up caution tape, and markers all over the driveway indicating spent shells. That left only three vehicles in our driveway; much better than the ten that responded and blocked off our street. More caution tape was stretched across the driveway, a grim scene indeed.

I called the station and related a story about burglars attempting to get into the house. They downplayed it as a small story, but to our neighbors, it was big news; the sort of thing that doesn't happen to people like us in a neighborhood like this.

I made coffee for those officers remaining. I know the detectives would be working for hours out there. The girls finally went back to bed. Christian fell asleep on the couch. Ian said he was going to try to get some sleep. He wanted to go to the hospital later today to check on his patient having trouble yesterday. I tried to convince him to stay home and let someone else check on the patient. Ian looked bad. "Your face is badly bruised, and you're banged up." I know the words are falling on deaf ears. Ian will go, no matter what.

I'm sure I'll get no sleep. I tried to work, thinking it would help take my mind off the fact someone came to my home with a gun. Keeping my mind on my job was the problem. My mind kept wandering to what happened. I sat in front of my computer and prayed. I'm so thankful the mayhem this morning was over, and no one was hurt or killed. Well, they were injured, but not permanently. Why does this kind of terror follow us?

Twenty-five years ago, Ian and I ran into trouble. We changed our lives and moved thousands of miles away to protect ourselves and the ones we love. Leaving all that behind only to have this happen here now.

I can't help but wonder what would cause someone to come after my son in this manner. It should have ended with Brian. He didn't steal from them or do anything personally to harm them. Christian told them he wouldn't be a problem for any of them.

Did they still think he talked to the cops? I wonder if they thought it was worth coming here because they're all going to jail anyway. Was this extreme behavior caused because he wouldn't be selling their weed? He wouldn't be selling anyone's marijuana after this if I can help it. I can only hope he won't. I want to believe he learned the consequences of this type of lifestyle. Everything he did involved all of us, and I pray it won't happen again.

Over the next few days, we went downtown to answer more questions about that night. They questioned us separately. I wouldn't let them ask the girls anymore after that first night. Two girls who thought they were safe in their own home. I argued that they were minors, who have told everything they knew the night of the incident. I said I didn't want them scarred by this horrific nightmare, but they already are. They were huddled on the floor, scared to death, listening to gunfire in their own front yard. They couldn't supply any more information. Since they couldn't help, I was adamant they needed to heal mentally. No one pushed after that.

The DEA knows more than the local cops and are a tricky group. They drilled Christian, reminding him they knew about him and all his friends. They dropped a lot of names and said the others were already talking. They told him if he would name names, they could protect him.

Christian was smart enough to know if they had anything on him, they would've used it already. The best thing he could do is keep his mouth shut and go back to school.

During Christian's interrogation, he finally admitted recognizing one guy who came to the house. He told them about his run-in with the guy at a club at the beginning of summer. The guy wasn't a friend, and he didn't know how he knew where we lived. My son also stated he didn't know anyone who might be dealing drugs. He never admitted to smoking weed or selling it himself. They told him they would be watching. He didn't care, because he was going back to school.

We all talked about what was said to the police. I reviewed everything Christian struggled with this summer. I was hard on him because I felt it was his fault but reminded him the whole family went through this. My reason for being so stern is I want it all to stop. He has a great future most people will never have. He could have blown it all this summer.

Ian took Christian's side because Ian made a lot of bad decisions before he became a doctor. Feeling bad for Christian wasn't going to help him. I love him and want him to live a full life, having fun and being successful.

"At some point in your life, you need to decide if you want this kind of grief or you want the right things. You and Jamie get along well; you might want marriage and a family. You're at a pivotal moment in your life. I'm not saying you should get married or make that decision today. I'm saying if that's something you want, then start preparing for it. Going to jail would take it all away."

I know Ian thinks I'm a hypocrite. I don't want Christian or the girls to make the same mistake we did; running from a past they don't speak about. Accepting this behavior is worse than being a hypocrite. Ian feels we should tell Christian what we did and why we moved here years ago. We left our friends and family to start a new life; close the doors on the old. I refused and said, maybe when he's older.

Ian and I talked about all the things we did and how it was a simpler time, that it was easier to run, but was it really? Or did we just survive it only to relive it in our children's lives? I say some things are better left unsaid. Ian and I decided to bury that life many years ago. I think telling the kids would only make my opinion implausible. I'd have no authority with them, and how can I discipline any of my kids when I can't judge right from wrong. My word won't mean anything.

We let it go. I won this battle. Again, we kept our skeletons in the closet. I hope we never let them out.

Ian wasn't happy with the decision, but I don't feel it's the right time. I don't want him to focus on the fact we got away with it, but maybe I'm wrong. Maybe when Christian graduates, if he stays out of trouble, we can sit down and compare war stories.

CHAPTER 24

Christian returned to the University of North Carolina, promising to focus on school and his team. He also said he wouldn't sell marijuana ever again. I believe him. This summer was horrible. A few days after he went back to school, I called my sister. I needed sister time, even if it's just a phone call.

I tell her the summer was miserable. I describe the shooting in our front yard, telling her Christian was selling weed. I don't say to what extent, but now it's out there. I tell her I'm not going to tell my brother. I would die if he knew. What if Mike didn't invite us to his home for holidays anymore?

She tells me I don't need Mike's approval. Why am I acting as though his opinion is so important? She reminds me I'm an adult and as a family we discuss things without judgment.

"Right," I say. "When have Mike and I been able to talk without judgment?" We both laugh. Mike and I have always been on opposite ends, even as kids, still blaming each other for everything. "This is different. Telling Mike would ruin Christian's relationship with him."

Kathy said she disagreed, but I think she knew I was right. She also said my secret was safe with her. She vowed one day we would all talk about it. Secrets in the family are never good.

I never told Kathy or Mike the truth about the Columbians. How would I ever be able to talk about all of that with them and Christian?

Our conversation lasts for an hour; we talked about everyone in the family. It's always fun to catch up on everyone's summer. We laugh a lot. Our family has a history of funny antics.

I found out Kathy had bad news. I could tell that truth was hard for her to say as well. She admitted Daniel is struggling with his addiction and is back in rehab. "Daniel wants so bad to be clean." Her voice cracks. "For some reason, the drug never let's go of him. It's the third time he's gone back. I hope it's the last."

I tell her I'm heartbroken hearing about Daniel's struggles, and will keep him in my prayers. I just don't know what a family can do in this situation. We talk about the other kids and how well they're doing, which brightens the conversation. Each one is doing so well.

Kathy is excited about Brook. She's been dating an attorney, and Kathy thinks they'll get engaged soon. I'm so happy for her. We chat for a while longer, then hang up.

We shared our worries about our sons. The situations are different, yet the same. No one warned us how much anxiety and stress our kids would cause.

Ian talks to Darryl. They laugh and carry on, talking about sports and new strains of weed Alan is creating. He's cross-bred a kind of cookie/Kush plant concoction. They laugh at how different marijuana is today than in the seventies, when a bag of Columbian Gold was a hit.

Ian tells him what happened over the summer, and that Christian is back at school. He laughs and says, "we literally dodged a bullet, but I think we're okay now." Ian knows it's not funny, but what can he say? Darryl says he talked with Sherry about everything, but she denied most of it. Sherry and Winston are expecting a child.

Ian tells him he's happy for everyone. They're all excited about a grandchild, especially Renee. She's so pleased with the idea of a grandbaby. Ian says he'll tell me the good news, and we'll see everyone on Thanksgiving when we come to visit. They hang up on a good note this time; no one left angry by the conversation.

I check in with my brother, and all is well at his house. Both my nephews are great and following in his footsteps. How exciting; more cops in my family. I'm happy for them all. Now would not be the time to come clean to my brother. He says he and Sean are doing better. Sean is coming around and able to talk about Jill, but it's been hard. I'm sorry for Sean still trying to come to terms with his mother's death all these years, and hope he can move forward, but grief is a terrible thing. No one can understand another person's struggles.

We laugh and talk about the family. I tell him what a great summer we had, and wish we had more time together. Mike and I promise to make time. What a friendly fake call to my brother. One day I will fix that, but it better be sooner than later. I think of Walter Scott, "Oh, what a tangled web we weave, when first we practice to deceive."

Isn't it amazing how different, yet similar, our lives are in this big family? We all have things that drive us and things that break us down. If you think about it, all families are alike in this way. Many won't divulge their secrets, preferring not to face the facts. All the things that happened to us happen to others every day.

In my life, I've learned no one is better than the next. You may be faster, smarter, funnier, or richer, but no one is better than another person. Each day you think your life is perfect, something happens to remind you it's not. While I feel lucky to live this life, it certainly has been crazy, but what's normal? My experiences are vast. No matter how hard I try to live, my ups and downs are not what most people perceive as normal.

We know Ian and I have brought on some of our troubles ourselves. Others, we had no control over, but no matter what, we persevered. I can only pray my children will be happy and satisfied with the life they choose for themselves.

Halfway through Christian's sophomore year at the University of North Carolina, we called him to meet us in New York. His cousin Daniel had died of an accidental overdose. They said it was a heroin and fentanyl mix. We all cried at the news. Christian was sad, but angry. I hated calling him to tell him he lost his cousin.

He at first didn't want to go, and I was afraid he wouldn't, but in the end, he changed his mind and met us in New York. Ian's brothers attended the funeral as well. I was so happy to see them there. They flew in together to be a part of the celebration of Daniel's life. My best friend Shelly and Keith came too. We hadn't seen each other in years, but still talked on the phone. Many old friends of Kathy and Michael came to help them celebrate Daniel, while sharing the pain of loss.

On the day of the funeral, Christian stood at the podium and talked about his cousin. I was so proud. He was no longer angry. Filled with grief, he spoke of better days. He talked of his time with Daniel when they were growing up and all the things, he learned from him. Even today, on this sad day, he would take this as another lesson from his beloved cousin. "Show up for the ones you love," were his final words, and then he took his seat beside Ian.

All the kids got up and spoke. Kathy talked of all the things Daniel did, from his first step to his motocross days. We all smiled at the beautiful memories. Brook was amazing. She planned her eulogy and spoke eloquently of her time with her brother and how they would all be together again one day. We all celebrated his wonderful life. Knowing he struggled with drugs while still being a beautiful person, was hard to imagine. Daniel was now at peace with his demons, and we believe God would take it from here. He was and will always be in our hearts, knowing this did not make it easier to say goodbye.

Unfortunately, our stay was a short one. We had to get back to Florida, and Christian had to get back to school at UNC. My girls had school as well. We regretted leaving Kathy, Michael, and the rest of the family. The airplane ride home was quite somber. I had a hard time wrapping my head around the reality I would never see that boy again. Suddenly, my thoughts were of him as a child. I picture the little boy that could do anything. Though he'd been grown for a long time, he was a fun little character as a child. As an adult, Daniel was so handsome, kind, and an all-around fun guy. He had so many friends.

Taylor and Anna cried off and on for weeks when they thought or spoke of Daniel, it was so sad he was gone, and our lives went on. The girls returned to school and continued their classes. The loss was rough but returning to school and keeping busy was helpful to us all.

I hoped Kathy would be able to find a way to deal with this loss. She and my brother-in-law had a hard road ahead of them without their youngest son. No amount of time would help them; keeping busy was only a temporary fix for the heartache they would carry.

As weeks turned into months, my girls returned to their routines, and both took driver's education. I survived riding as a passenger with them while they learn to drive. I'm exaggerating; they're both doing well as drivers. I finally stopped leaning in on the passenger side, because the mailboxes looked too close to the car.

It appears our lives are returning to normal in every aspect. Ian is working, I'm still working from home, and all is well. We didn't see Christian for Thanksgiving. We did, however, attend a lot of his games this season.

Christian did as promised, dedicating his days to school and his team. He played point guard and earned his place among the starters. The bench didn't see as much of him this year.

He and Jamie are still an item. She attends the games with us, and he drives down here to see her some weekends.

I learned Christian would become a father at 20 years old this year, and me a grandmother. I never expected this. Ian had a freak-out moment at the news, but he recovered nicely. The child will be a blessing, another little Conner. I can't wait to find out whether it's a boy or a girl. Maybe twins; they're common on my side of the family.

You never know what life has in store. Just when you think you have it all worked out, it surprises you.

CHAPTER 25

We've been fixing up the in-law suite for Jamie and the new baby. She decided to live there until she and Christian can find a place of their own. The in-law suite is twelve-hundred square feet, with a small alcove off the bedroom we enclosed to make a nursery for our grandbaby. It's looking fabulous, with a large bay window that makes the room bright and sunny. My father was a pilot, and we found some of his pictures of old bi-planes and decided to wallpaper and trim with an airplane theme.

The molding around the top is painted to look like clouds, and we found different types of model planes and toys to decorate the room. We also found out they're having a boy. He's due in June, perfect for Christian to come home and spend time with during the summer. His name will be Liam Christian Connor. I'm so excited. Jamie's mother, Megan, and I, have been working together to get everything ready for our first grandson. Liam is Jamie's grandfather's name, who died recently.

Jamie moves in this weekend. Taylor and Anna have become close to Jamie over the last year. We all spend a lot of time together. We attended Christian's games and cheered him on as Jamie's belly expanded with each visit.

I go up to the nursery and stand in the center of the room. Who would've thought we'd be having a new baby in the family this soon? At first, we were in shock, but everyone loves babies, and we were happy and excited. The girls were delighted when they heard the word pregnant.

A few years ago, I talked to the girls about how we'd handle it if one of them got pregnant. Now they see how a real family deals with the prospect of a new baby.

They were so excited to call the family and tell everyone we would also be having a child. Sherry's baby is a year old. His name is Justin. We haven't had the pleasure of meeting him yet, but they plan to introduce our little guy this summer when she and her husband, Winston, visit.

The girls are planning a baby shower inviting all their friends, and Megan and I have asked some family members; it will be a good time. I forgot how fun it is to buy little tiny baby things such as strollers, toys, tee shirts, onesies, and booties. Little Liam will be spoiled, no doubt.

I spend my day working on the news show airing in the morning. The girls went on a day trip to Daytona Beach with friends. The day is beautiful. I take a break and walk out back and look up and down the coast. The water is a pale green, and the waves are flat, but still beautiful.

The smell of the ocean fills my senses. I stand there, thinking about how lucky I am to be here. I recall doing this in California on the beach so many, many years ago. A moment of déjà vu strikes.

I spend a few more minutes of peace before going back to work. I am just about back to my desk when my phone starts ringing. Megan called to tell me she needed to take Jamie to the hospital; her blood pressure spiked, and they're worried. The hospital may induce labor, and it's way too early.

I tell her I'm coming up. She says not to, but I want to be there. I send a group text as I head out the door for everyone to check-in. I'll fill them in once I get there and find out what's happening. I put in the address to St Vincent's Hospital on my navigation system, and head over there.

I'm traveling on the highway away from the beach on Butler, where it passes over the intercoastal waterway. The speed limit is sixty-five, and I'm driving just under seventy. I notice a car speeding up behind me. I'm in the fast lane, so I signal to move to the slower lane. As I move over to let the car pass, it swerves into my lane. I'm thinking the driver is an idiot for passing on the right. They must have seen my signal. Signs on both sides of the highway indicate slow traffic to the right.

The car behind me is too quick for me to recover, so I stay my course. As the other driver realizes his error, he jerks his car back into the left lane, hitting the back left of my bumper. My car goes into a spin, so I ease off the gas but don't brake—defensive driving 101. Another vehicle suddenly hits the passenger side of my SUV, causing it to flip over. People say everything moves in slow motion, and your life flashes in front of you, but mine did not. The accident happened too fast. I see the street coming up to the side of my SUV with the first flip. I don't have time to be scared. I remember thinking I hope I don't flip over the guard rail and end up in the river.

I bang around, and all the airbags deploy. I thought it would never end, but it finally does, and when the vehicle stops, I'm hanging upside down, restrained by my seatbelt. The roof of my car is crushing me, and I feel a warm stream of blood run down the side of my face and drip into my hand.

I feel as if I'm dreaming. I can hear voices, but they seem far away. I feel someone take my hand and telling me, "you're going to be okay, help is on the way." She continues talking softly, trying to encourage me to stay with her. I fight to remain conscious, but the pain is so intense, I cannot, and it goes black.

Everything is dark and has been for a long time. I hear voices but can't wake up. A constant beeping is driving me crazy. I want to open my eyes and tell someone to shut it off, but I'm too groggy. I don't know how long I've been like this. I know I'm lying down, but I must be in the hospital, since I remember the accident.

I must be on strong medication because I can't open my eyes or move. The room is dark and lonely. I dream about my family all the time; I wish I would wake up from this dream. I want to go home.

Ian is holding my hand. I can feel it in my dream so real. He's saying, "wake up, Luv, I need you. Please don't leave me. I would take your place in a minute if I could." He starts crying.

I tell him, don't cry, but he can't hear me. I want to stroke his face and tell him I'm fine, but I can't move. I hear music. He put the headset over my ears, and I hear Chicago. "If you leave me now, you'll take away the biggest part of me.... Ooo baby, please don't go." If I could wake up, I'd tell him how corny that is. "I love you too, Ian, even if you are a sap."

Time passes, but I'm still in the dark. My girls are holding my hands this time; both crying and asking God to wake me up. I ask God to wake me up too. They talk to me through their tears, and I want to hold them both and say I'm here and love them. I can't reach for them for some reason. I don't understand why I can't snap out of this dream. They too play music for me. Hearing it is nice, but I'd rather talk. They play happier songs—"You're Beautiful," by James Blunt. "You're beautiful it's true, I saw your face in a crowded place..."

Everything is the same. This reoccurring dream where my family comes and talks to me. I can't touch them, but they all held my hand or brushed the hair out of my eyes. I can hear each one and feel them. Why is this happening?

Christian is in my dream now, and he wants me to wake up. He tells me Liam will be here soon. I thought my grandson was born already; that's why I was going to St Vincent's; they were going to take him early. Liam will be here soon.

I hear Ian and a doctor arguing about my care. Other than my erratic blood pressure, Ian says I'm doing fine. I've been lying here for weeks with no sign of improvement. Weeks? That can't be true. I was driving my car and had an accident. "Oh, my! Am I in a coma?" No way: I can hear everything they say, I can feel every touch.

"I want more tests run," Ian says. "I want an EEG." He wants them to check for brain activity. They must think I'm brain dead. What if they pull the plug on me?

"We're scheduling all those tests," the doctor says. We had to make sure your wife is strong enough to move. She's recovering from a broken pelvis, broken ribs, and head trauma, but she's healing well. We'll start the tests next week."

Ian is back, holding my hand, asking God not to let me have brain damage. I want to assure him my brain function is fine; the only thing working at the moment. I concentrate on movement all the time. I want to move something, anything. They need to know I'm here inside this shell that is my broken body.

I lay here in the dark, hoping I can open my eyes. I try all the time; I just can't. The kids are all here, and they're playing music for me again, I wonder what day it is. They put together a mix of my favorite eighties tunes in Pandora.

The Police are playing, and I want to laugh, the song is "Every breath you take... I'll be watching you." It isn't funny, though. My kids are here all the time, trying to wake me with conversation and music. I hear them talk among themselves. I can tell they're getting used to hanging out with me like this, but it's not normal for them. I don't want this to be their life, so perhaps pulling the plug and moving on is for the best. That thought saddens me.

The nurses encourage them to talk to me and play my favorite music. The activity will stimulate my brain. So, they do almost every day. They tell me everything they've been doing, and I'm happy to listen. I want so badly to say to them, "I hear you." I love them all so much.

Taylor and Anna hold my hand as I listen to music. I feel warm tears on my wrist, and it breaks my heart.

I need to move or move something. No matter what I do, I want my family to know they're helping me. I don't feel as alone when they're here. With every bit of strength, I can muster, I concentrate on moving my fingers. It seems hopeless, but I continue to try. When at last Taylor and Anna squeal with delight and say, "DID YOU FEEL THAT?" I can't see their reaction, but I can hear and feel the excitement.

"Dad, she moved," Taylor squeals again.

Anna excitedly says, "I saw it too. Her fingers moved."

The next thing you know, the room buzzes with people's voices. Doctors and nurses are checking me out and looking for signs of waking, but I'm still too tired. Later, Ian stands at my side, and it's quiet again. He tells me he loves me, and he'll never give up on me, and I must try harder to wake up.

"I am, Ian; I truly am."

Ian talks about our family and his love for me. He lists all the reasons why I must wake up.

"I know, Ian, I really want to, but it's hard. I couldn't love them any more than I do." He can't hear me, of course, because I'm speaking in my head.

The hospital has run test after test and can find no reason why I haven't woken up. Eight weeks have passed, and my injuries are all healing nicely. I've been receiving physical therapy to keep my muscles from atrophying. The doctor is telling Ian I don't appear to be brain dead, but in a couple of days, they need to move me to a facility specializing in comatose patients.

Eight weeks I've been lying here. Although I can't move, and haven't since the day I moved my fingers, I feel fine, so why can't I wake up? I try constantly, but nothing happens.

Ian asks if they can move me home. He will hire a nurse to take care of me. For some reason, he doesn't want me to be taken to the facility. "I will not have my wife put away in some facility miles from here. She's breathing on her own, and there's no reason we can't set her up at home."

The doctor doesn't like the idea. He says if something happened, Ian and one nurse wouldn't be equipped to take care of me. Ian continues to argue about the facility and home. She hasn't needed anything. She's breathing on her own and hasn't required resuscitation.

So now I know they extubated me. I don't remember, but at least I'm breathing on my own, and no plug pulling will be necessary. I need to make myself wake up.

He says, "let me look into what we'll need before you move her. We can have a therapist come to the house daily, and the nurse can be a full-time caregiver." This doctor is always negative. I call him Dr. Gloom and Doom.

Dr. Gloom and Doom reminds Ian of the cost of something like this, and "we have no idea when Mrs. Connor will wake up. She may never wake up."

Ian's furious; I can tell by his tone of voice. "Let me worry about that, Doctor."

I hear Ian's shoes on the linoleum floor as he walks swiftly away. "Mr. Connor, please be reasonable," Dr. Gloom and Doom says.

I hear footsteps in the hall; Ian making his way back.

"I'm *Doctor* Connor, and you will call me Doctor when addressing me. I won't let my wife be shut away from her family." He then turns and walks off again. Dr. Gloom and Doom has been saying, Mr. Connor since I got here.

For a long time, the room is quiet. Someone turns on my music, and I listen to one of my favorite Cure songs, "A Letter to Elise." "It doesn't matter what you do, I'll never get inside of you." I feel like crying, I've become such a burden to my family. I wish I could wake up, or at least understand why the hell I can't wake up.

I hear my son talking as my earbuds are softly removed from my ears. "Mom, it's time to wake up. Liam is coming today. He's early, but Jamie isn't doing well; she's still having blood pressure problems, and they feel it's best to induce her labor. They put it off as long as they can to let Liam grow."

High blood pressure, how terrible, she's so young. Jamie and I both seem to be struggling with a similar problem, making things difficult for us both.

"I wish you could be there with us. I'm taking your picture in with me." Christian takes my hand and places it on a photo; I can feel its corners. "You'll be there in my pocket, Mom." He breaks at that moment and chokes up a bit. I wish I could tell him how proud I am of him, and I want to be there. He hugs me and tells me he loves me, but he must go.

The earbuds are placed back in my ears, and I hear U2, "With or Without You, I can't live with or without you." I'm missing one of the biggest brightest days of my life; my son becoming a father. I have no choice but to let him do it without me.

Later, I sense a lot of movement in my room. Feeling the vibe, I assume they're preparing to move me, but no one has touched me. I hear Christian come in and talk to Ian.

They're moving my grandson to Wolfson's Children's hospital; something is wrong. I feel frightened but can't do anything.

I hear a lot of talking back and forth about little Liam, and then Christian leaves. From what I could understand, my little guy can't breathe on his own. Lord, please don't let anything happen to that baby boy. I would go to sleep forever if it meant he would be okay.

"I don't know if you can hear me, but I need to talk to someone." Ian holds my hand and rests his head on my shoulder. It breaks my heart I'm unable to talk or comfort him.

"Liam is three weeks early and is having complications," Ian says, through tears. "Christian is so grown up about it. He's going over to Wolfson's now to be with his son. I would go, but we're taking you home today." He rubs both of my arms. "I want you to be in our home. I'm setting up our room to accommodate you and all the equipment it will take to keep you comfortable. They, meaning the hospital, doesn't want me to, but I don't care what they want. You're my wife, and I say what happens to you. I love you, Dee."

I feel his tears on my arm. I feel so helpless, and it breaks my heart that my family is so broken without me. I hear the nurse softly say to Ian, "it's time, Dr. Connor, and the team is here to take your wife home."

He thanks her. Ian would never want anyone to see him cry. I'm sure this has been hard on him as a man. He sniffles a bit, lets go of my hand, then they begin to move me.

CHAPTER 26

The trip home in the ambulance was a bizarre sensation. I can tell I'm somewhere other than the hospital, and I smell the difference. I'm happy to be home but know what a strain it will be on everyone to take care of me. I'm sad, knowing I missed so much time with my family.

I can only imagine what this is costing Ian. And what about my job? I'm sure I was replaced a long time ago. I hear everyone moving about the house and my room all the time. It feels like an episode of the Outer Limits. I don't think there's anything as bizarre as being here but not being here. I know it's silly, but I can't help worrying about my appearance. I must look awful. My hair, what am I wearing?

My family is wonderful. They talk to me as if I'm awake. Each is focusing on treating me as they would under normal circumstance. They're doing everything for themselves. I'm so lucky to have such a loving family.

They're planning a surprise today, and I'm so excited. Even though I can't see or move, I know the surprise is for me. What though? It doesn't take long to find out.

Christian and Jamie are standing next to me. "Mom, I want you to meet your grandson, Liam. He's almost three weeks old. He's doing great, and they let us bring him home today."

I've been in the dark another three weeks and have no sense of time. But this is terrific news. Liam has overcome whatever health issue he had at Wolfson's, and now he's home with his family. I feel them move my arm, and they place little Liam in the crook, as if I'm holding him. I can hear him coo, and it's the most beautiful sound in the world.

"Dad," Christian calls.

I'm crying tears of joy. "Look," Jamie says. Christian adds "tears, Mom has real tears."

Ian, Taylor, and Anna all come in to see me holding the baby with tears streaming down my eyes, which remain shut.

"What does that mean?" Anna asks.

"Your mother must be able to hear us," Ian says. "She can feel Liam in her arms."

The nurse comes in and agrees with Ian. She tells them this is unusual, but not unheard of in coma cases.

At this point, everyone in the room is crying. My family finally has something to hope for, and today they celebrate. I've always known, so I'm not surprised to hear and feel them. It felt good to share something with them today; to be a part of this occasion and not have them talking around me.

As time passes, Christian and Jamie bring Liam to me and let me hold him often. I can't wait to see him. I feel hopeful.

I look forward to everything and pray I won't lay here like this forever. Lord, let me come back to my family.

I listen to music every day, and Ian professes his love for me each time he talks to me. I long to tell him I love him too. One morning after he tells me he's going to work, kisses my forehead and leaves, a Brian Adam song starts to play "Everything I do I do it for you." I feel a tingle in my legs I have never felt. "Don't tell me it's not worth fighting for…" the song continues to play.

The tingling moves to my arms, and I wonder what could be wrong now. My breathing is irregular, setting off my heart monitor. I hear the beeping I haven't heard in a long time. "There is no love, like your love," Brian Adams still singing in my ears on my headset. "Look into your heart babe…." Am I having a reaction to this song? My heart and pulse seem to be escalating as the words of the song echo in my ears.

Somewhere in the distance, a hear a woman saying, "Dee, can you hear me. Are you waking up hon, Dee?" She removes the buds from my ears. "Mrs. Connor, can you hear me?"

I feel as if I'm saying, "hell, yes, I'm waking up." I feel odd, but suddenly, my eyes want to open. I feel my hands and feet, and for the first time in forever, I'm aware of my whole body. I feel tremors throughout my body, and it's a little scary.

Suddenly, I'm looking into the face of a woman I don't recognize. My eyes blink rapidly, but I can see her. She has a phone to her ear. "Dr. Connor, you need to get back here as quick as you can. Your wife is waking up."

My girls are standing behind this woman. I hear Anna say, "Momma?" and Taylor runs into my line of vision. She reaches for my hand. "Momma?"

I can't tell you how grateful I am at this moment to see these beautiful girls of mine. They sound so young as they call out for me.

The nurse is asking them to step back so she can check me out. I just want to see them.

Christian and Jamie are next to run in the room. "Mom, you're awake, you're really awake," Christian says, with a big smile. I'm so happy to see them.

I feel groggy, but I'm back. I can see my family, and I think I'm reaching for them. They're all trying to get into my line of vision, and it's the best day of my life. The nurse says I'm doing fine.

Ian runs into the room. "How is she? Everything okay?"

"Yes," the nurse says, "she appears to be fully conscious, but we'll all need to take it slow. Let's not excite her."

I'm having a hard time speaking, and they're all looking at me strangely.

Taylor turns to Ian. "Why can't she talk?"

"I don't know yet, sweety. Let mom have a minute; she's been unconscious for a long time. We may have to work with her to get all her functions back."

This upsets my girls. I can see the disappointment in their faces. I try to speak, but the words won't come. To my family, I'm just making noises. I'm trying so hard to let them know how happy I am to see them. I can't imagine what my life would be like if I lost the ability to speak. But I'll cross that bridge later.

Christian pats my hand and rubs my arm. "Take your time, Mom."

I can smile, so I do, and the tears flow again. It's my way of reaching out to them. I feel as if I can do anything, knowing I've been out of it for so long, but am finally back.

I try to reach for them; but it's harder than I expected. I can move my hands and feet only inches, and it feels incredible. They all comment that my movement is a good sign.

My nurse asks them all to step back while she checks my vitals. She's studying me and doing all the things nurses do. She tells Ian she'd like me to go to the hospital for an examination to be on the safe side. She knows something, because she's looking at Ian seriously, before she steps out of the room to make the arrangements.

When she returns, my heart monitor is beeping steadily. I feel okay, but my heart is racing. She tells me my blood pressure is too high, and she called an ambulance.

"No, I'll be fine," I try to say, but it's a mumble. I want to stay here and look at my children; it's been so long since I laid eyes on them. I try to reach for them. Why is my blood pressure a problem? My monitor is going crazy, and I can't see them. "No, I want to see them." I hear them screaming, why are they screaming? Then all turns dark, but not the same dark as before. Funny, I'm not frightened, but this time feels as if something has changed. Going to sleep feels different this time too. Maybe I keep going this time.

Great! I hear that constant beeping again. Damn it. I want quiet.

"Open your eyes, my love. You can do it," and just like that, I'm looking into Ian's eyes. He kisses my lips, and I can kiss him back. I try to speak, but what I'm thinking and what comes out of my mouth are two different things.

"You scared me, Luv. You wake up for me, the nurse, and the kids, only to turn around and die before the ambulance gets to the house. We performed CPR until they got there, and then on the way to Mayo. We owe a debt of gratitude to the EMTs who came to the house and shocked you back to life."

I mumble, and he explains to me, in time I'll get my speech back. "You rest now. I'll bring all the kids tomorrow to see you.

I love you, and Dee, don't ever do that to me again. If there's a life without you, I don't want to live it."

"I'm here to stay, Ian. I love you too, with all my heart." He doesn't hear that, but he knows what I'm trying to say. His face shows so much stress, and his hair has turned a little more gray than I remember. I hope I can help him get back to his old self. My accident and coma have been hard on my family.

The hospital keeps me here for observation for a week, and my kids visit every day. Everyone is saying over and over I'm the miracle patient, and I believe them. My room is full of flowers from the station, my friends, and family.

They say I can go soon and start my recovery at the Rehabilitation Center near our house.

I'm excited to start walking. The nurses let me sit in a chair, but I'm weak, and can't sit alone. I don't care, I'm awake, and will work hard to return to good health. Everything, no matter how small, is a victory of which I'm grateful.

The days at the rehab are hard and often painful. I work every day on my leg and arm muscles, not to mention core strength. I'm so thin, those days not long ago when I was thinking about diets; this isn't what I had in mind. It takes weeks before I can take steps, but my speech is rapidly returning. My stay at the rehab center is longer than any of us wanted, but I need lots of assistance. I'm frustrated, but it's also wonderful.

Finally, my doctor tells me I can go home in another week. A nurse will be at the house during the day while Ian's working. My sister will be there as well to help around the house and get us a new housekeeper. I can continue my therapy at home. I'm excited, because this means I'm closer to independence and getting my life back.

CHAPTER 27

I can hardly believe another summer is almost over. My kids will all be going back to school. Jamie will be living in the suite, and Christian will return to school as well. Kathy went back to her family, and life goes on.

I'm walking with a cane and spend a lot of my convalescence in a chair out back. The kids have been so helpful during my recovery. They've all grown up so much over the summer; taking care of me and helping me get my life back. It takes Ian, Christian, and my twins to get me down to the beach, but they do it because they know I love it so much. I've been on a surfboard but can't stand yet. I'm okay with that; at least I'm in the water and riding a wave, no matter how much of a kook I appear.

The girls are making tacos tonight. We'll all sit down for dinner. Today is Sunday, and we never miss a Sunday dinner if possible. Christian has important news to share. I'm sitting in the family room, watching Taylor and Anna prepare the meal. We chat idly about what this year entails for them as juniors at their school.

They're both excited to go back. Both are talking about not driving two separate cars this year. We bought them Scion cars for their sixteenth birthday, one red, one blue. Now, since they're over the excitement of driving their own cars, they've decided they don't both need to drive every day. They'll alternate driving, and ride together unless one needs to do something after school.

Ian comes into the house in the middle of this conversation. He gives me a quick kiss and goes to change into shorts and a tee-shirt. Dinner is good, who doesn't love tacos, but I'm anxious to hear Christian's news.

Jamie looks over at Christian. I think she's giving him a sign to start the conversation.

"Well," he begins, and for some reason, I sense nervousness. "I wanted to tell you all, there's a change in my education plans. I won't be returning to the University of North Carolina. I'll finish my degree at the University of North Florida. Before anyone says anything, please let me explain." He looks at me and Ian before continuing.

"We all know I love basketball, but it's not my future. The fact is, fewer than two percent make it to the NBA. So, I'm changing my major to Accounting. I've always been a numbers guy." He and Jamie giggle, but I know he's always been a mathematical wizard.

"I've been offered a paid internship at Mayo in the accounting department under Mr. Hartman. My education is covered partially, as well." He pauses for our reaction. "He and I talked several times when mom was in the coma."

"Are you sure, son?" Ian asks. "You're giving up a lot, and you might regret not finishing what you started."

"Yes, Jamie and I discussed it. My quitting school isn't an option, but I want to stay here and be a family. Jamie needs me, and Liam needs his father."

Jamie smiles and reaches over to hold Christian's hand. They're a united front. I look at her, feeling sad they might've been afraid to tell us their plans.

"Besides, the coach at UNF says I can try out for the team. He seemed happy to have me come to the Ospreys. I feel I'm not giving up anything."

"Will you still live upstairs?" I ask. Hoping they will, I can't do a lot, but can help watch Liam during the day.

"We would like to, if it's okay," Christian says, and Jamie nods. "Jamie wants to finish school too."

"Well, of course it's okay," I say, smiling at them both. Both Christian and Jamie need to know we'll support them as they start this new life.

Taylor and Anna have been quiet, and I wonder if they're holding their breath. Finally, they both breathe a sigh of relief and applaud. I think they already knew about this plan.

Random Summer Storms

"It's settled then," Ian says. "Everyone stays, and you'll all finish school." He stands and extends his arms. Christian and Jamie jump up and run around the table to hug Ian and me.

"I have one more surprise," Christian says, and then kneels on one knee, takes Jamie's hand, and asks her to marry him.

She appears so surprised, it takes her longer than I expected before she answers. Her mouth forms an 'O', and then she nods her head and says yes. The twins are hooting and make whoop noises.

"Looks like Jamie's mom and I have a wedding to plan," I say, clapping my hands and laughing with joy. We hear Liam squawking from his pack and play. "Looks like Liam is happy too," I add, and everyone laughs.

The decision is bittersweet. Christian is giving up his basketball scholarship to stay home and be a father and husband, and I'm proud he's willing to give up The University of North Carolina for his family. The fact he might play ball at UNF is a plus. Ian and I did well with our son. He's turned his life around from last summer.

My girls are fine, and I know they'll do well. They haven't let me down yet. The time for a new chapter in our lives has arrived, and I couldn't be more excited. With one door closing and another opening, I need to do something else.

Since my accident and recovery, I've decided I need to let the skeletons in our closet run free. I don't want any secrets or lies coming between my family and me. We need to be truthful about the past, so we're prepared for the future. While I fear to tell the tale, I know it's necessary for us to move on.

I call my sister Kathy to let her know I'm breaking my silence and telling Mike everything. She gives me much needed encouragement, reminding me we're all family, and we struggle with things as one. "It will be good, you'll see," she says, and tells me it's great to have me back and to talk on the phone. I tell her I appreciate everything she did for me while I recovered. Ian and the kids appreciate her too.

She acts as though it was nothing, but we all know it was a lot for her to drop everything and take care of us for weeks. Our family unit is strong. I'm so fortunate to have them all.

I decided to call my brother and tell him everything about the past. He's happy when I call. The last time he saw me, I was in a coma. We've never been mushy in our relationship, but we cried on the phone this time, and he told me how he felt. Mike said he cried when he left and called Ian often to check on me. He said it was as hard as losing his wife.

I cried too, then told him everything. I laid out the long horrible story of how Ian and I got messed up with drug traffickers, and they attacked us at sea. Although he never let on, Mike never believed the whole story about the pirates, he is after all a cop. He laughed and told me how he investigated it for a long time, but it was a dead-end case, and he finally dropped it.

"Mike, there's something else," I say. "Christian got himself into some trouble the summer before last. We didn't want to tell you because, well, you're a cop and so are your boys."

"What happened?" he asked.

I rehashed the whole summer with Christian selling weed and the shootout in front of our house. Mike's tone of voice indicates he's angry and reticent; I guess that's the cop in him.

"So, what is Christian doing now?" he asks.

I tell him Christian isn't returning to UNC; he's giving up that dream. He has a family now and is getting married in the fall. We'll have a small ceremony here on the beach and would love for them to come. "We're all different people who have survived from our mistakes," I insist.

He's more forgiving than I gave him credit, because he reacted opposite from what I expected. "The boys and I will be happy to come. Everyone deserves a second chance. Look at you. You turned out okay, I guess. You've been kinda lazy lying around and sleeping for months, but I don't know. Your life hasn't been so bad."

We both start laughing; he's never been one to give compliments, so the fact he said I turned out okay is good.

We talk about the upcoming event, then Mike blows me away by saying, "by the way, I'm seeing someone. I think I'll bring her for the family to meet."

I'm so happy his life is changing too, and no one will ever forget Jill, but Mike needs someone also, and deserves to be happy.

I ask how Sean is. I worry about another woman in Mike's life affecting him. Mike tells me he's well, and both Sean and Mike Jr. get along great with Sarah. She's been good with Sean. "Talking about Jill doesn't bother her, and seems to help Sean a lot," Mike says.

"I'm glad to hear that," I say, as we get ready to hang up. Before we do, I say, "I love you, Mike." I've never said that to him.

"I love you too, little sister," he says.

We hang up, and I smile, then laugh aloud. He sounded like John Wayne, but I got some emotion out of him. He's always been a tough guy, but today he was my big brother Mike who loves me.

A few days later, we all sat down as a family, and I retold the story of the pirates in their true form as Cartel members and murderers. Ian and I related the real story we felt ashamed to tell the kids most of their lives. I hope they learn from this. At first, they thought it was remarkable what we did, and the fact we got away with it.

"The criminal masterminds," Taylor says, and Anna laughs, but it sounds fake.

Christian says excitedly, "It's hard to picture you guys doing all that. It was a crazy plan, and you two pulled it off."

I reminded them we didn't; their father almost died from a gunshot wound and we fled the state leaving our home and family. They finally knew the whole ugly story, but I don't know exactly what they thought. The girls were quiet, not saying much. After an uncomfortable silence, Taylor said, "Sounds scary, I'm glad you survived."

Anna brooded about the whole thing. She had a big crease in her forehead, and I was worried about her. A few seconds passed, then she added, "what a freaking crazy ass family we have! Oops, I mean..." We all know she didn't mean to say "ass," so I let that slide it certainly was appropriate.

"I'm sorry. We're not proud of any part of it, so I never wanted you to know." I searched their faces for forgiveness.

Anna and Taylor smiled an identical half-smile.

"It needs to stay buried," Anna said, "but I'm glad you told us. I don't want to talk about it anymore, and sure don't want other people to know."

We all agreed to leave it in the past.

"I agree," I said, "I'm tired all of a sudden. I'm going to go lay down for a bit." I felt sad, because the idea of telling my children I'm not the smart, strong woman they thought, is heartbreaking. I have faults and imperfections, and now they know the extent of those imperfections.

Christian hugs me as I limp off to my room. "I love you, son, learn from our mistakes," I say.

"I've learned a lot Mom, what you did back then has nothing to do with what I did. You coming clean to us is for you, remember that. I've learned from you and dad that we'll make our own way, mistakes and all. Clearing the air is good for the soul."

"How did I have a kid like you? So wise." I smile and shake my head. "Forgiveness is good for the soul too."

He smiles and rubs my shoulder as I head towards my bedroom.

My girls tell me they love me, and that warms my heart.

Christian heads out the door to see Jamie and Liam, upstairs in their little home. Christian seems happy, and that pleases me; I'm content with his decisions. He's grown to be a good man, and is a new dad.

This is my family. None of us are perfect. We all aspire to great things, and sometimes we fall short. The expectations we have of ourselves and others can be overwhelming, but in the end, we'll be who we choose. Truth or lie, the path is ours. I feel better with the truth out in the open. My son is right—confession was enlightening. My soul and conscious is clear. Nothing will change the fact we did these things. Our path since that time is what makes us who we are.

Being judgmental isn't a good thing, and I'll never lightly pass judgment on others. I hope my children won't judge us

Random Summer Storms

or others lightly as well. I hope they continue to be the honest, loving people they are with everyone. We're no better than the next person, and our troubles aren't any worse than the stranger walking past us on the boardwalk.

What a day this has been. I don't like it when I need to rest. I feel I've rested enough for a lifetime, but my body tells me otherwise.

I look forward to being awake and with my family; more than anyone will ever know. I know we all say we should live each day to the fullest, but tomorrow isn't a guarantee. It often takes real trauma in your life to appreciate what that truly means.

My whole family experiences things that have hurt them, and things that make them stronger. Such is life, and we all strive to live it the best we can. Grateful, loving, and hope to get through each day.

After I rested, I sit out back on the deck next to Ian, and we hold hands while watching the beautiful sun set. He tells me he feels blessed things turned out the way they did. He has a lovely wife, a handsome son, two beautiful daughters, a beautiful soon to be daughter-in-law, and a little grandson. Ian tells me his cup is full, and mine is too. We could not be luckier.

We can hear our kids in the house, talking and laughing, with our grandson in the mix of those voices, cooing and gurgling. This moment is what life is about, family weak or strong together. I'll never forget these days or take them for granted.

The sky is deep purple with orange slashes through the clouds. We love the calming effect of the surf as it rolls in. We sit and enjoy what we call our heaven by the sea. The ocean is a reminder of one last thing to conquer, returning to surfing and the feeling I get from dropping into a wave again. I know it will all come back to me. My life is full.

I think of a song I love and hum the tune in my head.

"There are places I'll remember all my life, though some have changed, some forever, not for better, some are gone, some remain. All these places had their moments with lovers and friends, I still can recall. Some are dead, and some are living, in my life, I've loved them all."

—THE BEATLES

WWW.SBPRABOOKS.COM/DENISEANNSTOCK